DEATH OF A

DUNWOODY

MATRON

Somebody's Dead in Snellville
Murder on Peachtree Street
Murder in the Charleston Manner
Murder at Markham

DEATH OF A
DUNWOODY
MATRON

PATRICIA SPRINKLE

A PERFECT CRIME BOOK

DOUBLEDAY

NEW YORK LONDON TORONTO SYDNEY AUCKLAND

A PERFECT CRIME BOOK
PUBLISHED BY DOUBLEDAY
A division of Bantam Doubleday Dell Publishing Group, Inc.
1540 Broadway, New York, New York 10036

DOUBLEDAY is a trademark of Doubleday, a division of
Bantam Doubleday Dell Publishing Group, Inc.

Library of Congress Cataloging-in-Publication Data

Sprinkle, Patricia Houck.
Death of a Dunwoody matron / Patricia Sprinkle. —1st ed.
p.   cm.
"A Perfect crime book."
I. Title.
PS3569.P687D4   1993
813'.54—dc20   92-38574
CIP
ISBN 0-385-42485-X
Copyright © 1993 by Patricia Houck Sprinkle
All Rights Reserved
Printed in the United States of America
May 1993

First Edition

1   3   5   7   9   10   8   6   4   2

Designed by Bonni Leon-Berman

To the lovely matrons of Dunwoody,
and to those who sent the jokes

DEATH OF A

DUNWOODY

MATRON

Running Ridge Road

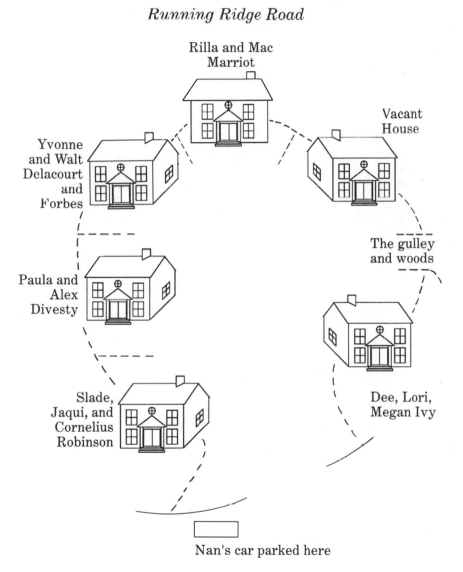

Rilla and Mac
Marriot

Vacant
House

Yvonne
and Walt
Delacourt
and
Forbes

The gulley
and woods

Paula and
Alex
Divesty

Dee, Lori,
Megan Ivy

Slade,
Jaqui, and
Cornelius
Robinson

Nan's car parked here

"There are a lot of fences in Dunwoody."

Dunwoody, Georgia, is a prosperous
Atlanta suburb.
Beside cash registers, cups bear signs:
Need a dollar? Take a dollar.
Got a dollar? Leave a dollar.

FRIDAY MORNING

In Atlanta, June is a temptress. Her cool mornings seduce you into forgetting that by noon she may fry your socks off. Yvonne Delacourt was like that, too. Fragile, lovely, helpless. About as helpless, in Alex Divesty's eyes, as a female barracuda.

This morning Yvonne stood on the half-acre of Bermuda grass between their two houses, wearing a clinging pink sundress, dainty hot pink sandals, and a look of bewilderment. "Oh, Alex, was that a loan? I thought it was a gift!"

A breeze flitted down the one block plus cul-de-sac that was Running Ridge Road. It ruffled Yvonne's soft black hair and carried her floral scent to Alex like a kiss. He nearly weakened and offered to cancel her debt in exchange for a weekend in the Bahamas. What would she say if he did? Before he could find out, she added in the tone of one being kind, "I can pay part of it next week, when I close on the Halstead house."

His face grew as red as his hair. "What do you mean, close on the Halstead house? That was *my* contract!"

"I know, Alex. I feel *so* bad about that." She reached out and touched his forearm with her fingertips. Her nails were painted a dusky, virginal rose. "My clients didn't decide they wanted to buy it until right after your contract expired. I'm sorry."

He flung off her hand. "Like hell they didn't! This is the fourth time you've sold a house right after my contract expired. It's once too often, Yvonne! I'm the guy who got you started in Dunwoody real estate—remember? You *owe* me those commissions. And you pay that loan Monday—in cash or a cashier's check!"

He pivoted on one toe to make a grand exit. Instead, his running shoe slipped on the dew-damp grass and he fell heavily onto his left knee, the sore one he'd begun to run on again only this week. He clenched his jaw on the pain and hauled himself to his feet. "Monday," he growled. "I have bills to pay."

"Poor Alex, of course you do." Her voice was as soft with forgiveness as her violet eyes. "I understand."

He limped across the grass and up his own walk. Usually he felt a small surge of pride when he approached the large Tudor-style house with its dark brown trim and small turret. He felt like a king pushing open the arched oak door. Today he was too pained in body and spirit to feel anything but annoyance. His wife, Paula, her gorgeous body hidden by a terry-cloth robe, stood at the open front door, sipping coffee. She must have heard him shouting, but not until she'd brought him a painkiller and hot coffee did she speak.

"You gave her money, didn't you?" Her voice was harsh with unshed tears. "But you don't have a penny so Craig can—"

"Craig's *your* son, Paula," he reminded her. "You need money for that crazy kid, ask his father."

It was so cruel—and so unlike him—that her eyes widened in surprise and she pressed her mouth with one fist. Contrite, he pulled her to him. "Paulie, I'm sorry. I didn't mean that. I'm just under a lot of pressure right now. The market's bad, and—"

She pulled away. "You gave Yvonne—"

He waved her to silence. "A *loan*, Paula. Besides, that's my affair, not yours." He went upstairs to shower and change for work.

She crossed to the kitchen window, and stared unseeing at the soaring teardrop of a Bradford pear tree. "That's what I'm afraid of Alex," she whispered. "That it's your affair."

Yvonne pulled a white clematis from the vine climbing her streetside mailbox and stuck it in her hair. Then she bent gracefully to pluck her morning paper from the day lilies. On her front walk she stood for a moment, admiring the way sunlight touched the tall brick house with taupe trim. At a slow, sultry pace she climbed the four steps to her own front door.

Back inside the house, however, her languor turned to haste. Almost frantically she turned pages until her own face smiled up at her. *Yvonne Delacourt, pouring tea at the Dunwoody Garden Club benefit.* She smiled back—not at herself, but at the bank president's wife beside her. If she had been a cat, she would have purred. Before she was through, Yvonne Delacourt wanted her name to be familiar to every Atlantan who *really* mattered.

It would be.

But not this morning. This morning she was just another Dunwoody matron with a child in preschool, a maid to clean her house, a yard man to manicure her lawn, and a tennis match at ten.

Down at Georgia Tech, Harley Sanders didn't realize he was tapping his pencil against his teeth until another student hissed at him to stop. He shrugged, slid lower in his seat, and further tuned out the lecture. He had more important things on his mind this morning than qualitative analysis.

Once more he reached into the pocket of his unironed shirt and pulled out the picture he'd ripped from the morning paper. He had unfolded and refolded it so often that a white line creased the woman's face. He laid the picture across his notebook and traced the line with one almost-clean forefinger, so lost in thought that he was startled when the student on his left jabbed the picture with his pen. "Better-looking than the prof."

Harley automatically looked from the photograph to the dark, squat young woman at the lectern, then refolded the clipping and

shoved it back in his pocket. "Concentrate on chemistry, man."
He fixed his blue eyes so intently on the professor that she stumbled midsentence in surprise.

She would never know that the notes Harley scribbled so virtuously in the last fifteen minutes of class consisted of two words, written over and over again: YVONNE DELACOURT.

Yvonne ran toward the net and returned a lob. "Good shot!" her teammates cheered. Flushed and perspiring, she looked more feminine than any of the others waiting to play.

"Why does she do it?" asked a woman sipping diet Coke on the sidelines. "Walt's crazy about her and he's got plenty of money. Why does she bother to sell real estate?"

A friend raised one shoulder and let it drop. "Why does any woman work?"

"Some work because we have to." Dee Ivy dropped into a vacant chair—breathless, as usual. Seldom could she leave her interior design office early enough to arrive on time. "You know what they say"—she gave a short, mirthless laugh—"most women are one man away from work or welfare. I learned the hard way."

Embarrassed, the others took quick pulls on their drinks, fiddled with their tennis bracelets, or found Yvonne Delacourt's match suddenly fascinating. "Come on, Vonnie!" two called simultaneously as Yvonne effortlessly returned a difficult serve.

Dee's mouth was sour with triumph. She'd won that battle, but she would lose the war. An old joke flitted through her mind: *Why were two women kicked out of the Dunwoody Junior League? One had an orgasm and the other got a job.* Actually a good many women in Dunwoody worked these days, but they didn't try to play on a morning tennis team. Dee would have to quit soon. Last week she had overheard one team member wondering if Dee "considered her damned decorating business more important than the team." Of course she did! What else *could* she do?

Her mind raced around the same old track she'd been on since Dave left five years before: bills, bills, bills. His child support was little more than a partial food and clothing allowance. Whoever set the figures had forgotten that people who raise children also have to pay for lights, water, heat, air-conditioning, and cars. Dave thought he was so generous keeping their membership in the Dunwoody Country Club, conveniently forgetting it was Dee who had to pay the monthly tab—just like he thought he was generous buying Lori that bright red Miata and paying the insurance. "All you have to pay for is maintenance and gas." Dee clutched the arms of her chair and breathed deeply, fighting down panic. She could scarcely buy her own gas, much less Lori's. What *was* she going to do?

When a hand dropped to her shoulder, Dee jumped. She peered up at Ava Settis, who from her viewpoint looked like a giraffe in sunglasses, she was so tall and bony. No giraffe, however, could afford Ava's stunning new tennis dress or the diamond tennis bracelet sparkling on one tanned wrist. Neither could Dee.

"Dee, honey!" Ava's smile was wide but apologetic. "I'm sorry, but I've decided not to do the bedroom over just yet. I'm not sure what I want. Okay?" She gave Dee's shoulder a quick squeeze.

"Sure. No problem. You can get back to me." Dee managed to smile until Ava moved on, then gripped her lower lip with her teeth. That was the second cancellation this week. What was going on? She'd worked hard to build her reputation, prove she had a flair. She had decorated some of the most prestigious homes in Dunwoody—including Yvonne Delacourt's. Her business had been growing until recently. What was different?

She caught the two women beside her exchanging glances. They knew something she didn't. Well, let them! She got up as casually as she could and strolled over to buy a Coke. That meant she couldn't afford a Burger King on her way back to work, but nobody had to know. They wouldn't believe it, anyway. How could she live in upper Dunwoody, drive a silver BMW, and not afford a Whopper?

Because the man who had stood between Dee and welfare wanted his children raised in Dunwoody. Wanted it badly enough to lease their mother a BMW and keep up the house payments until their younger daughter's eighteenth birthday. Then, for nine years of raising children, taking good care of her cars, paying utility bills and maintenance companies—just last week, the air-conditioning man—Dee would get half the equity they'd had in the house when he left.

Figuring it out kept her awake at night. No matter how she twisted the figures, her share always came out less than she would need to make a down payment on another Dunwoody house and buy a decent car. Meanwhile, Dave had bought a bigger house up on the Chattahoochee River and took nubile young women to the Bahamas for long weekends. He could afford it, damn him! When Dee protested that it wasn't fair—that nine years of taking care of a house ought to count for something— her ex-husband and two male lawyers looked at her as if she were a moron.

If her business failed now . . . Her chin started to quiver, and she knew she was going to bawl again. She hurried into the bathroom, hid in a stall, and sobbed.

She was scrubbing her eyes and cheeks with toilet paper when she heard two women come in.

"That's the tackiest thing I ever heard of! After all you've done for her!"

"Well, I *was* a bit surprised." Dee recognized both the high, squeaky voice and the soft drawl that replied. Carolyn Cameron and Yvonne Delacourt had finished their match.

They turned on the water, so Dee missed a few words until

they turned it off, then she heard, "—wouldn't decorate it for me." Yvonne sounded gentle, patient, and long-suffering. She sighed. "She must just be too busy."

Her companion slammed something—probably a hairbrush—down on the counter. "Well, she won't be busy working for me! I've been thinking of redoing the downstairs, but I'll try that new place down Mount Vernon Road. The nerve of Dee Ivy!"

"It felt like poison ivy to me," Yvonne admitted, then hastened to add, "but I don't want to criticize. She could have a good reason for turning me down."

Heedless of her tousled blond curls, flaming cheeks, and still-wet lashes, Dee flung open the stall door. "A damn good reason, and you know it!" She turned to Carolyn. "She wanted me to decorate that house for free—even give her client a discount on fabrics and paper. She'd get her commission, the client would get a lovely home, and what was I supposed to get?"

Yvonne crossed the small marble space and held out one hand, violet eyes as wide with concern as Dee's blue ones were with fury. "Oh, Dee! I wouldn't have hurt you for the world!"

Meanwhile Carolyn, whose husband's travel agencies supported her more than comfortably, said in a reasonable tone, "The advertising, Dee. John says a business has to advertise."

"John has an enormous advertising budget. I—I don't!" Dee raced from the room as fast as her Reeboks could carry her. She'd miss her match, but she didn't care. She didn't plan to ever return. Maybe if she were lucky she'd crash the car on the way back to work. Or maybe the earth would open and swallow her.

The last thing she heard was Carolyn's titter and two gently drawled words, "Poison Ivy." She knew the name would stick.

Rilla and Mac Marriot never got up before ten, since they no longer had to. While Dee Ivy was hurrying back to work, they were finishing a lazy brunch on the sun-dappled deck overlook-

ing their wooded backyard. Theirs was the large house at the
bottom of the cul-de-sac that ended Running Ridge Road. Rilla
stretched, basking in the sun filtering through the glossy leaves
of Mac's magnolia. It was an enormous tree, older than Sherman's notorious march through Georgia. When Mac built this
house, he had made the architect design a deck shaded by the
magnolia each morning and by a huge walnut at the other end of
the house each afternoon. Whenever the weather was pleasant,
he insisted on eating outdoors. He had spent too much time in-
doors at one point in his life. In retirement he soaked up sun
whenever he could, until his pale blue eyes peered from a tanned
face with sun-bleached hair, lashes, and eyebrows, giving him
the look of a person seen in a photographic negative. A very
handsome negative, Rilla thought. He didn't look nearly sixty.

She sipped her coffee with an appreciative "ummm."

Mac grinned. "Is that for me or the coffee?"

She patted her short curls, which she carefully bleached to
match his, stretched her legs beneath her red-and-white-striped
sundress, and wiggled tanned toes in tomato-red sandals. "Both.
Your shirt just matches your eyes, and I'm always grateful for
that first surge of caffeine. Isn't this a gorgeous day?" She
reached arms high above her head and closed her eyes to let
sunlight caress her lids.

Mac watched her indulgently. Even after thirty-five years of
marriage, there was no woman who could come close to Rilla.
She was cute, perky, a good manager, and fiercely loyal. He took
her hand across the table. "You ready for tonight?"

"I think so. Sue Ella's got the food under control. How about
you and Richard?"

"Under control, but not ready. Feel like a bit of sun?"

She chuckled and glanced at her well-browned arms. "Don't I
look like I need it? But the mailman comes at two, remember."

He checked his watch. "We've hours before then."

Their conversation might have been cryptic, but Mac and Rilla
knew exactly what they were saying. They'd been speaking in a

private code for several years now, since Mac retired and they had started spending so much time together.

Mac stood up, sucked in his already-trim waist, and beat on his chest. "Me Tarzan, you Jane?"

She rose and kissed him lightly. "No, me Cleopatra, you Caesar. Me watch Nile, you go to Rome. Five minutes to clear the decks."

She carried their dishes into the kitchen, where a tall tan woman was washing pots. Beneath her gray uniform, rounded shoulders spoke eloquently of years at a sink. Her flat black shoes were run over at the sides. Her hair was gray-black, like steel wool, and had been dragged into a bun at her neck. Only two spots of bright pink rouge and a few wisps of hair frizzing about her head softened her drabness. Her eyes were a curious light gray and large, bulging behind half-closed lids. She turned and gave a small jump.

"You startled me, ma'am! I didn' think you'd be done so soon."

Rilla set her dishes on the counter. "Sue Ella," she chided her gently, "I've told you a hundred times. Use the dishwasher!"

Sue Ella wiped her hands on her white apron. "Sorry, Miss Rilla. I keep forgettin'. I'm used to washin' up when they's just a few. I'll use the dishwasher when I start to cook in earnest."

Rilla peered into the refrigerator. "You have everything you need? We may have more than fifty here tonight, and even though we're starting late, they'll probably be hungry." She crossed the kitchen and gave the other woman a quick hug. "Soon they'll come to our little gatherings just for Sue Ella's good cooking." Sue Ella made a small inarticulate sound—disavowal mixed with deep pleasure.

Rilla drew away and pushed the woman gently by the shoulder. "Go on up to Mama Di's now, and change her bed. Give her room an extra good polishing, then you can finish down here. Mac and I will eat out tonight, so we won't bother you again."

Sue Ella dried her hands more thoroughly on a fluffy yellow towel and held it briefly to her cheek. "I jus' love workin' here, ma'am. Everythin's so sunny 'n' bright. These three weeks've seemed like heaven! I'll have that room ready in a minute, I sure will. In just a minute."

"Take your time," Rilla told her. "If you need me, I'm going to sit on the front stoop and meditate for a while. Give Mama Di's bathroom a polish while you're at it."

"I sure will, Miss Rilla, sure will." Sue Ella almost curtsied as she backed out of the room, and Rilla heard her running up the stairs like an awkward hare.

Sue Ella would do, Rilla thought, as she made her way to the front stoop and settled her skirts about her in a patch of sun on the top step. An immaculate housekeeper, an excellent cook, dumb, plain, obedient, and adoring—what more could any woman want?

Rilla was scanning the sky for clouds when she heard a shout from Mama Di's room. "Hey! You there! What are you doing?"

Rilla hurried down the steps and around the house. The fence blocked her view of the backyards, but above her she saw her mother-in-law at an open window, shaking a pointed finger toward the Delacourts' roof next door. "Come down at once!" the old woman commanded imperiously. "You'll break your fool neck!"

Unperturbed, a man on the Delacourts' roof wasn't even looking at her. "I'm cleaning the gutter. Your tree messes it up." He jerked his head toward the Marriot walnut.

Rilla craned her neck to peer up at the huge tree. Did its leaves really blow into gutters that far away? That was the least of her worries. She hurried nearer to the house and shouted up, "Oh, do be careful. The roof is so steep!"

His grunt might have been a short laugh. "I'm careful."

"You're the Delacourts' new yard man, aren't you?" Rilla kept her voice pitched loud, hoping Mac would hear.

The man gave her a brief, insolent nod. "Yeah." He fumbled at the gutter, but she did not see any leaves.

"Get down!" Mama Di ordered. "You Peeping Tom!"

Again he ignored her.

Rilla leaned back and shaded her eyes. "I guess you get a good view up there, don't you?"

He straightened briefly and looked around. "Yeah."

"Be very careful!" she called again, then turned to her husband's mother. "Go back inside, Mama Di, before you catch cold."

"How can I catch cold in June?" the old woman demanded. "You tell him to get down off that roof, or I'll shoot him!"

Sue Ella appeared and gently pulled her back inside.

The Delacourts' gardener was surly as the dickens, Rilla thought, watching him for a moment, but he was a handsome devil—if you liked your men tall and dark with one curl falling over mirrored sunglasses.

"When he is good, he is very, very good, and when he is bad, he is horrid," she chanted. She wondered if Mac and Richard could see him up there, and where Yvonne had found him. Mac would find out. He liked to know everything there was to know about his neighbors.

Thelma Hardwick always had her dinner at noon.

Two years earlier, when she had moved into a high-rise retirement home in downtown Atlanta, she had elected to hire a woman to cook and wash dishes rather than eat in the congregate dining room. Swollen feet made walking difficult some days, and besides, Thelma liked her food cooked the way she liked it. She also liked to eat at her own pace—savoring each bite, finishing her meal just before her favorite soap opera at one.

Today, however, she scarcely noticed whether she was eating baked chicken or green beans. Finally she raised distressed eyes, and her wasted hands fluttered beside her plate. "I'm sorry, Lucky. I didn't hear what you said."

"I axt if you want dessert befo' or after yo' story, Miss

Thelma." Lucky cocked her head in equal distress. Miss Thelma was sometimes contrary and often forgetful, but today she was just plain out to lunch—and Lucky didn't mean the lunch that was before her. "What's the matter wit' you?" she demanded.

Thelma pushed herself back from the table and struggled to her feet, wincing at the pain as they took her full ninety pounds. "I am just weary, Lucky. I think I'll take a nap."

"Is yo' baby comin' to see you later?" Lucky darted a quick look at the small boy with dark curling hair in a silver frame.

Thelma's sigh seemed to come from the soles of her feet. "Not today, Lucky. You go on home when you finish the dishes."

As the bedroom door closed, Lucky shook her head. "Weary, my hind foot! You ain't never been too weary to watch yo' story before." She cleared the table, still muttering. "Spilin' fur a stroke's what you are, 'lessen you tell somebody what's botherin' you. It's sumpin' to do wit' dat woman. I know it is!"

After a cautious listen toward the bedroom door, Lucky moved to Thelma's desk, picked up a worn Bible, and took out a clipping. "Huh! Stuck in there like I wouldn't see it. Doan you know Lucky knows ever'thing goes on in this place?" She smoothed the picture and considered the face smiling up at her. "Pretty woman. Hard mouth, though. I wouldn't work for her."

Lucky traced words under the picture with one gnarled brown finger and gave a small sigh of regret. If she had stayed in school long enough to learn to read, maybe she could have been more help to Miss Thelma now. As it was, all she could do was wait and pray.

While Lucky was studying a photograph in downtown Atlanta, Jaqui Robinson was parking her silver Nissan 300 ZX in the first drive on Running Ridge Road, gathering an armful of bags, and heading for her own front door.

Up at the head of the cul-de-sac she saw Rilla Marriot perched on her front stoop. Why would a woman with a perfectly good deck spend so many sunny mornings sitting on that sorry excuse for a porch? Someday maybe Jaqui would get up the courage to ask her.

Jaqui herself never sat anywhere it was sunny. Her skin was light, the color of café au lait, and she had no intention of letting it darken. Slade liked it the way it was.

She hoped Slade would like her new coiffure—sleek against the scalp, curls cascading from her crown down her back. She touched it, then started up her front steps. In one bag she carried the jump suit she'd bought for that night. Crimson and gold, it made her feel like an Ethiopian queen. She'd had her nails painted to match, and sculpted especially long.

Before she reached the door, Slade opened it—wearing not slacks and an expensive jacket like any other well-paid baseball player, but scuffed tennis shoes, a pair of khaki cutoffs, and a Braves T-shirt he'd had long before he signed a Braves contract. "What you doin' lookin' like some low-class nigger?" Jaqui said in an exaggerated drawl, pushing past him to drop her parcels in a chair.

"Trying to look like a low-class nigger," he told her sourly, closing the door behind them. The drapes were pulled, the room dim in the light of one small lamp. "I'm hiding from my darling fans. Seems like I can't step out my door or walk down a sidewalk without somebody wanting me to sign a baseball or a scrap of paper."

"You've been pitching good this year," she reminded him, opening the drapes and switching off the light.

"That doesn't give people the right to expect me to sign my name all the time," Slade grumbled. "Would you believe, one woman stretched out a used Kleenex yesterday and wanted me to scribble my name on it?"

She shook her head, disbelieving. "You can't write on a Kleenex, Slade. It tears."

"That's what I told her. So she gave me her old grocery list instead. It had been in her pocketbook with the Kleenex. God's truth, Jaqui! I'm getting sick and tired of it."

"Go on!" She threw back her head, and her rich laugh filled the room. Then she moved close and began to scratch his chest with her inch-long scarlet nails. "You adore it, Slade Robinson," she purred. "Admit it. That's why you decided to play ball."

He circled her with the Braves' newest and best pitching arm, and for a few minutes neither spoke. Then he murmured, "I decided to play ball, beautiful, because I love playing ball. And I love getting paid for it. I do not love smearing my name across somebody's snotty Kleenex."

She glided to the white velvet sofa, sat down, and crossed her legs, careful not to wrinkle her emerald silk pants. One gold sandal dangled from her toes and slapped against her sole as she talked. "I'll tell you what *I* do not love, Slade Robinson. I do not love living in this snooty white neighborhood where not one single woman gives me the time of day."

"There aren't any single women in this neighborhood, honey— except Dee Ivy, and she probably stuck her old man for plenty. Otherwise, how could she afford it? And Dunwoody's not all white. Five percent of us are something else."

"I'm tired of being something else! Other Dunwoody wives play tennis, shop, eat lunch out. Nobody has even invited me yet."

"You don't know how to play tennis."

"I did in college. I'd pick it up again if they'd ask me. And I already know how to eat." She let her sandal fall to the thick blue carpet and pulled her knee up to her chest. "I'm lonely, Slade." She rested her chin on her knee and gave him what her mirror assured her was a pitiful look. "I have lived on this street for six months, and I do not really know one person. Dee works, Paula's always doing volunteer stuff, and Rilla's always with Mac."

"What about Yvonne Delacourt?"

Jaqui shook her head. "We don't have a thing in common except little boys. Please think about moving, honey. Please?"

"Maybe you'll meet somebody new at the Marriots' party tonight," he said hopefully.

She shook her head again. "We both know we get invited to those parties because you are a baseball star. They don't care a thing about me. If you were plain Slade Robinson, do you think they'd ask us? Unh-unh!" She tossed her gleaming curls in firm denial.

He chuckled. "They might ask us to serve or wash dishes. Look on the bright side. Wouldn't you rather eat caviar than serve it?"

She threw a pillow at him, but her mouth curved in a reluctant smile. "You and your bright sides. I will stay here six more months, Slade, one year to the day when we moved in. But if we haven't made friends by then, we are moving. I want friends for me and Cornelius both."

"Cornelius has friends!"

Jaqui felt a surge of triumph. She'd gotten to him. That boy had wrapped his daddy around his tiny finger one minute after he'd been born, and for four years he'd been wrapping him tighter.

She pressed her advantage. "He plays with Forbes when Forbes's mama doesn't keep him in day care all day so she can show houses. Maybe one afternoon in two weeks. That's not much, honey."

Slade bent and brushed her cheek with his fingertips. "We'll think about it, baby. Really we will." He brightened. "Maybe somebody we know could buy that vacant house down the street."

"The one next to the Marriots?" She shook her head. "We couldn't do that to a friend. Dee Ivy said it's been up for sale for nearly three years, but it's priced high even for this neighborhood, and the seller refuses to come down."

"Then they aren't likely to come down for a black buyer. I will think about all this, honey, I promise, but right now I need to get dressed. I'm due downtown."

At the foot of the staircase he turned, saw tears leaking beneath her lids, and crossed the room back to her. "Is it that bad, hon?" he asked, cupping her chin in his palm and gently forcing her to look up at him.

She spoke thickly through her tears. "I thought coming to Atlanta would be like coming home, Slade, didn't you? But this isn't like any home I ever had before. Here we are where Martin Luther King, Junior, lived, a city that's had a black mayor for years, has a black former U.N. ambassador, and a city council that's almost all black—and I can go for days without ever seeing a black face!"

He knelt before her, took her hands and framed his own face with them. "Here's a black face. Will this one do?"

"You know it will, sweetheart. I do love you so!" Jaqui held him close for a moment, then pushed him away. "Go work for a living, man! Bring home some bacon—and caviar!"

He hummed as he trotted lightly up the stairs to change.

In a penthouse high above Atlanta's Peachtree Street, a tiny woman cocked her silver head and regarded an old friend across the lunch table. "All right, Rip, tell me what's bothering you." Her voice was deep and full of gravel, her tone imperious.

The big man wheeled his chair closer to the table, ducked his head to avoid her gaze. "Nothing."

"Pshaw. You're just fiddling with that pecan pie. Mildred baked it just for you. What on earth is the matter?"

His smile was lopsided and he spoke in the thick, slow voice of one recovering from a stroke. "I can't fool you, can I, Mary?"

"Not for a minute. What's the matter?"

"My daughter-in-law. She worries me."

"I saw her picture in the morning paper. She looks charming."
He struggled to speak clearly. "Like a damned sawdust pile—
smooth and soft outside, rotten underneath. Fall in, you
smother."

"Who's smothering?" Mary Beaufort asked shrewdly. "Walt?"

"No, he seems to be okay. Adores her. But she's sly, Mary. Up
to something. If I find out what it is, I'll deal with it!" He
slammed his good fist on the arm of his wheelchair. "I will, by
gum!"

That off his chest, he attacked his pecan pie with gusto. Now it
was his companion's turn to be disturbed. The doctor had
warned Rip about getting excited. Right now, she thought, he
looked downright murderous.

Some women put lemon slices in finger bowls. Dunwoody matrons put lemon slices in toilet bowls.

At ten o'clock that evening, two people shared a booth in an Underground Atlanta pub. The woman was dark, long, slender, and elegant in dark green. The man was large and perspiring heavily, and having a hard time making himself heard over a huge piano player crooning Elvis's southern medley.

"Your problem," Amory Stirling Travis shouted across the table, "is that you don't have enough to occupy your mind."

"My *problem*," thought Sheila Beaufort Travis wearily, "is what I'm going to do with you, dear Amory, for a week. Especially if you don't change your tune." What she called back, however, was "Isn't the music good? But I'm getting tired. Have you had enough culture for one evening?"

"Don't go yet! The evening is still young." A couple paused beside their table.

Sheila looked up—surprised, then pleased to see one of her favorite coworkers. "Tom Settis! What are you doing here?"

Tom grinned, his Adam's apple working. "Like you, getting culture."

"Hey," Amory exclaimed. "Has anybody ever told you you look—"

"—just like a skinny Richard Nixon? Yeah." At Sheila's unspoken invitation, Tom eased his lanky frame into the booth beside her and gestured up at the woman, who was still standing.

"Have you met my wife? Ava, this is Sheila Travis, from Hosokawa."

Ava Settis was as tall as Tom, and golden. Golden brown hair, golden skin, even golden eyes. As Amory shifted to give her at least a third of the bench, she pushed sleek wheat-colored hair off one cheek and smiled. "Glad to meet you, Sheila. Tom's always singing your praises."

Sheila indicated her companion. "This is my nephew Amory."

Amory chuckled at their evident surprise.

No one, looking at them, ever took them for aunt and nephew. Where would a woman not yet forty, with long limbs and black curly hair, get a ruddy nephew of thirty-five with jowls like a basset, hands like hams, and shoulders like a thick oak door? When Sheila had first met Amory just before her wedding eighteen years earlier, she'd wondered, too. All the Travises she'd met were uniformly tall, slender, and handsome.

Amory shared one trait with them, however: tenacity. Nothing Sheila had said all evening had persuaded him to change the subject. Now, with relief, she watched him summon a waiter. Maybe for a while he'd talk about something besides his plans for her life.

Since his surprise arrival at five-thirty, Amory had harped on one theme with several boring variations: how shocked he was to find Sheila, "after your lovely embassy home," living in an apartment; how unfortunate that she was working instead of playing tennis and lunching with friends; how lonely she must be since his uncle Tyler's death, living alone.

"I'm not alone!" Sheila had insisted in her apartment, bending to pat the Sheltie curled at her feet. "I've got Lady."

Amory had dismissed the dog with a wave of his hand. "And just look at your fridge!" He had held the door wide for her inspection. "Not a thing for a proper meal!"

That she had conceded. She had been out of town for two days, had planned to spend her Friday evening at karate class and the grocery store. She had been delighted, instead, to put on her dark green dress and Japanese pearls and let Amory buy her dinner.

Her delight, however, was short-lived. Over broiled fish he had blinked through thick lenses and restated his theme. "You spend too much time with your aunt. Miss Mary is a sweet old thing, but you need to stop running her life and live your own."

"I don't run Aunt Mary's life," Sheila had protested. "I just try to keep her from running mine. How's the banking business?"

Trying to turn Amory from his chosen subject was like moving a grand piano with one finger. "You need to get out more. Don't just sit in an apartment and brood about Uncle Tyler's death. Buy a house. Get your furniture out of storage."

"I don't need a house. I travel too much." When he started to rumble again, she'd ordered cheesecake and watched his nose twitch.

Amory's nose was long and unusually thin, and when he was enthusiastic about something—like solving Sheila's problems—it twitched magnificently. Until she met his mother and grandfather Stirling, Sheila had wondered if his nose had come from the wrong box. She had discovered, however, that a heavy face and thin nose were as much a part of the sterling Stirling heritage as a string of Mississippi banks. The Stirlings, Sheila's aunt Mary had once remarked, were "nearly as rich as they are ugly."

Poor Amory was no exception. But since he had no idea he was ugly, he carried and enjoyed himself with the joie de vivre of any attractive, wealthy bachelor. Usually Sheila enjoyed his company. He was not always this tiresome.

When she'd finished her cheesecake, she'd ordered coffee and tuned him back in. He was insisting, "Get to know some neighbors!"

She had nearly choked, swallowing a laugh. What would he say if she told him how involved she had gotten recently with her nearest neighbor—and that neighbor's three family murders?

She'd had just enough wine with dinner to make the notion tempting, but common sense won out. If she told Amory, he'd tell his dad. All she needed was Wyndham flying in from Mississippi to save his baby brother's widow from snooping around any more murders.

Not that she intended to have anything to do with homicide again—unless she murdered Amory.

It might kill him, she had mused over her second cup of black coffee, if she told him the truth about her marriage. What if she said, in a reasonable tone, "Amory, what you need to understand is that your uncle Tyler was a wonderful diplomat but a less-than-perfect husband"?

That's when she had suggested Underground Atlanta—as a fit penance for herself. How could she even think of saying such a thing? Amory had adored his uncle, that giant of Far Eastern diplomacy. He also shared with Tyler the illusion, still common to a few southern males, that women exist to flutter around their menfolk. Amory would never understand Sheila's pleasure in reading a book without waiting for a peremptory command to do something else, her joy in living simply with a few favorite things instead of catering to Tyler's obsession with appearances, her pride in being an executive with a multinational corporation instead of arranging flowers and seating for Tyler's latest important dinner party. If sometimes in the privacy of her own home she wept for loneliness, she still preferred her present situation to that she had had married to Tyler. She would not, however, tell that to Amory—unless he got even more obnoxious.

Amory had called for the dinner check and waved away any notions Sheila might have had about paying. When the waiter had borne away the credit card, he had leaned confidingly over the table, face pink with earnestness. "You haven't said . . . I mean, are you all right, Sheila? Do you, ah, need anything?" She had appreciated what he was trying to say. It was probably the closest a banker could come to giving money away.

Tempted once again, she had almost replied: I could use a good man, Amory—mature but not dull, intelligent, who makes me laugh. She had pushed that thought down and told him what he wanted to hear. "I'm fine. Tyler left me well provided for." To forestall more questions, she added firmly, "I work for the same reason you do: because I want to."

Now, over the piano player's music, Tom Settis was trying to explain to Amory exactly what Sheila did, and why it was so important to Hosokawa International to have a person on board who was completely bicultural. Amory was making appropriate social noises, but Sheila had no illusions that her nephew was really impressed. She might be flying to Japan in sixteen days to oversee the visit of ten U.S. senators to Hosokawa's major factories in Japan. She might be participating in top-level trade negotiations to make certain no one got insulted in either language. Amory had already expressed his opinion earlier, in the car: "Dammit, Sheila, you've got better things to do! Let them get themselves another girl."

Sheila was remembering that remark, and thinking up things she wished she'd said, when another couple paused by their table and greeted Tom and Ava warmly. "Mac and Rilla Marriot," was Tom's casual introduction. "Friends of ours from Dunwoody."

When the Marriots dragged up chairs to fill the narrow aisle and Tom suggested they all take a nearby vacant table for six, Sheila agreed amiably, grateful that someone else was giving Amory such a good time.

She could just hear him when he got home. "Atlanta's not the least bit stuck up. Folks are just as friendly there as they are here in Tupelo."

These new people, however, were unusually friendly for Atlanta. Mac's chair was pulled too close to her own, and Rilla was prattling to Amory as though she'd just found a long-lost cousin. Were they married, Sheila wondered, or twins? They were identically petite, with short curly yellow hair, tanned faces lightly wrinkled, and wide sky-blue eyes. Both wore white silk pants, a yellow silk shirt, and sandals. Both were hung with enough gold chains to feed a family for several months. One of few visible differences between them was that she wore lipstick. As they raised their glasses in a toast, broad gold wedding bands gleamed in the light from the bar.

Amory hitched up his bulk to give Rilla an inch more room. "You all seem to know everybody!" He added to Sheila, "They've talked to almost everyone in the place. Are you the owners?"

"Wish we were. We just come in here a lot." Mac waved toward a passing waiter, who hurried to his side. When he'd ordered refills all around, he asked the predictable southern question. "You folks from around here?"

Tom explained Sheila and Amory, then added, "Mac and Rilla live around the corner and down the street from us."

Rilla looked at her watch. "Gracious! And we're supposed to be having a little get-together at our house, starting soon! We're having such a good time, I almost forgot. It's partly business, but mostly just a few friends dropping by for a bite. Won't you come, too—all of you?" She gave Amory and Sheila a special smile to let them know they were included. "We'd love to have you."

Tom and Ava enthusiastically accepted. What Sheila would love would be to fall into her own bed for twelve straight hours and forget her latest business trip, Amory's lectures, and the smell of stale smoke, but she was beginning to feel very hungry. As she weighed facing Amory and an empty refrigerator at her own place versus losing Amory in a crowd and eating the bounty of a Dunwoody party, she decided the latter had definite advantages.

"Sure," she said with what she hoped was a bright smile. "Okay with you, Amory?"

Amory was charmed. Delightful new friends and a spontaneous midnight party didn't often come his way on the same day.

Ava went to the ladies' room while Amory and Tom took care of the tab and the Marriots made their way to the door. Alone at the table, Sheila noticed that on his way out, Mac stopped by several tables, passing out business cards. "Hope to see you later." "Don't forget to come, now." "We'll be seeing you there. Just give my card to Norris, who'll open the door."

Sheila wondered what Mac's business might be, and hoped they had enough food for the city of Atlanta.

After all he'd had to drink, Sheila insisted that Amory let her drive her own Maxima, pointing out that she knew Atlanta better than he did. She didn't tell him that Dunwoody was as foreign to her as Reno. She could follow the taillights of Tom's Lexus. In his current state, Amory could scarcely follow his own belt buckle.

"How far is it?" he asked as they pulled out of the parking lot.

"Far," Sheila told him. She flicked on the radio. Joy! Chopin études ought to lull him into silence for a while. "Rest," she ordered. His head was already leaning against the window, and a light snore rippled his lips.

The subdivision, near the Dunwoody Country Club, seemed a forest, with streets rolling up and down hills and around so many curves that Sheila hoped Tom would lead her out when the party was over.

Running Ridge Road was only one block long, but even it curved downhill. There were three houses on one side and two houses and a wooded gulley on the other. The Marriots' house was at the bottom of the cul-de-sac. Expensive cars lined the street, and clusters of people were already making their way down the walk as Mac's Continental stopped in the drive and the driver, a stocky short man, helped Rilla out. Sheila took Tom's wave of advice and parked up the hill, in front of a big Tudor-style home. She nudged her nephew gently. "Come on, Amory, we're here."

Tom parked just ahead, and together the four of them made their way downhill. The streetlights were far apart, but in their glow Sheila felt the hovering presence of tall trees and saw manicured, landscaped lawns surrounding large, gracious homes. Like three of its five neighbors, the Marriots' house was an enormous neocolonial with shutters and a fanlight over the door.

"That house next to Mac's has been for sale for over two years," Tom murmured at her elbow. Of modern design, the cedar and stone house was almost hidden behind a thick stand of trees. A sign in front was a blur of whiteness in the dark.

At the Marriots' they were greeted by a towering man who looked like a gorilla in a tux. "This is a private party," he announced.

Tom clapped his muscular arm. "They are with me, Norris. This is Amory Travis and Sheila Travis."

Norris peered down at them, wiggling brows like brown fuzzy caterpillars. Mac appeared behind him and welcomed them genially, putting a hand at Sheila's back to guide her into the living room. She could hardly hear him over the din of a small jazz band. "You folks make yourselves at home. Bar's in the den and food's in the dining room." He turned to beam at another couple and exclaim, "You old devil, I *heard* you were back in town!"

The Marriots' "few friends" turned out to be a horde of people shouting to make themselves heard over the music and consuming great quantities of food. Sheila need not have worried. There seemed to be no end to caviar tucked into tiny boiled new potatoes, chutney cheeseballs on crackers, shrimp mousse, marinated mushrooms, watermelon and honeydew with cherry-honey cream, crab claws, shrimp dip, and delicacies she could not even begin to name. Some guests were beginning to concoct sandwiches of roast beef or ham carved by the same man who had driven Mac's Continental. He now wore a white jacket that bulged over his wide shoulders.

Amory ignored the food and headed for the bar, where he

found bourbon and a Suwannee classmate. Sheila left them deep in reminiscences and accompanied Ava to the buffet.

When Ava drifted off to greet other friends, Sheila remained, trying not to appear like she was eating all the crab claws and shrimp and wondering how Miss Manners would eat a caviar-stuffed new potato and a slice of beef with a toothpick. Suddenly Mac appeared and took the knife from the stocky carver. "One of our guests needs assistance, Richard," he said softly.

"Right." Richard cracked his knuckles as he went.

Mac carved in his absence. Sheila noticed that while he laughed and talked like a man who had drunk too much, his carving hand was perfectly steady. He had ordered several drinks after joining their table in Underground Atlanta, but had he ever finished any of them? She had not noticed.

In a few minutes Richard returned, gave Mac a nod, and took the knife without a word. Mac went back to his guests.

Rilla drifted by with a very thin woman in red on her arm. "You simply must see my roses," Sheila heard her say.

A beautiful light brown woman in a striking gold and red jump-suit helped herself to crab claws. "Aren't they delicious?" Sheila asked, helping herself to another. As long as she could eat, she might not fall asleep.

"Very. Let's eat them all! You live around here?"

Soon they were chatting lightly but happily as two women do at a party when they know no one else and find a kindred spirit. A big ebony man came from the living room with purpose in his eye. "Honey, Paula Divesty wants to talk to you about maybe donating some clothes to the battered women's shelter. Can you spare her a minute?"

A moue of reluctance twisted the other's bright mouth, but she turned to go with him. "I'll be back," she promised Sheila. "Don't eat all the crab claws. By the way, my name is Jaqui Robinson."

"Like the baseball player?"

"Yeah. Except I spell mine J-a-q-u-i and *he's* the baseball player." She poked one thumb talon into her husband's arm.

With a practiced smile he stuck out his hand. "Slade Robinson. Glad to meet you."

Sheila gave him a smile of apology. "I'm glad to meet *you*. Do you play for the—" She stopped, appalled. Her mind was totally blank! What *was* the Atlanta team called?

His chuckle was deep. "I am delighted to meet somebody who doesn't know a thing about baseball. It's a treat."

She actually loved baseball, she just hadn't been to a game since Tyler's death. Maybe she'd get Amory to take her to a Braves game—that was it! the Braves!—next week. But for now, having been identified as "the wife of Tyler Travis" for years, she understood Slade's pleasure—and wouldn't spoil it.

"I'm Sheila Travis," she said, returning Slade's shake.

"Can that be Sheila *Beaufort* Travis? It is!" A man quickly crossed the room, holding his glasses by the left side as if trying to get a better look. She knew that habit—and the shy, insecure person who went with it.

"Walter Delacourt!" She swallowed a last bite of crab, wiped her fingers with a napkin, and gave him both her hands with delight. "Have I seen you since high school? How'd you know my married name?"

She scarcely noticed when the Robinsons drifted away. She was trying to bridge two decades since she and Walt had been close friends. He didn't seem quite as tall as he used to when he first reached six two. Perhaps he had added a few ounces to that beanpole frame. But his wrists still seemed about to grow out of his jacket and he still mumbled slightly when he talked.

His eyes shone with pleasure behind his glasses. "I've kept up with you through Dad. He and your aunt Mary have stayed good buddies. She's really something, isn't she?"

"She is *something*," Sheila agreed, "but exactly *what* depends on how hard she's trying at any given moment to run my life. I see you're still crazy about birds." His tie tack was a small silver mockingbird.

He nodded. "Just got back from birding at the Grand Canyon. It was fantastic!" He sobered a little. "I don't get away much, though, since Dad had his stroke."

"How is your dad? I haven't seen him lately."

Walt chuckled—his best feature and once a very familiar sound. "The same old Rip. He's in a wheelchair, though, and doesn't come down to the office much. I pretty much run things now."

It was hard to imagine. Walter Winwood Delacourt had always looked and talked far more like a banker than poor Amory ever would, and had probably voted Republican long before it became fashionable. No one would suspect by looking at Walter that his family fortune came from the Winsome brassiere factory in southeast Atlanta. He worked hard in high school to conceal the fact. Did he ever summon up courage nowadays to mention his product in public?

Not so his father, Rippen Delacourt. "I'm in the meat-packing business," he would tell strangers, then guffaw heartily at their chagrin when they discovered what his business really was. Once, after too many mint juleps at a Derby Day party, Rip had joked about being in a "hands-on" business. Walt's face had burned all evening.

But it was beaming now, and he still lightly held her hands, as if to clutch this special moment. Sheila and Walt had never been romantically involved, but had often attended dances and parties together. Probably, she thought with a wry grin, because we were both so tall and skinny.

"Weren't we gawky stringbeans in those days?" he asked, echoing her thoughts. "But you've gotten beautiful! I haven't changed much." A deprecating wave dismissed his long body, then he peered about the crowded rooms. "I want you to meet my wife, Yvonne." He said her name almost reverently. "Wait right here. I'll get her."

While he was gone, Sheila tried to picture what the woman would look like: plain, probably tall, with a debutante stoop and impeccable southern antecedents. Her hair might be drab, but it would be beautifully styled, her face expensively creamed and painted. She'd wear a black sheath, black heels, and one string of perfect pearls. She would extend one bony hand and drawl through her nose. . . .

"I am so glad to meet you. I do hope we are going to be friends."

The gentle voice dripped magnolias and honeysuckle, and Sheila took a step back in surprise. This was Walt's wife? This *child?*

Years before, Sheila had been given a storybook doll in a box. It, too, had dark hair floating around a heart-shaped face, a perfect nose, brows arched above deep violet eyes, and long black lashes. Although Yvonne's pink dress was not ankle-length with yards of organdy ruffles falling in tiers, it certainly gave that effect, and she wore a perfume that evoked gardenias after rain. Sheila half expected to see her dangling a wide-brimmed hat from one hand. Instead, the hand was slipped confidingly through the crook of Sheila's arm, linking them. "I do hope we will be friends," Yvonne Delacourt repeated.

"I hope so, too," Sheila murmured automatically, but she was puzzled. How on earth had shy, plain Walt landed such a beauty? And when? Yvonne could scarcely be thirty, and looked younger.

"We were married last year," he said with pride. Clearly the man was still besotted. No wonder! Almost every man at the party hovered hungrily in the archway, waiting for Yvonne to conclude her conversation and return to charm them.

All except two. Across the room Sheila saw a man with thick red hair watching Yvonne intently. His eyes were narrowed and his jaw clenched. Sheila was glad he wasn't fixing that smoldering gaze on her. If Yvonne noticed him, however, she gave no sign.

Near the bar, a rangy dark man in a black suit was also watching Yvonne. He was lean and handsome, and his gaze held none of the intensity of the red-haired man's, but it reminded Sheila of her father's expression watching sumo wrestlers on television.

"Do you like it, Daddy?" she had asked once as a child, feeling a bit queasy and wishing he would change the channel before those two gargantuan men crushed each other.

"No," he'd replied, "but I can't help admiring their skill."

The man across the room wore that same look of reluctant admiration. When his eyes met Sheila's, he swiped a dark curl from his forehead, and one corner of his mouth twitched, as if he were about to smile. Just then Rilla Marriot entered the living room with a short man on her arm. To Sheila's surprise, the dark man turned abruptly and strolled toward the hall.

"You having fun?" Rilla asked as she passed Sheila and the Delacourts. Without waiting for a reply, she murmured, "I am off to show Glen my roses."

"You simply must see those roses sometime," Yvonne told Sheila as Rilla moved on, "but you'll have to be very good. Rilla shows them only by special invitation." Her laugh rippled after her hostess. Rilla must have heard her, but did not reply.

Sheila was getting thirsty from all the crab legs she'd eaten. She was about to suggest that they move toward the bar, when a man with a flushed face hailed Walt from a circle of cronies. "Hey, Walt! Come over here and tell these jokers that I really did beat you on the back nine last Monday. They don't believe I birdied that last hole. Come tell 'em!"

Walt hesitated. His wife gave him a little push. "Go on. I'll introduce Sheila around." Walt joined his friends, and Yvonne guided Sheila gently by the elbow, like a tugboat steering a liner.

At Sheila's request they went first to the bar. Then Yvonne led the way to where Jaqui Robinson was talking with another woman. The stranger was as tall as Sheila, but far more austere. Her black skirt reached almost to the floor, her white blouse had a high neck and long sleeves. A gold locket was her only ornament. In a roomful of southern women painted and dressed like butterflies, her olive skin was free of cosmetics. Her hair was thick, and a rich chestnut, but it was pulled to the nape of her neck and tied with a black bow as if she couldn't be bothered with it. She looked like a woman who insisted on and valued her privacy. But she could not completely control her large brown eyes. They would always betray what she was thinking, Sheila decided.

They smoldered now as Yvonne drawled, "Paula, Jaqui, this is Sheila, a friend of Walt's from high school. They went to the prom together!" Sheila felt like a prize exhibit at some bizarre women's fair. Yvonne's tone proclaimed, "This is the girl who didn't get my husband!"

"Glad to meet you." Paula spoke in a flat, uninterested voice. If that was glad, how did she look and sound when she was not?

"Sheila and I met over a mutual obsession." Jaqui gave her new friend a conspiratorial wink. "Say, Yvonne, could Forbes come play with Cornelius Monday? I'll be home all afternoon."

"Sure. I'll tell day care to bring him home at two-thirty." For Sheila's benefit, Yvonne added, "Jaqui and I both have four-year-old sons. They are darling together! Paula doesn't have a little boy at home, so she volunteers a lot. She works somewhere almost every day. She's the little red rooster of our neighborhood!"

It was a silly gender error, scarcely worth correcting, but it made Paula Divesty choke on her drink. By the time they had patted her on the back and made certain she was all right, it no longer mattered.

Making no attempt to introduce Sheila to any of her male admirers, Yvonne towed her toward a petite blond woman sitting alone in a flowered chair. "Dee? I've got somebody I want you to meet. Sheila, this is Dee Ivy."

Dee had an almost-empty glass in her hand, and from the way her head lolled against the chair, Sheila knew this was not her first vodka. A much-smeared plate beside her indicated she had also made several forays on the Marriots' delicious buffet. She rolled her eyes in Yvonne's direction, then deliberately turned her head away.

"Dee?" Yvonne touched her shoulder lightly. "Be sweet."

The woman shrugged her off with a snarl. "Leave me alone, Yvonne! I've had enough of you for one day."

Yvonne favored her with a gentle, forgiving smile. "I just want you to meet a friend of Walt's, Sheila Travis. I think you'll like Sheila. She's alone, too. Her husband was that wonderful diplomat in Japan who was killed climbing Mount Fuji a couple of years ago. Now she's come back to Atlanta to work, and she hasn't bought a house yet. She might be looking for a decorator sometime soon."

Even while making proper noises to Dee, Sheila was considering Yvonne in silent amazement. How had she known that much about someone she had never had reason to meet?

"Glad to meet you." Dee spoke brusquely and thrust out a damp hand. "If you want a decorator, Yvonne knows how to get me." She buried her nose in her drink, staring pensively at a bank of potted hydrangeas in the empty fireplace. Then she raised her head and glared at Yvonne. "I know how to get you, too."

"There you are, Sheila!"

Amory loomed out of the crowd like a genial giant. "I've been looking all over for you!"

It couldn't be true. She hadn't traveled twenty feet since he left her. Then she caught his expression and knew why she was suddenly so dear to his heart.

"Amory Travis, may I present Yvonne Delacourt, the *wife* of an old *friend* of mine." Given how much bourbon Amory had downed, she felt her nephew needed all the emphasis on certain words she could give. "And this is—"

"He doesn't want to meet me." Dee turned her back and slid deeper into her chair.

"Of course I do!" Amory promptly sank into the opposite chair, nose twitching violently. Sheila turned to hide her smile. Poor Dee! Amory never passed up an argument. Dee had lit his fuse, so she'd be stuck with him for quite a while. This time it was Sheila who exerted pressure to move Yvonne away.

Across the room, the red-haired man had joined Jaqui and Paula. From the way he hovered at Paula's elbow and speared an olive from her plate without a word, Sheila deduced they were married.

Yvonne headed straight for him. "Hello, Alex. I didn't know you were here. I want you to meet Walt's friend, Sheila Travis."

He mumbled a greeting, but was so obviously uninterested that Sheila again pressed Yvonne's arm to move on.

Before she poured Amory into her car for the long drive home, Sheila remembered to ask Walt how his wife knew so much of her own history.

"Vonnie collects people," he said proudly, "and she loves to know things about them. Me, for instance. Before we got married, she insisted on looking at all my old school annuals. She read old letters I had saved, went through our family albums, anything at all to get to know me better. When she found our old prom picture, she asked about you. I told her a little, then when Dad mentioned you one day, she asked more. She even knew you had moved to Atlanta. Read it in the paper or something. I've been meaning to call you, but . . ."

Sheila waved away his apology. "We all get too busy to do the things we mean to. By the way, do I understand you're a stepfather now?" It was hard to picture.

Walt shrugged. "Not a very good one yet, but I'm learning." He bent his head so close to hers, she could smell his most recent scotch. "I tell you, Sheila, Yvonne is the most loving woman I have ever known. I'd have married her if she'd had *twenty* kids! I don't know how I got so damn lucky."

Sheila did not know, either.

She did know, however, why she agreed at the door to let Yvonne Delacourt show her the vacant house next door on the following Monday after work.

She had no intention of moving to Dunwoody, especially into a five-bedroom contemporary house. But she had seen Paula, Dee, the redheaded man, and the strange man with that one rebellious curl following Yvonne all evening with eyes that ranged from cautious to downright unfriendly. For Walt's sake, she wanted to try to find out why.

When you call 911 in Dunwoody, who answers? The BMW repairman.

MONDAY

At half past six Monday morning, Nan Jones Quentin parked her brown Toyota near one corner of Running Ridge Road, pushed back the driver's seat, rolled down both front windows, and prepared herself for a long, hot siege. She had enough pens, paper, iced tea, and fruit to last all morning. She also had a Georgia State notebook and research data form from a friend in the Sociology Department, in case someone asked what she was doing.

What she was really doing was beginning research for her first feature article, on Braves pitcher Slade Robinson. Normally Nan was a highly competent surgical nurse at Grady Memorial Hospital, but she dreamed of becoming a writer. Equipped with one journalism class from Georgia State and the soaring optimism of a budding writer, she hoped to place her article in a not-too-distant issue of *People.* She was shy, however, about saying she was a writer yet. She was also hazy about what exactly she needed to know before approaching her chosen subject for an interview. Her first step, she had decided, was to watch his street one morning to get a feel for what she termed its "ambience." Then she'd try to get up her courage to call Slade.

She could, she quickly decided, sum up the ambience in one word: rich. The lots were large. Some were prim with well-trimmed hedges, others a riot of flowers, but any of them could have appeared on the cover of *Southern Living.* Having recently bought impatiens for a window box, Nan was awed at what it must cost each spring to plant these lawns with crotons, hibiscus, begonias, and other plants too delicate to survive even Atlanta's short winter.

It was hard to see all the houses well from her parking spot, for three were downhill and one was hidden behind trees around a curve. Slade's was on the nearest corner. That was all that mattered. She could tell, however, that four, like his, were stately brick homes with shutters and small stoops, while his next-door neighbors' house had a pointed roof, dark brown trim, a curving stone walk, and a small turret that made it look like a modest castle.

She drew a quick sketch map, numbered the houses, and poured a plastic cup half full of tea. She was going to need it worse later when the air grew thick and hot. She could not afford to run her air conditioner all day.

In the next six hours Nan had little success in learning anything about Slade Robinson. He left in a maroon Jaguar at seven forty-five and never returned. He did, however, wave at Nan as he passed, which she hoped augured well for a future interview.

Otherwise, her morning was a procession of expensive cars carrying well-dressed people to work, school, and wherever the women went all day. Maids and yard men arrived and went about their work. A phone crew labored on lines for an hour. A lone male jogger trotted up and down the hill three times, slumped to the curb, and stared at house three for quite a while. He got a drink from the maid sweeping the walk of the big brick house at the bottom of the cul-de-sac. Finally he jogged away.

No matter how dull the events, Nan recorded them. Not only was it good practice in descriptive writing, it was habit. As a nurse, she had been taught to take precise notes. She knew how easy it was to forget minute details unless they were logged in as they occurred.

She had no idea at the time how valuable those notes would become.

She noted, for instance, when a man with red hair emerged from house two, rang the bell of house three, then pounded on the door. Nobody answered. He pounded again but finally went back to his own house, changed clothes, and went to work in a gleaming black BMW.

About an hour later Nan was surprised to see a woman leave house three. Why had she not answered earlier? As she passed in a cream Mercedes, Nan admired her hair. It was a soft dusty black, looked naturally curly. Nan's own was between red and blond, and frizzed when she had it permed. During the morning she found herself fantasizing about that woman and the leisured life she must lead. When the woman returned late in the morning, Nan flushed and ducked as if she had truly been invading her privacy.

At nine-thirty a large black man arrived in a small gray truck and parked in the Robinsons' drive. He lugged out a power mower, went in through the gate, and started to mow the backyard. The fence was low enough for her to catch glimpses of his red cap in various parts of the yard. When he came to mow the front lawn, Nan got out and offered him some iced tea in a spare cup she'd brought. He accepted, but it was tea wasted. He was not their regular yard man, and did not know Slade.

It was well past noon when a man she'd seen leaving house three early in the day with a small boy returned home alone. His dark blue Buick Riviera was the only American car Nan had seen. By the time he hurried away sometime later, everyone on the street had gone somewhere except the maid on the cul-de-sac. Nan was ready to leave, too. She was hot, hungry, and had more important things to do. She had never realized research could be so tedious. Besides, Slade Robinson might not come back until after that night's game against Los Angeles.

Dunwoody, she decided, starting her engine, was not half as exciting as downtown Atlanta. As she headed down the street, she wondered again what these women did with their lives.

At quarter to three, a beige preschool van delivered a small boy to his home on Running Ridge Road. Four-year-old Forbes was excited, for he'd been brought home early to spend the afternoon with Cornelius Robinson, and Cornelius's daddy was a *real* baseball player. He might pitch Corny and Forbes a few balls! Forbes had gotten a good bit of mileage out of that possibility all morning among his cronies. Now he couldn't wait to get to Corny's. Trailing his small red backpack, he jabbed the doorbell with an impatient finger. "Mama! I'm home!"

She didn't come to the door.

Forbes jabbed the bell again, then shoved the door with his shoulder. It swung open. Maybe she was on the phone and had left it open for him.

Dropping his backpack in the hall, he trotted toward the kitchen. "Mama? I'm home. It's me, Mama!"

Still no answer.

Forbes took two cookies from the jar and got a box of grape drink from the fridge, then made a circuit of the downstairs, careful not to spill crumbs. No Mama. She might be napping. Should he waken her, or go straight to Corny's? Which would make her madder?

He tiptoed up the stairs and peeped into her bedroom. The bedspread was smooth, the room smelled of lemons. The ladies had come to clean. Maybe Mama had to show somebody a house. That happened sometimes, but he'd never been left alone before.

Puzzled, he wrinkled his nose. Somebody had used an upstairs potty and not sprayed. He hoped Mama wouldn't blame him.

In his own room he sat on the floor, forced the straw into his grape drink, and thirstily sucked. Then he set down the drink to collect his case of Micromachines. As he headed for Corny's, he reassured himself that Mama would see his backpack in the hall. She'd know where he was.

Jaqui was surprised to see Forbes arrive alone, but chided herself for a worrywart mother. After all, the boys were almost five, and this was a quiet, dead-end street. She sent them into Cornelius's room to play and switched on a soap opera.

An hour later Forbes stopped his Micromachine in the middle of a "zoom!" and clapped one small hand to his cheek. He had just remembered something terrible: he'd left the box of juice on his white bedroom rug! What if it spilled? Mama would be furious!

"Corny, I gotta go back home. I forgot sumpin'."

"I'll go wit' you." Corny stuck two tiny cars into a pocket and led the way downstairs. "We're goin' out for a while," he called to his mother.

"Don't go in the middle of the street," she answered.

"She always says that," Corny told his friend in disgust.

Forbes ran up the steps to his own front door and pushed. This time the door didn't budge. "I musta closed it too good," he called down to Corny, waiting on the sidewalk below.

"Ring the bell," Corny suggested.

Forbes considered. If his mother was home, had she found the grape juice? He'd know as soon as he saw her. If she hadn't, he could tell her he was going up to get another toy, then pour the juice down his toilet. If she had, she wouldn't yell as loud if Corny was there, and she certainly wouldn't hit him. She didn't let anybody—even Walt—see her do that.

He pushed the bell with all his might.

But though he rang and rang, nobody came. At last he turned, small shoulders sagging with defeat. "I'll have to wait till she comes to get me. I just hope she doesn't find it."

"Find what?" Corny wasn't really paying attention. He was trying to hop on one leg all the way down Forbes's walk. Since the walk sloped, it was pretty hard to do without falling.

"I left a box of juice on my rug. Grape," he added as one doomed. "If Mama finds it, or somebody kicks it, I'm gonna get killed!"

Corny finished his hop and came back sweaty with success.

"Can't nobody kick it until you get home and go to your room. Mamas don't kick grape juice on rugs."

"Walt might," Forbes said darkly. "He doesn't always look where he's going."

Corny considered the problem. "Want to pray about it?"

"Pray about grape juice?" Forbes's voice oozed scorn.

"My grandpa's a preacher, 'n' he says you oughta pray about *ever'thing.*" Corny folded his hands and bowed his head. "Dear God, please don't let Forbes get in trouble about that grape juice. He didn't mean to do it, he just forgot. Amen. Oh—nor don't let Walt kick it, neither. Amen again. There," he assured Forbes.

As the two little boys trudged uphill to Cornelius's house, Corny was light as a feather. He knew what God could do. Forbes, less experienced in prayer, wasn't so sure.

At half past five Slade Robinson told his wife, "I'm heading down now. You coming to the game?"

Worry puckered Jaqui's forehead. "I hope so, but I don't know what to do about Forbes. Yvonne usually picks him up by five, but she hasn't come or called."

"Call her."

"I tried, but nobody answered."

Slade, tucking in his shirt, suggested absently, "Maybe she had to show a house and is running late." He leaned down to give her a kiss, stayed until she pushed him away.

"Go! We'll come if we can. I'll try her again in a minute."

She didn't have to. As she finished speaking, the neighborhood was rent by roars of pain.

"Yvonne! My God, *Yvonne!*"

Jaqui and Slade dashed to their front door just as Alex erupted from his. Almost immediately Rilla and her maid appeared at the Marriots' door, and an instant later the Ivy girls dashed down their steps and huddled together on their lawn. Everyone gaped at Walter Winwood Delacourt.

He lurched down the steps of his house, arms waving like those of a giant marionette. His glasses dangled from one ear. His hair stood on end. His eyes rolled in their sockets, and he alternately clutched his head and flung his arms above his head. His white shirt was stained and spotted, his tie was askew. He staggered onto his lawn and peered helplessly up and down the street, bellowing in pain and rage. "Yvonne! God help me! *Yvonne!*"

Slade was farther away, but more used to running than Alex and he didn't have a bum knee. They reached Walt at the same time.

"Steady, man." Slade caught the distraught husband by one arm and gave him a shake. "Steady. What's going on?"

Walt stared in horror from one to the other. His mouth worked soundlessly for a moment, then he cried, "Yvonne! She's dead! Oh, my God!" He fell to his knees in a day-lily bed, buried his head in his arms, and sobbed.

At her own door, Jaqui backed inside, turned the television volume up, and headed for Cornelius's room. "Forbes, you get to stay for dinner and maybe spend the night!" she called cheerfully. "Spaghetti suit you?"

With one last look at the two boys, she gently closed the bedroom door and thanked God that Cornelius slept in the back corner of the house. Maybe the boys would not notice what was going on down the street.

Meanwhile, Slade started for the Delacourts' door, but Alex held him back. "You can't go in there! This is a matter for the police!"

An hour later, Sheila Travis braked her Maxima and peered, puzzled, at a crowd milling at the corner of Running Ridge

Road. "What on earth is going on?" she asked herself aloud.

"Pull over here and park. I'll find out." Amory was already opening his door. "I see Mac Marriot over there. I'll ask him."

Sheila, too, had glimpsed Mac's blond head in the crowd clustered around a tall, uniformed officer. A blue DeKalb County police cruiser blocked the street's entrance, lights flashing.

Sheila was ashamed to feel thankful as well as curious. All day she had felt like kicking herself for agreeing to view a house she had no intention of buying—and for mentioning that fact to Amory. Of course he'd insisted on coming along. "As long as you know from the first that I am not interested," she had repeated as he climbed into the car.

"So you say," he'd rumbled, "but you're a woman. If you change your mind, I want to make sure the structure is sound."

Sheila had considered kicking him, too.

All the way over she had sworn under her breath. How could she have forgotten what Mount Vernon Road was like at rush hour? The world's longest parking lot. Now, whatever was going on, it had one silver lining. If she could somehow get a message to Yvonne, she and Amory could go out for a leisurely dinner and celebrate *not* having to view the house.

She let her head fall back on the headrest and closed her eyes until Amory returned. "I didn't get to Mac," he said, lowering himself into the seat, "but we may as well leave. We can't get in there tonight. Some woman's been killed."

Sheila felt as if she'd just jumped out of a plane without a parachute. She'd met the women who lived on that street the previous Friday night. She knew only one who had gotten murderous looks. "Who?"

Amory shook his head and turned to peer over the back of the seat. "Nobody seems to know. You can pull out after this next car."

Instead, Sheila cut the motor. "I think I'll go see if that policeman can get a message to Yvonne. I wouldn't want her waiting for us. I'll be right back." She headed for the crowd at an awkward lope.

Only years of experience at embassy functions made it possible for Sheila to elbow her way through the crowd. The nearer she got to the police tape, the closer people pressed together, leaning slightly forward to peer down the hill. At last she could see over the sleek dark hair of a short woman in front. Her stomach tensed. While several officers seemed to be examining various lawns, it was the Delacourt house that had police cars in front and a news crew from WSB-TV scuttling about on the Bermuda grass.

As Sheila froze, taking it in, a man ran down the Delacourts' front steps to a police van, shaking off reporters as a child shakes off water at the beach. He took a small black case from the van and hurried back inside.

Sheila resolutely pushed through the front row of the crowd and found Mac Marriot trying to attract the attention of a tall police officer—who seemed equally determined to ignore him.

She touched Mac's shoulder. "Mac? I met you Friday night—"

His blue eyes lit up and he stuck out a hand. "Good to see you again!" She could have been his best friend—except he hadn't called her by name. "Isn't this awful?" He must be just back from a run, she thought. His white shirt and shorts were damp and his hair curled above beads of sweat. Had he chosen blue earphones for his Walkman to match his eyes? And why did those eyes watch the officer so warily?

"What's going on?" Sheila asked. "I had an appointment with Yvonne, and—"

He put a consoling hand on her arm. "Yvonne's dead, honey." His light, husky voice vibrated with concern, so his question surprised her. "What was your appointment about?"

"We were going to view the house next to yours." It was so

trivial, she hated to mention it. What mattered at this point was
Walt. Where was he? Was someone with him?

Mac, however, was diverted. "You don't want that house. It's
poorly built, overpriced, the basement leaks—"

She cut him off. "I know I don't. What happened to Yvonne?"

"I don't know. I was out for a run, and when I got back that"—
he paused, changed whatever he'd been about to say to—"officer
refused to let me past the corner. Says the Ivy girls saw a
strange man jogging around here this afternoon, so they're looking for clues." He swore vehemently. "What clues do they hope
to find in people's front yards, for heaven's sake?" Suddenly his
anger evaporated into a sunny smile. "Hey! Maybe if you'll
vouch for me, I can get home, and come back to fill you in."

Before she could object, he'd tugged her by the arm and presented her to the handsome specimen of DeKalb's finest. The
officer listened impassively to Sheila's assurance that Mac did
indeed live in the house at the end of the cul-de-sac, then shook
his head. "Nobody goes in or out at present. Sorry."

"Look, man," Mac jogged in place, "do you know what happens
to a man's bladder when he runs five miles? Let me get to my
house, or take the consequences."

The officer looked around—for a good bush? Finally he looked
over his shoulder at the house Mac was pointing to. "Okay," he
said dubiously. "I guess it's okay. But walk in the middle of the
street, and don't try to come back out."

"No problem, Officer." Mac jogged inside, turned, and jogged
back. "Any message for Walt if I see him?" he asked Sheila.

"Just tell him—" She stopped. The officer had taken out his
pad and pencil. "Never mind."

"You knew the deceased?" The officer shoved back his hat.

Before Sheila could reply, Amory appeared and thrust a business card toward him. "I am related to this woman, Officer, and I
assure you she knows nothing about this situation. We were
merely passing by—"

"Oh, Amory!" she snapped in exasperation.

The policeman looked from Sheila to her companion with increasing curiosity. "Exactly what was your connection with the deceased, ma'am?"

"None," Amory said just as Sheila said, "She was a realtor. She was going to show me a house tonight. It's down the hill behind some trees."

The officer's pencil was poised. "May I have your names and addresses, please?"

"Officer, I assure you—" Amory began.

Sheila shushed him. The policeman was only making up for not getting a more exciting post nearer the crime scene. She fumbled in her purse for her driver's license.

Five minutes later, when he had taken down what he needed, the officer left them to greet the Channel 5 news team and usher them around the cruiser. Amory took that opportunity to melt farther back into the crowd, pulling Sheila with him. "Let's go," he growled.

"Not yet." Sheila was waiting for the officer to return. "I want to find out if Walt needs anything. I can't just leave him."

"Of course you can!" Amory's plump face was flushed with irritation. "You hadn't seen the man for years until Friday night. He's not going to expect you to do anything for him now."

Amory was right, of course. Walt would not expect anything from her. He wouldn't even care that she was there. But years earlier her maternal grandmother had explained why she bothered with a cranky neighbor. "Some people are given to us, Sheila. We may not know why, and they may be terribly inconvenient, but they are our responsibility. We have to do the best we can by them."

Sheila felt like that now. Friday Walt had been given to her. She had no idea why, but she had to do the best she could by him.

"Come on!" Amory interrupted her thoughts by jerking her

arm hard. Caught unawares, she lurched forward and stumbled, causing a nearby man to step forward and demand, "Do you need help?"

Sheila turned and saw her own reflection in mirrored sunglasses. Behind them, she was pretty sure, was the dark-haired man she'd seen watching Yvonne at the party. Tonight his curl fell over a yellow sweatband. He wore red running shorts, and a dazzling white sleeveless shirt that showed off tanned, muscular arms. This close, she could smell clean sweat and a spicy aftershave—and see that he wasn't as handsome as she had thought. His nose was a bit long, his chin unexpectedly square.

"Do you need help?" he repeated, looking from her to Amory.

Amory let go of Sheila's arm and took one step back.

Sheila shook her head. "No, I'm fine. My *nephew* is eager to go. I will leave," she told Amory firmly, "as soon as I know Walt is okay."

Amory subsided, but stayed close to her right side, one hand infuriatingly near her elbow. The other man moved to her left side. "What's happened here?" he muttered.

"I don't really know. A woman has been killed, we heard."

He looked around, then asked so softly she almost didn't hear him, "Know who she was?"

"A woman named Yvonne Delacourt, I think."

She felt rather than saw him tense, heard urgency behind his terse "How?"

"I don't know. Did you know her?"

"I did her yard. Guess I'll have to find another job." Abruptly he turned and melted into the growing crowd. Sheila watched him go, bemused. Did all Dunwoody yard men wear Rockport running shoes and a Rolex watch?

Rumors swirled through the crowd, which still peered in horror down the placid-looking street.

". . . stabbed five times!"

"I heard twelve!"

". . . raped and beaten"

". . . house just ruined!"

". . . *not a stitch on!*"

Sheila could not help conjuring up the picture: Yvonne's home in shambles, a nude figure sprawled bloody and bruised on the floor, Walt standing over his wife's battered body in shock and horror. She swayed, was grateful when Amory caught her arm again and steadied her, but he repeated with annoying persistence, "I think we should leave, Sheila."

"Not *yet*," she told him fiercely.

Amory let go of her arm and backed into the crowd, disgusted. When she next glimpsed him, he was chatting with a thin young woman with reddish-blond hair and freckles.

At last the officer returned to his post. Sheila went to confront him. "Pardon me, but I have changed my mind." Shades of Amory! she thought as she realized what she had said. "I must get a message to Mr. Walter Delacourt, the victim's husband. Could you send it by radio or something?"

He considered. "What's the message?"

"Tell him Sheila Travis is out here. Ask if he wants me to call his father or if there's anything I can do for him."

The officer went to his cruiser and made the call, listened, said something she didn't hear, then motioned her over. "The chief gave him your message. He said he doesn't need anything tonight, but thanks very much."

She turned away, feeling a little let down and more than a little embarrassed. The officer probably thought she was a publicity seeker. Maybe you are, she told herself wryly as she searched faces for Amory's.

He was concluding his conversation with the young woman. "—my aunt's phone number," she heard him say. "Feel free to call me."

Sheila never remembered where they went to dinner, or what she ate. All she recalled was how her heart ached for a gangly man who had waited so long to find happiness, and lost it so soon.

At eleven-thirty that night, Harley Sanders hunched over a pay phone on the Georgia Tech campus and tried to shut out the noise of students passing by. "I tell you, Mom, I'm *sure*. It was just on the news." He listened intently, shook his head even though his mother couldn't see him. "Of course I'm not going to the cops! Why would I do a dumb thing like that? Nobody here even knows I . . . she . . . oh, hell, you know. She was married to some guy named Delacourt, and lived in a big brick house." He paused, listened. "Yeah, once or twice. I went running up there. . . . No, nobody saw me. . . . Of *course* I'm sure!" He listened, then spoke urgently. "No, Mom! Don't tell anybody, *especially* Granddaddy! What if he told one of his golf buddies? If the cops here ever made the connection— Look, just don't say anything, okay?" He listened again, brushed away a fellow student who had shaken his shoulder impatiently. "In a minute, buddy! I'm almost done. Listen, Mom, I've got to go now. Somebody wants the phone. Yeah." His voice dropped. "I love you, too, Mom. Sleep well. Finally you can."

A few blocks away, a woman sat on her living room couch and stared at the sportscaster on the television screen while her lips moved in silent prayer. The news story she had just seen replayed vividly in her imagination: the dead body of Yvonne Delacourt being carried, wrapped in plastic, to a police van. If she had spoken aloud, her words would have surprised even her dearest friend. "Thank you, Lord," Thelma Hardwick whispered over and over. "Oh, thank you, *thank* you, Lord!"

One Dunwoody matron writes: "I love Perrier. I not only drink it, but also use it to fill my iron. And it's terrific for cleaning up my dog's mistakes from the carpet. Really!"

TUESDAY

Early the next day, Sheila carried the *Atlanta Constitution* and a steaming cup of black coffee out to her apartment's second-story deck and sank into a wicker chair, grateful for a sheltered outdoor spot to welcome the dawn. Amory wouldn't be up for hours. He'd stayed up late playing her old Beatles records and reading a new history of the Civil War, and left her a note that he planned to stay in bed until lunchtime. A light rain was falling, and the world was silent except for two quarreling bluejays and three mama ducks instructing their ducklings on a small pond down the hill.

Usually this was Sheila's favorite time of day. The morning was fresh and cool, with the rich scent of wet honeysuckle wafted up by a light breeze. But Sheila's pleasure was snuffed out as soon as she picked up the paper and saw the smiling face on page one. How *unfair* that Yvonne Delacourt was not alive to see this day!

Sheila shook out the paper and scanned the story. It used a lot of words to say very little: Thirty-one-year-old Yvonne Delacourt had been found sprawled on her guest room bed the previous afternoon, stabbed through the heart with a brass letter opener. Her husband Walter Delacourt, forty, found her when he returned home from work. So far there were no suspects.

Whenever Sheila had gotten involved in a murder case previously, someone else had urged her in while she hung back with considerable reluctance. Today, even hampered by the presence of Amory—who would surely tug her back at every step—she found herself considering each of the people she remembered glowering at Yvonne last Friday and wondering how she could best interview them.

She had scarcely raised the possibility when her phone rang. She hurried in to get it before it woke Amory. She was not totally surprised to hear Walt on the other end.

"Sheila? I've got a problem."

"You sure do," she agreed.

He sighed. "It's Forbes, Yvonne's son. He's four. I hate to admit it, but I completely forgot him last night. He spent the night with a neighbor, but I don't really know them. I can't impose on them any longer, and I don't know what to do. I'm no good with children."

The same old tunnel-vision Walt. His wife might be brutally murdered, but at the moment he was focused on finding someone to take care of a four-year-old. It would never occur to him to bring the child home.

"Does he have aunts or uncles? Grandparents?"

"None that I know of, and I've got so much to do . . ." He didn't so much end the sentence as let it trail off.

Sheila knew what his silence meant. Walt might not like to impose on neighbors he knew slightly, but his conscience would trouble him not one whit for imposing on a friend he had not seen for twenty years.

Her own conscience wriggled a bit as she said, "Maybe you could take Forbes to Aunt Mary's for a few days." She was not certain whether her strongest motive was concern for the child, a desire to stay in touch with the case, or a willingness to impose on Aunt Mary to make up for past grievances.

He jumped at the offer eagerly, but good manners compelled him to ask, "You don't think she'd mind?"

"No, she's leaving for Asheville tomorrow. But she's visiting a friend before going up to her own place, so her housekeeper isn't joining her for a week. Mildred adores children."

Sheila ought to know. She'd been one of the children Mildred adored.

Walt hesitated, then blurted out, "Would you ask them and take him? I have so many things to do here, and I don't think I can face him just yet. I don't even know if he knows about . . . you know."

Telling a four-year-old his mother had been murdered was not one of Sheila's favorite things, either.

"You did ask if there was anything you could do," Walt reminded her peevishly when she did not reply.

That had not been remotely what she had in mind.

By the time Sheila reached Running Ridge Road, the rain was falling steadily. Walt had suggested she come by for Forbes's clothes before picking up the child at Jaqui Robinson's house, but when she arrived, he stood blocking the doorway instead of inviting her in. Unshaven and pale, he looked as if overnight he had shed a few pounds from his already skinny frame.

Clutching his glasses by the left rim, he adjusted them on his long nose and peered first over Sheila's right shoulder, then over her left, never directly into her eyes. "I'm glad it's you. The detective is coming again, too, in a little while."

The air was fragrant with wet boxwoods and Confederate jasmine, but a drip from the roof was splashing her as it hit the stoop. "Can we go inside?" she suggested. "I'm getting wet."

"What?" he asked blankly, then nodded. "Oh, sure." But he still did not step aside.

She was dismayed to find him so dazed. Even when his mother died in his junior year in high school, Walt had stayed in control. Tied his tie and polished his shoes. Today his hair fell limply into his face and his clothes looked like he'd slept in them. His navy

pants surely belonged to a good suit, and it was hard for Sheila
to imagine the Walter Delacourt she knew putting on that green
polo shirt with them—or going barefoot. His toes looked white
and fragile.

Ignoring his feet—and the rain—he stepped onto the small
stoop to join her and looked up and down the quiet street like a
man about to make a dash for freedom. "I don't think I can stand
much more of this!" He seized a large blue silk magnolia from the
wreath on the front door and pulled it between his fingers. Without that flower the wreath became a study in mauve and pink.
"Who could have killed her, Sheila?" he cried, his voice hoarse
with grief. "Who would have done a thing like that?"

"Let's go inside," she asked again. "We're getting wet."

In the hall, her ankles sank into soft white carpet and her eye
moved from one mahogany reproduction to the next. No family
heirlooms were woven into this decor, no favorite art or chairs
given a place from love. She couldn't help thinking of the house
Walt grew up in, furnished by generations of Delacourts. It
would never have occurred to Walt's mother—or to Sheila's aunt
Mary, either—to let a decorator choose a picture or an ornament.
Theirs were pleasures and investments, not decorations.

Sheila turned from trivialities to essentials. "You need a bath,"
she told Walt with the frankness of an old friend.

He glanced down, surprised, as if he had never seen his body
before. "Yeah, I guess I do. I haven't changed since I got home
last night, except my shirt. I—I got some of her blood on it when
I tried to lift her." His voice was almost a monotone. "I guess I
forgot to dress this morning." He turned toward the stairs.
"Forbes's room is upstairs at the back, on the left. Take whatever you think he needs." She wondered, but did not ask, why he
assumed a childless woman would know what a child needed
better than the child's stepfather.

"Are we allowed upstairs?"

"Yeah. They've finished dusting the house." Surveying the

results, she thought "undusting" would have been more accurate.

"Have you had breakfast? Coffee?" When he shook his head, she pushed him toward the kitchen. "Come on, let's both have a cup of coffee, then you can shower and I'll get Forbes's things."

He didn't make the coffee, but he pointed her in the right direction, then sat at the breakfast room table, clutching his mug as if his very bones needed warming. "I still can't believe this. I just can't believe it."

"Do you want to talk about what happened?"

He shook his head. "I don't *know* what happened. I played golf in the morning, dropped by here a little after noon to shower and change, then went to work. Vonnie was fine when I left. When I got home, her car was in the garage, but she wasn't downstairs, so I went up, looking for her. She has an office upstairs, and sometimes has a radio on and doesn't hear me come in. She wasn't in her office or our room, and there was a stink . . ." He trailed off into a horror Sheila could scarcely imagine.

"Had she been dead long, do you think?"

He glared at her. "How would I know that? I'm not a coroner. But I knew she was dead. Dead!" He buried his face in his hands.

While he recovered, Sheila carried their mugs to the dishwasher. Seeing that it was already partially filled, she bent to survey the contents: two pottery cereal bowls, three juice glasses, two coffee mugs, two goblets, two luncheon plates, silverware, two cups and saucers, and two dessert bowls. Just what you might expect from a small family that had not yet eaten dinner—although some families might not use Royal Doulton china and Reed and Barton sterling for lunch. Still, Walt and Yvonne were practically honeymooners. Perhaps she set an elegant table for an infrequent tête-à-tête lunch. The ornate Francis I silver was exactly what Sheila would have expected from Yvonne.

To give Walt more time, she wiped the counter—which was

already spotless except for an empty Perrier bottle beside the sink. Finally she touched him gently on the shoulder. "Get me a small suitcase, then go shower and change. I'll pack a few things for Forbes."

He had barely disappeared up the stairs when the doorbell rang. The visitor on the doorstep was the redheaded man Sheila had noticed at Friday's party, wearing a tentative smile and holding out a plate covered with a dishcloth. "Hi, I'm Alex Divesty. We live next door. My wife baked some muffins. . . . Is Walt in?"

"He's showering." Reading Divesty's face, she felt compelled to add, "I came by to collect a few things for Forbes and take him for a few days. I'll tell Walt you sent the muffins. That was very kind."

She reached for them, but the man kept them and pushed past her. "Don't bother. I'll just take them in."

He set them on the newly wiped kitchen counter and picked up the Perrier bottle, holding it in the dishcloth. Catching her eye, he polished it, held it aloft, and said jauntily, "I'll take this. I collect and recycle glass for my neighbors."

Sheila had no authority to keep him from taking it, but her expression must have given him second thoughts. He set the bottle back on the counter. "Yeah. Well, it can wait."

When he had gone, Sheila headed upstairs.

Forbes's room was a decorator's dream and a child's nightmare: thick pale carpet—easy to soil and impossible for cars, trucks, or blocks; a large bed with shams, difficult to make; rows of toys that looked like they sat in place most of the time; an enormous mahogany dresser with brass pulls and a high mirror. The bathroom next door, which he shared with the spare bedroom, was papered in adult and very feminine florals and had no stool to help a small boy reach the sink. Sheila put Forbes's toothbrush and comb in the small case Walt had left on the bed, chose clothes and toys at random, and poured an open box of grape juice from the rug down the bathroom sink. At the last minute she grabbed his green vinyl raincoat and draped it over one arm.

By the time she was finished, Walt was downstairs, talking to a man hidden by the back of a big chair. The police detective? She paused in the foyer. "I'm leaving, Walt."

The man rose and turned with a smile of welcome. "And who are you, ma'am?" He stuck out a hand. Sheila shifted Forbes's bag to her other hand and offered her own, with her name.

He was short, probably less than five five, and plump, with a round face as pink as the rosebud in his lapel. His head was almost bald except for a shaggy fringe that must have been blond before it grayed. At a distance he might have looked like a jolly monk in a baggy gray suit, but beneath shaggy eyebrows his gray eyes were mere slits—and cold. "Sheila Travis," he murmured blandly. He turned to Walt with an inquiring look.

Walt roused himself from misery. "Sheila's a friend of mine. She's taking Yvonne's son to her aunt's for the day. Sheila, this is Captain Drake. He's in charge of—" He stopped and turned away.

Drake interjected smoothly, "A friend of yours, eh?" His tone was pleasant, but Sheila had to resist an impulse to step back from his gaze. His eyes met hers for several seconds that felt like minutes. Feeling as if he were sucking her mind, she found her own gaze dropping first.

"It's always good to have a friend." He pulled a notebook from his pocket. "Just tell me where you live, Ms. Travis, and what you're removing from the house, then you can be on your way."

Reminding herself that this was his job, Sheila opened the duffel bag and held up each garment. He watched without saying —or writing—a single word until she'd showed him every article of clothing and each toy. "That's it?" he asked. His tone was fatherly, but his eyebrows were slightly raised, making her wonder if he suspected her of concealing Yvonne's jewels on her person.

She nodded. "As Walt said, it's just a few things for his little boy."

"And you two have been friends"—he rolled the word in his mouth like spit—"for how long?"

Walt was no help. He was methodically breaking fireplace matches into inch-long pieces. "Since high school," she told Drake evenly, "but we lost touch. We met again last week. I was coming by last evening so his wife could show me a house—" She mentally congratulated herself for *not* saying *the house across the street*. What would he have made of that? Fortunately, he took her pause for emotion.

He waved her toward the door. "Okay. I didn't mean to upset you, ma'am. Take the kid's things and go. I need to talk with Mr. Delacourt here."

Sheila left quickly. Drake had been perfectly courteous. So why did she wish she were heading to the showers? As she drove up the street, she murmured a prayer that he would solve his case quickly. It was a strictly selfish petition. She did not want to have to work either with or against those cold gray eyes.

She rang Jaqui's bell, ashamed that her knees were trembling. What did one say to a small boy at a time like this?

"Why, come in! I didn't know it was you Walt was sending. Don't you look great in that gray suit! And I like your yellow umbrella." Jaqui herself was gorgeous in a silk caftan patterned in the jewel tones of tropical birds. Red satin slippers peeped from beneath the brilliant hem. "Come on in," she repeated, stifling a yawn. "Let me give you some coffee. Forbes is just finishing his breakfast."

"Does he know?" Sheila asked softly.

Jaqui shook her head. "The boys were playing upstairs when

Walt found Yvonne. I kept them up there all evening—even fed them supper in Cornelius's room. I told Forbes his folks said it was okay for him to spend the night. Slade went up and told them stories and said prayers with them, and he said Forbes never asked about his mother at all. He still hasn't, if you want to know the truth, and I didn't have the stomach to tell him."

"Me, neither," Sheila agreed, "but looks like I get to do it anyway." She followed Jaqui into a breakfast room that was cheerful even on a dreary day.

Two small boys in underpants sat at the table, heads bent, earnestly scraping the last sugar from the bottom of their cereal bowls. Forbes had the uncombed, tousled look of a child who has gotten to do as he likes for hours. Nevertheless, he was handsome, with Yvonne's heart-shaped face and black curls and eyes as dark and round as the bottoms of Hershey kisses.

Jaqui went to the refrigerator. "What can I get you, Sheila? Juice? Coffee? Perrier?"

"Coffee would be fine." Sheila leaned against the counter to sip it and gave her charge a tentative smile. "Hello, Forbes. I'm a friend of your daddy's."

"My daddy's dead," he said matter-of-factly. "Now I have a *step*daddy."

"You better not step on *my* daddy," Cornelius warned him. They both went into gales of giggles over the joke.

Jaqui smacked her son lightly. "Come on, monkey, and get dressed."

When they had gone, Forbes raised dark, curious eyes to Sheila. There was a stillness about the boy that made her want to bend down and hold him closely. Instead, she met his gaze and spoke slowly and gently. "Forbes, Walt sent me to take you to visit somebody. A woman named Mildred. I think you'll like her."

His eyes widened in sudden terror, and he shrank against the back of his chair. "Please don't!" he whispered. His lower lip trembled. "I won't ever do it again!"

Puzzled, she moved closer to ask, "Please don't what, Forbes?"

He shrank farther away. "Don't kidnap me! Please! I'll be good! Honest I will!"

Shocked, she stepped back, protesting, "I'm not kidnapping you, Forbes! What made you think I was?"

His dark eyes were pools of anguish. He inched his chair away from her, obviously poised for flight. "M-m-mama says b-b-bad children get k-k-kidnapped. She says people pr-pr-pretend to be friends and t-t-take you away. They *never* bring you back. But I didn't m-m-*mean* to do it! I really didn't!"

Now he trembled all over. Huge tears threatened to spill over. "What did you do?" She was terrified of what he might say.

He was suddenly wary. "You don't know?"

"No."

"Then I won't tell you. And I won't go with you. I won't!" He took a deep breath and shouted, "Miss Jaqui! Mr. Slade! Don't let her kidnap me!" His arms flailed the air, his face grew red.

Slade came in from the next room. "What's going on?"

Sheila explained. Slade bent over the small boy, who was now clinging to the chair for dear life. Gently prying his fingers loose, he lifted the child and held him close. "Miss Sheila's not kidnapping you, Forbes," he murmured into the child's ear. "She really is a good friend of your mama and daddy. I promise you. And she has something to tell you. Something important. Would you like to sit on my lap while you listen?"

Forbes hesitated, lips trembling, eyes full of tears, then nodded. When Slade got them both comfortably arranged, Sheila joined them at the table and began, "I have some very bad news for you, Forbes. Your mother—"

She stopped, mentally cursing Walter. What had they taught the child? Did he believe in heaven? Did he know what dead was? Of course—his daddy was dead. "Your mother has gone to be with your real daddy."

"My daddy is dead," he pointed out.

She nodded. "I know."

His dark eyes held hers. His lips still trembled, but his gaze didn't waver while he sat there, taking it in. Then he asked in a voice which tore at Sheila's heart, "Is Walt dead, too? Is that why he didn't come?"

"Oh, no! But Walt is very, very sad, and has many things to do. That's why he asked me to take you to visit my friend Mildred."

"I'd rather stay here." Forbes burrowed deeper into Slade's arms.

"We'd rather you did, too," Slade assured him, "but not this time, son. Today you have to go with Miss Sheila to see her friend. Soon you can come spend another night with Cornelius. Fair enough?"

Forbes shook his head decisively. "No. I won't go with her."

Slade's troubled eyes met Sheila's across the tousled dark head.

Stymied, she bent to her purse with a vague idea of offering Forbes some gum. Then she had an inspiration. Deftly she reached toward Slade. "What's this, Slade Robinson? Are you keeping quarters in your ears?"

As Slade's face lit with a grin, Forbes turned slightly to look.

"Turn around, Slade," Sheila commanded. "I think you've got one in the other ear, too."

When the ballplayer complied, Forbes edged one small ear toward her. "Look in mine," he demanded.

"Yes!" she exclaimed. "You've got a dime!"

"No I don't." He stuck his finger in his ear and wiggled it. "You are fooling me."

"That's right," she agreed. "When I was a little girl, a magician taught me that trick—and a few others, too. I'll show you when we get to Mildred's, and you can play them on Cornelius."

The child paused, then gave her a reluctant nod. "Okay. I guess so."

She put out one hand and stood. Slade rose, too, sliding the child down one muscular thigh with practiced ease. "Let's get you dressed, fellow. Can't go meet a lady in your underpants."

Forbes was chuckling when they returned, but when he and
Sheila left the house, Sheila saw tears in the pitcher's eyes.

Mildred accepted Forbes as Sheila had known she would.
When the boy gravely informed her, "My mama is dead," she
bent down and gave him a hug. "Mine is, too, honey. Why don't
we make us some brownies? There's something mighty comforting about licking a brownie bowl." They went to the kitchen hand
in hand.

Sheila poured two cups of coffee and carried them to a dainty
bedroom done in Wedgwood blue and ivory. Aunt Mary, working
a crossword propped on several pillows, peered at her over half
spectacles, but said nothing.

Sheila handed her one coffee, set its twin on a mahogany table,
and went to open the drapes on the leaden sky. "Good morning!
Time to rise and shine and find those wonderful wooden par-
quetry blocks you used to pull out when I was little. They must
be around somewhere."

"Sheila Beaufort Travis, have you gotten yourself fired?"

"No, ma'am, thank you, ma'am. I'm going to work in just a
minute. First I brought your coffee."

Aunt Mary frowned and took a considering sip. "Where's Mildred? She knows just how I like it."

"I know just how you like it, too, and Mildred is busy. I've
brought her a small boy for a day or two. Now, don't get that
expression on your face—it's the least you can do. He's Rippen
Delacourt's grandson, and his mother was murdered yesterday."

Aunt Mary took off her glasses and primmed her lips. "He is
not Rippen's grandson, he's Walter Delacourt's stepson, and I do
not remember volunteering to baby-sit."

"I volunteered for you," Sheila told her cheerfully, "or, rather,
for Mildred. You're leaving tomorrow—aren't you?" she added,
noticing a certain flicker in Aunt Mary's eyes.

Aunt Mary was suddenly busy looking for something on her nightstand. "I don't know, dear," she murmured absently as if discussing something of absolutely no importance.

"Can't bear to miss the excitement?"

Aunt Mary lifted her chin. "Don't be vulgar, Sheila. I am merely postponing a trivial trip for a day or two to support an old friend in his time of need. I trust you will not be difficult."

"Meaning, you expect me to get involved if asked? Well, surprisingly, this time I will—if asked. But so far the only thing Walt has asked me to do is keep Forbes. *Unless* he asks," she added warningly, "I can't butt in."

"Ummm." Aunt Mary sipped her coffee again and frowned. "Not enough sugar, dear."

"It's practically syrup, Aunt Mary. Far more than's good for you. Now I really must go to work." Sheila started to the door. Aunt Mary stopped her by holding up one petite hand.

"Walter is a mouse, Sheila. Always was. Takes after his mother. But you stay in touch with him, dear. Poor boy, he may need more help than he knows."

Rain fell all day long, as if the very skies grieved for Yvonne Delacourt. Amory arrived at Sheila's office late that afternoon, dripping wet but triumphant, having secured tickets to a popular play and reservations at one of Atlanta's favorite restaurants.

"I don't feel much like—" Sheila began.

Amory waved away her objections with a grand gesture that showered her whole office. "We didn't know the woman, Sheila, and you don't need to sit at home and mope. Now, get a move on. Miss Mary wants us to drop by her place before we go out."

Sheila tidied her desk with a reluctant sigh. "Forbes doesn't really know me, but at least I knew his mother. He may want to talk about her."

Forbes, however, seemed to have forgotten his mother, or at

least her untimely demise. Sheila and Amory found him in Aunt
Mary's kitchen, just finishing a game of Go Fish with Mildred. "I
beat her again, Miss Sheila!" He crowed, clapping his hands with
glee. His eyes were shining.

"Sure did," Mildred agreed glumly. "Beat me at dominoes, too.
He got real lucky at matching those dots." She slid Sheila a
sideways look. Sheila wondered if she, too, was remembering
how often a small Sheila used to win at dominoes on rainy afternoons.

Mildred slapped her cards on the table and pushed back her
chair. "I've got to work on supper now, honey. We can play again
later. Sheila, Miss Mary wants you to join her for sherry."

To Sheila's amazement, Amory scooped up Mildred's discarded
cards. "Do you know how to play Old Maid, fellow? I'm a whiz at
that."

"I can learn," Forbes assured him solemnly.

"If you'd like, I'll play one hand," Sheila offered, "then teach
you that magic trick."

Forbes gave her a look of scorn. "You can teach the trick, but
you can't play, Miss Sheila. Old Maid is a *man's* game."

"And your aunt wants you," Mildred reminded her.

Doubly dispatched, what could she do but go?

She found Rippen Delacourt with her aunt. The sight of her
aunt's old friend in his wheelchair gave her a pang. Rip had aged
greatly since Sheila last saw him at Easter. How much had he
aged in the past twenty-four hours?

He clasped her hand between his two big ones and gazed up at
her with wet brown eyes. "Bless you, Sheila, for wanting to help
my boy. Bless you." His voice was still blurred from his stroke,
his tongue hard to manage. His once-bulky body no longer filled
his chair, and he sat slightly sideways, favoring his weak left
side. "We've got ourselves a real mess." His tongue twisted on
the last word, and he wiped his eyes with his good hand.

"Has something else happened?" Sheila looked from him to
Aunt Mary, who waved her toward a chair.

"Sit down and have some sherry, Sheila." Not until Sheila had sipped the amber liquid did Aunt Mary continue. "Rip is afraid Walter is going to be arrested for the murder of his wife."

"Why? What motive do they think he had?"

Aunt Mary was refilling her own glass, so her brown eyes did not meet Sheila's browner ones as she replied. "They don't have to prove motive, dear. You know that. His prints are on the murder weapon. Walter told them he pulled it out when he found her."

Sheila's heart sank. It was exactly the kind of dumb thing Walt would do. He'd once tried mouth-to-mouth resuscitation on a dog who'd been hit in the road. But what jury would believe he'd pulled that letter opener out instead of pushed it in?

Aunt Mary interrupted Sheila's stricken reverie. "Rip wants you to see what you can find out about this murder. What do you think, dear?"

Her expression was wholly innocent, but they both knew whose idea it was for Sheila to be "asked" by Rip—and who was doing the asking.

Rip clutched his bourbon with such force that Sheila feared the crystal glass would shatter in his hand. "That woman tried to borrow money from me two weeks after the wedding," he rasped. "Needed to pay some old bills, said she didn't like to worry Walter. Never paid me back, of course." He drained his drink in one gulp.

"How much did you give her?" Financial matters could always divert Aunt Mary, even from contemplating murder.

"Few hundred. All I had on me at the time. She"—a dull red stained his cheeks—"she hugged my neck for it." His eyes were bloodshot with worry and weariness. "Walt didn't kill her, Sheila. Frankly, he doesn't have the gumption. Find out what really happened. Please? For an old man?"

It wasn't an old man she saw. It was her friend's boisterous father, who could always be counted on to host a swimming party, cookout, or even a formal dance for his son's high school classmates. "Let's ask Mr. D.," someone would suggest when they ran out of ideas. Mr. D. always came through—providing lavish food and entertaining pranks, roaring with laughter, and having as much fun as any teenager. One spring night he had even flown ten of Walt's friends in his corporate jet to Alabama so they could watch migratory birds arrive on the beach at dawn. Having just crossed the entire Gulf of Mexico in one heroic flight, the birds collapsed to the sand, exhausted, numb, and very vulnerable. Tonight Rip Delacourt was very like those birds.

Her voice was not quite steady as she replied, "I'll try, Mr. D. I'll really try."

*LOST MAN, ON OUTSKIRTS OF DUNWOODY, SEEKING
DIRECTIONS FOR A GOLF DATE:* "Please tell me how to get into the country
club."
DUNWOODY MATRON: "Well, first you would
have to submit an application to the
committee."

W ᴇ ᴅ ɴ ᴇ ꜱ ᴅ ᴀ ʏ : T ʜ ᴇ   ʜ ᴏ ᴜ ꜱ ᴇ

"**Y**ou are not going into that house alone. Absolutely
not!" Amory swallowed the last of his breakfast coffee and set
his mug down with a thump. "What could your aunt be thinking of?"

"Walter's father," Sheila told him. "She'd sacrifice a hundred
nieces for Rip. They've known each other fifty years, at least."
She picked up her purse and started for the door. "Besides, I
won't be in any danger. All I'm going to do is look around and
talk with a few people, ask if they saw anything. But if you insist
on coming, I'll pick you up about half past twelve."

Murder or no murder, she had an important meeting at
Hosokawa International at nine, and she was running too late to
properly argue with someone as pigheaded as Amory.

"Don't have anything better to do." He was right. Sight-seeing
in Atlanta would be tame when he could be having an exciting
visit to a murder scene. Of course, Sheila thought with a sigh as
she got into her car, he *could* be getting on a plane for Mississippi.

———

During a break in her meeting she called Frank McGehee, a young police officer she'd met the previous fall after a murder on Peachtree Street. Since then she had kept in occasional touch with him and his girlfriend, Crystal Robles. Recently McGehee had joined the DeKalb County police's Major Felony Unit.

After they'd exchanged greetings and a bit of chat, she asked casually, "Are you working on the Delacourt case, Frank?"

"Not working much. It looks pretty open and shut that Delacourt did it."

"On what evidence?"

He hesitated. "Is he a friend of yours or something?"

"We went to high school together."

"That's tough. You see, the door wasn't forced, and Delacourt himself says there're only three keys: his, his wife's—which was in her purse—and one his dad has. His father—"

"—is in a wheelchair and unlikely to commit murder. I know, Frank. But maybe Yvonne let someone in."

"Maybe." Frank sounded skeptical. "But Delacourt's prints are the only ones on the murder weapon, which was a brass letter opener he usually kept on his desk downstairs. He volunteered that information. Said it was a souvenir of their honeymoon in Hawaii. He also admitted he came home around noon to shower after a round of golf. Hard life, Hawaiian honeymoon and playing golf on a Monday morning." McGehee sounded wistful.

"The evidence, Frank," Sheila reminded him, hoping she didn't sound as impatient as she felt.

"Yeah, well, the M.E. fixes the death between noon and two-thirty, when the kid came home from school. If Delacourt left at twelve-thirty, like he says, that doesn't leave much time for anybody else to get in, stab her, and get away."

"Two hours? That's a long time!" she protested.

"Who else would know she'd be there alone at that precise time? *And* how to get in and out without being seen? It's an open street, Sheila. A stranger would be taking an enormous risk."

"What if it wasn't a stranger? How about a neighbor?"

"Well, we were checking them, but Drake—"

"The detective in charge? I met him."

"Watch out for him, Sheila. Jake Drake's a snake, of the biblical variety. Remember? 'The serpent was more wily than other beasts.' He's new in the department, and tough as nails. We don't wipe our—uh—noses without his permission. And in this case, he's pretty sure he's got his man, so . . ."

So they weren't looking for evidence other than what could be used against Walt. Detecting in blinders. Sheila had seen it before, in a case in Chicago. Detective Mike Flannagan had been difficult to work around then. Jake Drake would be almost impossible now.

"Any chance of my seeing what you've found so far—on the QT?"

"Well—" Frank paused so long, she wondered what he was doing. When he spoke next, she suspected he'd been looking to make sure nobody was around. "If you leave your trunk unlocked in your parking lot this evening between six and seven, you might find a surprise in it later."

"Jake Drake will eat you for dinner."

"Only if he finds out. Don't sweat it. Drake's in court most of today, and I owe you. Crystal has finally agreed to marry me. You deserve something for getting us together."

"I don't remember it being very difficult, but hey—anything to get copies of those reports. Congratulations, and thanks."

"It's not just a gift. I wouldn't do this ordinarily, Sheila, for you or anybody else, but you got lucky on the Peachtree case, and some of us feel Drake's rushing this case a bit. Delacourt swears the only time he touched the weapon was to pull it out. The scarcity of blood under the body verifies that it was in the wound for several hours after death, and there's only one clear set of prints on the weapon. One set, not two."

"Like someone wore gloves to kill her."

"Right. Drake's theory is that it was Delacourt both times, trying to throw us off his scent, so he's got us busy investigating Delacourt. If you want to scout around elsewhere . . ."

"I certainly do."

"Then be very careful. If you thought Owen Green objected to amateurs, you ain't seen nuttin' yet! Jake Drake doesn't even like other *officers* butting in on his cases—especially women. And if he finds out I gave you the stuff—"

"Not if he sticks pins under my fingernails," she promised.

"He might." She thought he sounded unnecessarily cheerful.

Amory was already complaining when he climbed into the car at noon. "I still don't think we ought to go in. Dad—"

Sheila sighed. "Amory, you may go with me, or I'll take you to a MARTA station so you can catch a train downtown and spend the day as you like. But you may *not* object to what I am doing, or mention your father again this afternoon. Is that clear?"

"I suppose so." His voice was huffy. He might have to give in, but he didn't have to like it. "I sure could use lunch first."

"We'll eat as soon as I finish," she promised. She did not, however, promise how long finishing would take.

As she braked the car in Walter's drive, Amory began another litany of complaint. "Are you *sure* we ought to go inside? Whoever killed that woman might come back. Besides, if the police find you . . ."

She gathered her last shreds of patience. "You can't have it both ways, Amory. Either the killer may come, or the police. Not both at the same time. In this case, from everything I've heard, I might prefer the killer." Leaving him to think that over, she slammed the door behind her.

A chipmunk scampered into a clump of azaleas. Otherwise the street was deserted. It would not be impossible, Sheila thought, for her to lure Amory inside, murder him, and escape without ever being seen. "Bad girl!" she chided herself, climbing Walt's steps.

Before she got Rip's key in the lock, Amory was on her heels. "Well, if you are going in, I am, too." The first mate, going down with a ship the captain had not needed to sink. She did not reply.

Inside, the air-conditioning was on high, a welcome change from the oppressive heat outside. Yvonne's gardenia perfume still lingered in the air. Looking around at the thick white carpet, new furniture in pastel floral prints, silk plants and floral arrangements, and expensive, meaningless bric-a-brac now smudged with fingerprint powder, Sheila once again wondered if Walt enjoyed coming home to this. How different from the deep, comfortable chairs, silky, jewel-toned Orientals, jungle of houseplants, and litter of three generations' collections, hobbies, and travel souvenirs he'd grown up with!

Amory echoed her thoughts. " 'I want a house that has gotten over all its troubles. I don't want to spend the rest of my life bringing up a young and inexperienced house.' Jerome K. Jerome. Can you imagine slurping your bourbon and grazing in that living room after a hard day at the office?" Amory himself lived in a rambling antebellum house he'd decorated with impeccable taste and castoffs from both Stirling and Travis ancestors. He'd filled it with so much Civil War memorabilia, however, that Sheila could not imagine any woman moving into it. She'd have to enjoy guns on every wall and cannonballs on the coffee table.

Amory headed past her, calling over his shoulder, "What exactly are we looking for?"

"I don't know," she replied truthfully. She felt a sudden urge to run back outside, jump in her car, and drive to her office, leaving Amory to find his own way home. What *was* she doing here? Rip had given her the key, told her to come. But what could she find that Jake Drake and his professional technicians had not?

Amory turned in the kitchen doorway, ever the harbinger of

cheer. "Does Walt know we're here? What if he comes home and finds us snooping around?"

"He won't. I checked with his secretary. He's locked himself in his office and told her he doesn't want to be disturbed." Just like he locked himself away when his mother died. Funny how some things never change. "Besides," she added with asperity, "we aren't snooping."

"Hmph," he grunted, disappearing into the kitchen. "*I* believe in calling a spade a dadgum shovel."

Walt probably would, too. And the thought of what Jake Drake might call it made Sheila prowl through the big pale rooms with one eye figuratively over her shoulder.

She quickly concluded that neither the living nor dining room contained any clues to the murder—or to Yvonne's past. Nothing looked more than three years old.

In the breakfast room she found Amory seated before a small plate heaped with chicken salad, a bowl of red congealed salad, and a glass of milk. "Don't look so horrified," he told her. "I just took a little. Walter won't mind." His confidence was impressive, since the two men had never met.

Sheila moved around the kitchen, opening drawers and cupboards. Here, too, everything was shiny and new. Had Yvonne moved to Atlanta with just the clothes on her back? Had she not brought one favorite omelette pan, one battered kettle? Apparently not. On a shelf near the stove Sheila found what might be a lone link with Yvonne's past: a shelf of gourmet cookbooks. Someone had doodled remarks beside some of the recipes: *Henry likes! Disaster! Don't try again!!!* But none of the books had Yvonne's name written inside.

"Not my favorite snack, but it'll hold me till lunch." Amory rinsed his dishes, then took a bottle of Perrier from the fridge.

"Why don't you just cook yourself a steak?" Sheila asked a bit acidly.

"I don't want to mess up the kitchen." He wandered into the

den and turned on CNN. She followed. That room, too, looked brand-new and, except for the fingerprint powder, like it had just been cleaned.

Walt's study next door, she was relieved to find, was cluttered with papers and furnished with a soft leather chair and a huge oak desk that used to be in his father's office. A worn blue and gold Persian rug was laid over the carpet. Bird pictures covered the walls and carved birds sat on a bookshelf with glass doors that Sheila recognized as one that used to be in his mother's bedroom. She suspected the books were Walt's, too. They had a rumpled, well-read look. A pillow was wadded into the chair. Mute witness to two sleepless nights since he'd found his murdered wife?

She climbed the wide carpeted stairs and went first to Forbes's room to collect what she hoped were enough clothes to last him a week. As she looked in the closet for another pair of shoes, she found a large duffel bag. She filled it with clothes and impulsively added a gray stuffed elephant that looked more worn than its companions. Then, dropping Forbes's things near the top of the stairs, she approached the guest room across the hall.

Immediately her eye was drawn to the bed, to a dark stain on the bare mattress. In spite of the air-conditioning, the air still reeked of stale blood. Hurriedly she pushed up the two windows and leaned against the screen to inhale deeply of fresher air.

This room, like Forbes's, was at the back of the house. Because of the angle of the windows and a huge walnut tree between the two houses, she could see only pieces of Rilla's maid sweeping their deck—a gray shoulder, the tip of one shoe, a broad hip. A movement drew her eyes to the Marriots' upstairs window, where a white-haired woman peered out, then quickly drew back.

Sheila turned her attention inside. The room looked as if it had never been used—except for a silver hand mirror on the dresser and that ugly rust-brown splotch on the bare mattress. No tissues in the wastebasket, no slippers under the bed. The drawers were empty and the smell of new wood rose faintly when they were opened. The closet contained Yvonne's winter clothes—expensive wool suits and skirts, cashmere sweaters. Her furs were probably in storage, Sheila thought—adding a silent "Meow."

Why had Yvonne Delacourt come in here at all? To dust? Unlikely. Surely she had a maid. To meet a lover? Again unlikely. Why use this room instead of her own? Why use her own house instead of a neutral, safer place?

Besides, Sheila reminded herself, she had no reason to think Yvonne had been anything but a happily married woman.

The most likely explanation was that she had been attacked downstairs, run up seeking to escape, turned automatically into the first door at the head of the stairs, and collapsed onto the bed. Had there been signs of struggle elsewhere in the house, which Walt had already carefully removed—or on her body? Sheila would have to wait for Frank's report to find out.

She left the scene of Yvonne's death and headed to the smaller front bedroom, which served Yvonne as an office. In spite of white ruffled curtains and salmon-pink walls, it was a serious place of business. The closet contained a filing cabinet and a small copier. The desk telephone was connected to both an answering and a FAX machine. An eelskin briefcase beside the desk contained two blank real estate contracts, business cards, and a case with essentials for redoing one's face in the middle of a workday. If it had also contained clues, Jake Drake had taken them away.

The desk contained the first mementos Sheila had found that Yvonne had kept from her past: a studio portrait of a sweet-faced woman, a piece of coral, and a glass from a Nassau hotel, used to hold pencils.

Sheila took a sheet from a small cube of paper and, after making sure there were no telltale smudges or indentations on it, jotted down the name of the hotel and *Mother?*, and thrust the paper into her jacket pocket.

The desk's bottom drawer was stuffed with photographs, while stacks of neatly banded correspondence filled the middle drawer. Everything was smeared with gray, so Sheila knew Jake Drake had probably found anything important there was to find. Only curiosity made her carry the contents of both drawers to a chair in the corner.

The chair, alas, was built for Yvonne's petite frame, not Sheila's longer one. Hopefully this wouldn't take long.

The photos were what she might have expected. The infant Forbes in his bath, covered with food in his high chair, and sitting in his mother's lap, playing with a small silver whale she wore around her neck. An older Forbes sitting on Santa's lap. The only surprise was that every other adult's face—even Santa's—had been neatly cut off the pictures. Yvonne's child would know no more about his own past than he could learn about his mother's.

The letters were recent invitations from friends and thank-you notes for parties Yvonne had given in Atlanta.

"Find anything?"

She gasped. "You startled me, Amory!"

"Shouldn't have. You knew I was here. Find anything?"

"Not unless you count bread-and-butter notes from Atlanta's rich and famous."

He chuckled. "Reminds me of a joke somebody told me when they heard I was coming to Atlanta. Do you know why Dunwoody matrons hate group sex? All those thank-you notes." Chuckling far more than the joke was worth, he roamed down the hall. "Is this the room where it happened?" he called. "Ah, yes, there's still blood on the mattress. I'd advise Walt to trash it and get a new one. He'd probably never get out that stain."

"Probably not," Sheila agreed. Not to mention the pain.

She rose and went to the last room, the gigantic master bedroom. The white-ruffled spread on the enormous mahogany fourposter was rumpled. A mound of pillows in white eyelet shams lay beside it on the floor. On top of the pillows sat a worn brown teddy bear with one eye. It was older than Forbes. Had it been Walt's, or Yvonne's? Why would Yvonne keep him when she had discarded virtually everything else from her past?

Amory strolled in to join her, paused at Walt's dresser to eye a litter of matchbooks, small change, and business cards. "Now, this looks fairly human. Most of this place is so shiny, it gives me the heebie-jeebies." He bent to pick up the bear. "Hey, little fellow, if you could talk, what could you tell us, huh?"

Sheila browsed through Walt's litter, but if there was a clue there, she missed it. Meanwhile Amory wandered, flexing his long fingers around the bear's stout middle. "Hey!" He whirled toward Sheila. "There's something in here!" She hurried to his side.

His hands were too clumsy. She took the bear by force and ran her fingers along each seam until she found a concealed opening. Inside was a small green book.

"It's mine! It's mine!" Amory grabbed for it. "I found it!"

Sheila backed away. "You can have it in a minute. Just let me look through first."

He glowered, then gave in with poor grace. "Oh, well, it's probably nothing." Still pouting, he clomped down the stairs.

Sheila perched on the bed, the bear in her lap, and examined his find—an inexpensive nine-year-old appointment book with spaces for three days on each page and Saturday/Sunday combined at the end of each week. She was surprised at how worn it was. What had been so special about that particular year?

Browsing through the pages, she paused at May 28. It had an unusually long list of entries. Was it significant that they were all written in different color ink? *Bert & Sue 4 Seasons* in navy blue, *5m* in pencil, *10m* in light blue, *Choose silver w/ R* in red, and *D no dice* in black, the first letter heavily shaded. Thumbing back,

Sheila found that no date with multiple entries had any two written in the same color. It almost looked as if someone had used this appointment book for several years, but why would anyone in Dunwoody be so frugal about a cheap appointment book?

If the book were Yvonne's, she had not used it to record real estate appointments, either. Jake Drake probably had her business calendar.

Out of curiosity Sheila sought the previous Monday's date, the day Yvonne died. It contained only one entry: *A200m?* Was it written nine years ago—or last week? And why the question mark?

She dropped the book into her jacket pocket. She would turn it over to Jake Drake, of course—but not until she had copied it.

In the master bathroom hamper she found a crumpled tennis dress, a purple skirt and coordinate knit top in white, purple, and turquoise, a pair of tennis socks, a pair of panties, two lacy bras, and Walter's clothes—including the green shirt he'd been wearing when she saw him the morning after Yvonne died. She did not see, however, what she was looking for: the shirt he'd worn when he found his wife. With a sinking heart she knew Jake Drake had taken it for a lab workup. She also knew exactly what he would find: Yvonne's blood.

A growl from her stomach made her check her watch. Two already? Amory was probably grazing the fridge again! It was time to go.

Carrying Forbes's duffel bag to the bottom of the steps, she went to look for her nephew. The den was empty, the large-screen television blank. Lifting one blind to scan the backyard, she was startled to see Yvonne's gardener calmly clipping the cedar hedge beside the fence separating the Delacourt and Marriot backyards. He had not been there when she looked out the bedroom window earlier. How had he gotten into the fenced yard without coming through the house?

She had to test three keys on Rip's ring before she found one that opened the dead bolt to the back door. Stepping onto the deck, she demanded, "Does Mr. Delacourt know you are here today?" The heat welled around her and began to thaw her bones. Until that moment, she had not realized she was cold.

Today he wore khaki wash pants, a red T-shirt, a Braves cap, and the mirrored sunglasses. His shirt was perfectly dry. He could not have been working long in that heat. "Did you hear me?" She crossed the deck and leaned over the rail.

"Yep," he drawled without turning around. "I usually come Tuesdays and Fridays, but yesterday it rained. I came by and he said to come work today." He punctuated his words with sharp snips at the foliage.

"How did you get in? Wasn't the fence gate locked?"

"Got a key." Whistling, he shambled farther down the hedge.

Sheila refused to be so neatly dismissed. "Do you have a key to the house, too?"

"Nope." He snapped off a particularly thick branch with obvious satisfaction. Was he pretending it was some part of her anatomy?

"What's your name?"

He looked her way but did not lift his sunglasses. "Who wants to know?"

"I do."

He shrugged. "You don't count. Sorry." He turned his back.

She persisted. "Have you worked here long?"

"Long enough."

"Weren't you at the party next door last Friday?"

He grinned over one shoulder, showing very white teeth. "You invite *your* yard man to your parties?"

She was getting hot, and knew her hair was beginning to frizz. "I don't have a yard man. Why were you at the corner Monday night?"

He shrugged again and raised the clippers malevolently. "It's a public street. Look, lady, I've got work to do. You want my advice? Go back where you came from. Stop asking questions. This is no place for you. Look what happened to—Mrs. Delacourt." Without another word of farewell he strode to the far fence and began to prune a tall camellia.

She had noticed his slip, though. He had almost said "Yvonne." How well had Yvonne Delacourt known her yard man?

She was startled by voices from over the fence beyond his darting clippers. "How could you be such a fool?" The woman sounded close to hysteria. "If the police find out—"

"Nobody's going to find out anything!" a man shouted. A door slammed. It was over so abruptly, Sheila almost thought she'd imagined it. But the poisonous words hung in the sultry air.

The gardener continued clipping without a word, his back to her. Thoughtful, Sheila returned to the kitchen and tore a piece of paper from Yvonne's kitchen pad. *Check on gardener and neighbors*, she reminded herself, and thrust the note into her pocket with the small green book and the first memo. Hopefully she would remember to take all this out when she took the suit off that evening. If not, her dry cleaner was accustomed to returning the odds and ends he found in her many pockets.

The house suddenly closed about her. Calling Amory's name one last time and receiving no reply, she quickly locked the back door and hurried to peer out the front one to see if he had gone to the car. He was up the hill and across the street, chatting with the decorator they'd met Friday night. Dee Ivy. Amory was still drinking his purloined bottle of Perrier. The woman clutched a bag that looked like groceries. Poor thing. Amory could talk long enough to cook her eggs. Sheila scooped up Forbes's things and hurried out.

On the doorstep she stopped with a sharp intake of breath. Standing on the walk, focusing a camera, was a thin, freckled young woman Sheila ought to recognize but didn't. Behind her, two slitted gray eyes watched from a blue police car at the curb.

Detective Jake Drake had arrived two minutes too soon.

*What are three words a Dunwoody matron
never hears?
"Attention, K Mart shoppers . . ."*

WEDNESDAY: THE PEOPLE

Drake left his car and sauntered past the young
woman on the walk without speaking to her. Today the rose in
his lapel was red, but he wore the same baggy gray suit. "We got
a call that somebody was here. Mind showing me what you've
got in that bag?" He flicked a toothpick into the liriope lining the
walk, mounted the steps, and held out his hand. Sheila leaned
against the iron rail while he fumbled among Forbes's clothes
and pulled out the elephant. "Cute." He retained the stuffed toy
but handed her the duffel bag, his face so close to hers, she could
smell onions on his breath.

Resisting a strong urge to step backward, she asked, "How's it
going, Detective Drake?" His steely eyes narrowed. "Captain
Drake, ma'am."

"Captain Drake. Are you making progress on the case?"

Frank was right. His smile was a direct descendant of one that
hung from a tree in Eden. "Certainly am, ma'am. Ought to be
making an arrest any day now. Don't suppose you have anything
to contribute, do you—like your plans for the little boy's future?"

Sheila shook her head. "My plans for his future are to give him
back to his stepfather as soon as possible."

Drake's smile widened. "Might be a while, ma'am. Be sure
you've got enough clothes to last him a good long time." He
handed her the elephant and turned back to his car.

"I will return him to Walt very soon," she assured him, arranging the elephant so he peered out the top of the bag.

She hoped it was the truth.

When the policeman had left, the thin young woman came hesitantly up the walk toward Sheila. In addition to the camera, she carried a huge shoulder purse that flopped against her hip as she walked.

About thirty, she was thin and moved in a loose, quick stride. She was pale, with short reddish hair, and the nearer she came, the more freckles Sheila could see. They spattered every visible inch of her body, making it difficult to say whether she was white with specks of tan or tan with tiny patches of white. Perspiration glowed on her face and neck.

She did not belong to this neighborhood, Sheila was certain of it. Nothing she had on was expensive enough—not the purse, nor her blue denim skirt, white cotton shell, or white canvas espadrilles. The camera was old and battered. An elderly brown Toyota parked farther down the street was probably hers, too.

"Do you live here?" the woman asked tentatively, shoving sunglasses onto the top of her head. Her eyes were so green, she must wear tinted contacts.

"Obviously not," Sheila told her with a wry smile. "Didn't you hear the detective practically order me off the property?"

"I didn't know who he was. I am Nan Jones Quentin." She put out one hand. A small gold monogram dangled from a slender chain to confirm it: NJQ.

"I'm a writer," Nan continued when they had shaken hands. "Just starting out, actually." Her words, like her walk and handshake, were staccato. "I hope to do a story about this case."

"The person you want to talk with, then, is that detective." Sheila felt only partly guilty, like a Roman tossing an eager

Christian to a lion. "I just came to fetch some clothes for the
Delacourts' son. Good to meet you," she called back as she hurried across the street to Amory.

Miss Quentin was already aiming her camera again. Cringing,
Sheila could imagine the caption: *Front door of murdered
woman.*

Amory's voice carried. ". . . mostly just painstaking routine."
The nerve of the man!

"Like standing around drinking Perrier," Sheila agreed, coming up behind him, "but somebody's got to do it."

He turned, gave her the smile he probably gave file clerks.
"Hello, Sheila. Did you get that information we needed?"

"Had a hard time getting it past enemy lines, but it's right
here, sir." She thrust the duffel bag at him, he pushed it
back.

The woman gave Sheila a smile that spoke chapters about how
much she believed what she was hearing. "I'm Dee Ivy, remember?" Dee was not only sober today, she was crisp and professional in a black linen dress with tiny white polka dots, a red
linen jacket, white stockings, and black patent heels. Sheila was
amazed. Amory must have hidden charms if he could entice such
an attractive woman to stand chatting in heels and jacket in this
heat.

Dee held a bag from Lord and Taylor and a small plastic grocery bag that was sweating beads of moisture. "I hope *somebody*
gets to the bottom of this, but I still can't believe anybody could
get killed on our street." She shuddered. "My girls are home
alone so many afternoons. Lori's only sixteen and Megan's just
twelve." Her eyes were full of worry.

"Were you here that day?" Sheila asked. No time like the present to begin questioning the neighbors.

Dee hefted her bags. "No, I had clients all afternoon."

"Did you know Yvonne well?" Sheila remembered Dee's snarl the previous Friday and wondered if Dee sober would remember, too.

If so, she wasn't letting on. "She was one of my very best friends!" Her eyes grew moist. "Vonnie lived over there for more than a year before she married Walt. When she first moved in, we did a lot of things together. Forbes was just a baby, so I helped her find him a doctor, get into the club, things like that. She'd had a rough time before she moved here."

"Oh, really?" Sheila hoped Dee would say more. She did.

"Oh, yes! She'd been married to an old man, a business associate of her daddy's. She didn't quite say so, but I got the idea that she'd sacrificed herself to get her daddy out of some kind of financial trouble. Then her poor husband died right after Forbes was born, and Vonnie found out he'd left her almost penniless! He'd gambled his money away, or something. Can you imagine? Bless her heart, she was so embarrassed that she packed right up and moved here to make a fresh start."

Dunwoody: haven for penniless widows seeking a fresh start. Sheila wondered if the chamber of commerce had considered the possibilities of that slogan.

Meanwhile Dee was gushing on. ". . . used to bring me flowers from her yard, have us over to dinner sometimes. I introduced her around, got her on a tennis team, and decorated her house—except Forbes's room. Yvonne . . . well, she wanted that more formal than I would have done it."

"It's awful," Amory said bluntly.

Sheila, meanwhile, was so busy considering the difference in cost between yard flowers plus impromptu dinners and a full-scale interior design that she missed the beginning of the next sentence. ". . . we didn't see as much of each other." Had Dee said, "After she and Walt got married," or "After we had a fight"? Perhaps Amory would remember, but Sheila doubted it. He wore an attentive expression, but she knew from experience that he seldom remembered what women said five minutes after they said it.

Dee looked at her watch and gasped. "Oh, dear, I really must go! I have a client coming at three."

"How about tonight?" Amory asked as if he'd asked before. "I've got those dinner reservations, and Sheila's going to complain she's got too much to do."

"I sure am," Sheila agreed.

"Well—" Dee clearly was tempted.

"You'd be doing me a favor," Sheila assured her. "Why don't I put Forbes's bag in the car, Amory, while you all make plans?"

As she had hoped, her return to the car put her on a collision course with Yvonne's yard man, who was now strolling up the street.

"Did you finish your hedge?" she asked.

He grinned. She was suddenly—and uncomfortably—aware of just how tall, dark, and almost handsome he was. He would look more at home swarming up a mast with a sword between his teeth than sauntering down the middle of Running Ridge Road. "You know how it is with hedges," he said laconically. "It will still be there when I get back."

"I don't even know that you *are* a gardener."

"Let me do your yard. You'll see."

"I live in an apartment with one small bonsai tree. Anything else I try to grow dies a pitiful death. Sorry."

His expression was hidden by his sunglasses. "A green thumb can be cultivated."

"I've been too busy cultivating a suspicious mind. How long have you worked for Walter?"

He shook his head. "It was Mrs. D. I worked for. Never saw him until yesterday. Used to see the little boy sometimes, though." He raised his sunglasses and stared pointedly at the elephant's soft gray head. "You got him?"

"No, he's with a family friend. I'm taking him some things."
He looked at her intently. "He's safe?"
His eyes were very blue, and compelled her to nod.
"That's good." He replaced the glasses. "That's real good.
Now, you run along home and don't come back."
"Is that a warning or a threat?"
"Whichever you prefer." Without a word of farewell he set off
up the street.
She watched him go, puzzled and more than a bit annoyed. A
strange gardener, one who gave orders but no name. He carried
no tools and had no truck. No bus lines ran near Running Ridge
Road, so how did he get home? And how had he managed to so
imprint their conversation on her brain that she could replay it
word for word?

"He makes me nervous."
Sheila jumped to hear a lifeless voice echo her own uneasy
thoughts. Paula Divesty had crossed her lawn, looking taller
than ever in black slacks and a silky white blouse. As it had been
at the party, her hair was pulled to the nape of her neck and held
by a black bow as if she couldn't be bothered with it. Again she
wore no cosmetics. She carried a black bag over one arm, her
long, slim feet were encased in black flats. In spite of her Quak-
erish appearance, however, she moved so gracefully that Sheila
could picture her in a flame-colored skirt and yellow blouse
whirling around a Gypsy campfire, chestnut hair loose and flying
about her bare shoulders.
Distracted by this image, she did not immediately reply. Paula
persisted. "Yvonne's gardener, I mean. He gives me the creeps.
He's not like a gardener at all, really."
"What do you think he could be?"
Even Paula's shrug was graceful. "He could be *many* things,"
she said with a meaningful smile, "but I don't guess it matters

now what he was to Yvonne—unless he killed her. He certainly looks capable of it!"

Sheila watched the gardener turn the distant corner. "Did anyone see him hanging around Monday afternoon? Did *you?*"

Paula fingered the bow at the nape of her neck. "I was gone most of the day, until very late. I work at a shelter. Are you interested in helping battered women? We're always looking for volunteers."

Right now Sheila was overcommitted to a stabbed woman. "Not at present," she said. She hastened to add, "Maybe later." She meant it. "By the way, are you married to Alex? I was there when he brought Walt some muffins. That was nice of you."

"It was the least we could do," Paula called over her shoulder, already climbing the hill toward Amory and Dee. Sheila could hear only the end of what she called back to Dee as she turned and started back toward her own house. "—order it, then, and count us in. I can't attend. I have a meeting that afternoon."

Did this woman ever stay anywhere long enough to finish a conversation, Sheila wondered, or was she perpetually moving on to the next item of business?

As Paula passed en route to her own house, Sheila fell in beside her. "Did you know Yvonne very well? Well enough to know who might have disliked her?"

Paula gave a ladylike snort of derision. "Most married women disliked Yvonne—but probably not enough to kill her." She opened the door of the navy blue Mercedes wagon standing in her drive. "Sorry to run, but I'm late. Good-bye." She started the car, backed quickly out, and waved at Dee and Amory as she passed them.

Sheila, watching Paula's car, heard Dee saying ". . . always going to some meeting or other. Poor Alex. Well, I'd better be going, too! See you about six."

As she turned, her foot must have caught on a stone. She

pitched forward and landed awkwardly on her knees, tumbling her bags and spilling their contents. While Amory helped Dee up, Sheila loped up the hill to retrieve groceries, a bra, and a pair of pantyhose, and return them to the bags from which they had fallen.

"Thanks. I'm okay," Dee assured them, clutching her bags and walking toward her big brick neocolonial with just the trace of a limp. The other two went down toward the Delacourts'—Sheila carrying the duffel bag of clothes and Amory dangling his empty Perrier bottle. He was a liberated southern male, willing to let women do it all.

Sheila did not hear a word he said on the way down the hill. She was too busy wondering why everything Dee had bought at Lord and Taylor's had K Mart price tags.

As they reached Sheila's car, the Marriots' maid emerged from the house at the end of the cul-de-sac and began sweeping their front walk. Quickly Sheila thrust the duffel bag into her trunk. "I'll be right back," she called to Amory over her shoulder.

The maid looked up in surprise as Sheila approached and greeted her. Sheila asked, "Did you prepare the food for last Friday's party? I thought the shrimp dip was especially good."

The woman's odd gray eyes brightened with pleasure, and she smiled, revealing a gold right upper incisor. "It's my own recipe. Folks usually like it."

"You had a lot of excitement here on Monday, didn't you? Too bad you weren't sweeping the deck that afternoon—you might have seen the murderer!"

That startled her. She backed up a step. "Oh, no, ma'am, I was inside all day and the Marriots were away. We never saw a thing." She began to sweep with vigor, moving back down the walk.

Sheila turned back to the car, disappointed. Frank McGehee

was wrong. Fifty murderers could have walked up this street
Monday afternoon unobserved.

Amory was once again deep in discussion with a female. This
time it was Nan Quentin. She'd finished taking pictures and was
taking notes instead. Heaven knew what Amory might be telling
her. Sheila arrived in time to hear him say, "I'm sure she'll tell
you whatever she's discovered so far." He pulled Sheila into the
conversation by grabbing her elbow and holding it. "Sheila, this
is the writer I was talking to Monday night down at the gates.
She was actually here all Monday morning, watching the street.
She might have some information!"

The woman flushed and said hastily, "I didn't really see anything important. I was trying to meet Slade Robinson, the ball
player, to get an interview, but he was gone all morning. I left
soon after noon."

Since Walt had seen Yvonne alive after noon, Sheila suspected
Nan Quentin's notes would be of little use to anybody—including
Nan—but Amory was already urging her, "Come get a bite with
us."

Sheila was too genteel to throttle him in front of a stranger.
She'd wait until they got home.

Amory had a radar for good food. He found a new restaurant
on Chamblee-Dunwoody Road, only a few blocks away, and
chose a table in the far corner. "We won't be overheard here," he
grunted portentiously.

Since it was well past most people's lunchtime, they wouldn't
have been overheard wherever they sat, but Nan was so impressed by his forethought that Sheila didn't point that out.

The neophyte writer chatted cheerfully as they discussed various menu items and made their selections, then she fell silent.

"Tell us about yourself," Sheila suggested to break the ice.

Nan blushed. "There's not much to tell. I grew up in South

Alabama and got out of high school with no money, so I joined the navy to get my nurse's training. For a little while I was married to an ensign, but that didn't work. I saw a lot of the world for several years until I finally decided two years ago I'd had enough. I've been working at Grady ever since. I'm not really a writer yet," she added, digging into her chef's salad with such gusto that a glob of French dressing spattered Amory's tie. "Oh, sorry! But"—she turned back to Sheila—"I've been taking courses at Georgia State, and I want to be a writer more than anything in the world! Amory says you are private detectives working on the case?"

"We're not—"

Nan didn't wait for the rest. "If you'll let me write it up afterward, I'll do any research you need. Anything! I'll dig in the library, visit the newspaper, cultivate some reporters, just anything. This is an incredible break for me!"

Amory was busy eating a hot roast beef sandwich. He couldn't possibly meet Sheila's eye. She glared at his balding head and considered how to reply.

The only time a library had been involved in one of her investigations, she'd found a body in its basement. Usually she tried to avoid, not cultivate, reporters. In fact, she usually tried to avoid poking around in murders. Since, for once, she had decided of her own free will to take this murder on, should she take on an amateur researcher, too? After all, she had lots of work back at the office. And Nan might save her some drudgery.

"Well," she suggested, tackling her shrimp salad, "you could try to find out something about Yvonne Delacourt's past."

Nan nodded eagerly. "I can try. What do you know so far?"

"She moved to Atlanta about three years ago, I think. Her neighbors may know from where. Try to find out if she has any family living, where she lived before Atlanta." Whether or not Nan turned up anything, that ought to keep her busy.

"I'll start checking this afternoon!" Nan's face was pink with excitement. "I'm off tomorrow, too. I'll call you if I find anything at all!"

Sheila swallowed a sigh. She remembered something Tyler often said. "God save me from novice reporters. The old ones are as bad as bloodhounds, but the pups yelp." Nan almost yelped in her eagerness to put her nose to the scent.

"Oh!" Nan reached to the floor and hauled up her enormous purse. "I almost forgot! These probably won't mean anything to you, but . . ." She shoved a wad of folded papers at Sheila, overturning a water glass in her eagerness.

After the spill had been hastily mopped up, Sheila spread out the sheets. They were closely covered in a cramped, minuscule script. "My notes from last Monday morning," Nan explained.

Sheila managed not to sigh, but she dreaded the thought of plowing through those crowded pages. "Could I possibly keep them to read tonight?"

"Sure. I have a copy at home."

"I wonder what *I* should do next?" Amory finished his sandwich and frowned like a man in charge of a homicide case pondering how well he had deployed his troops.

"You could spend some time with Forbes," Sheila suggested. Before he could protest, she added, "I'll bet he's never been to the Cyclorama."

She knew that would hook him. Amory never visited Atlanta without an afternoon in the old theater in the round which depicted the Battle of Atlanta. The temptation to show it to a child who had never seen it would be intriguing, if not irresistible.

Amory brightened. "Good idea. I can pump him on who his mother's friends were, too, and he might even know where Yvonne used to live. So," he summed up briskly, "Nan is going to the library and the newspaper offices and I'm taking Forbes to the Cyclorama. Where are you going?"

Sheila laid her napkin beside her plate and pushed back her chair. "I," she said firmly, "am going back to work."

What does a thoughtful Dunwoody
matron request for Christmas?
A Mercedes. She knows her husband
hates wrapping presents.

Since Sheila planned to work late, she let Amory drop her off at her office and keep her car. "I'll get a cab home," she told him.

Not until the cab drove away from her apartment at ten-thirty that evening did she remember what she should have thought about sooner: Frank McGehee's smuggled documents and her absent trunk.

He had been inventive, however. Propped against her door was a sheaf of daisies and a large box of chocolates. Inside the box were two chocolates—maple creams, her favorites—and copies of the police reports.

She munched the candy while she took Lady for a walk, enjoying the rumbles of thunder and the way light gray clouds scudded across the deeper sky. When the Sheltie had had enough exercise, Sheila returned home, turned off the air-conditioning, and threw open the windows to let in the freshening breeze. Exchanging her work clothes for a soft cotton caftan and slippers, she made a pot of coffee. Finally, mug in hand, she found a pencil and spread the documents around her at the table. Lady fell asleep on her toe while she worked.

She learned little from a list of hairs and unidentified prints at the crime scene, but was interested in how Yvonne had been found. Not nude, beaten, and raped (as Monday night's gossips

had claimed), but lying on her back on the guest room bed, wearing lavender panties. Her eyes had been closed, her hands
crossed at her breast, and a white silk lily had been tucked into
one hand.

Sheila was surprised to find the medical examiner's initial au-
topsy report in the file only two days after the crime. Drake
must be rushing other departments as well as his own.

Among other facts, the medical examiner noted that her skin
was soft with lotion (of course it was!), that she had not had
recent sexual intercourse, and that she had been killed instantly
by one thrust of the brass letter opener that pierced her heart.
There were no signs of struggle and almost no blood except what
had oozed from the wound and pooled under the body "indicating
that the weapon remained in the wound for several hours before
being removed." The killer would not have been spattered with
blood.

As she read the description of Yvonne's stomach contents,
Sheila couldn't repress a smile. Would Amory have eaten so
heartily if he'd known he snacked on leftovers from the dead
woman's last meal?

The murder weapon itself had been described by a cautious
officer with no flair for the dramatic. Jake Drake himself? She
could imagine him dictating the generic terms: "shiny brass-
colored letter opener eight-and-one-sixteenth inches long, shaft
five inches long, point very sharp, handle also brass-colored, top
curved in birdlike shape." Bird*like* shape? Sheila's lips again
curved in a wry smile. She knew the police had to be careful not
to come to conclusions, but surely either it was a bird or it
wasn't. That explained why Walt had kept the letter opener on
his desk, though—not just a sentimental memento of his honeymoon, but a bird. She wondered what kind of bird it was.

Tired, a little nauseated from considering horrors reported so
matter-of-factly, Sheila rubbed her eyes, stretched, gently removed Lady's muzzle from her toe, and went to refill her mug. In

the approaching thunder she could almost hear Aunt Mary's deep reprimand, "You drink too much coffee, dear."

"How else will I stay awake?" she asked the empty room.

The rain came suddenly, a torrent that streamed past her eaves and drummed on the concrete two stories below. Sheila rushed to shut the windows, leaving just a few inches open to let in the moist coolness. Lady whined and went back to sleep. Sheila returned to the table and read the description of Yvonne's body once more. Unless Yvonne laid herself down and patiently posed for death, someone had taken great care to lay out the body for burial. Why?

And where had the murderer gotten a white silk lily? A few of the many silk floral arrangements throughout Yvonne's house contained lilies, but all in shades of mauve, pink, blue, and cream. Had a police officer mistaken a cream lily for a white one? She'd ask Frank. But wherever the lily came from, it absolved Walt. He might conceivably stab someone in rage. He would never have thought of that touch.

You're just jealous, Sheila told herself, *because he forgot to order you a corsage for the senior prom.*

Maybe so, she replied, *but silk lilies and Walter Delacourt don't have much in common.*

Finished with reports, she went to recover the paper scraps and green appointment book from her jacket pocket. The little book still made no sense. It seemed that Yvonne had preserved her secrets in a code impossible to break without intimate knowledge of her life. Had anyone had that? Certainly not her husband.

The most crowded date of the year was April 23. Entries on that page had been made in nine different colors of ink. For nine different years? The green cover was certainly tattered enough to hold nine years of secrets. The first entry was brief: *H25, C500*. The sixth was the longest: *C1000, Mmb, J100m, S50m, K200m*. The ninth read *Wmb, R100!, C1500, A200m*.

Were the letters initials for names? If so, what could "m" stand
for besides meter and million? Neither seemed likely. Why that
curious repetition of *C?* Did *A200m* in April relate to *A200m?* in
June—possibly written the day she died?

On other pages, the letter *C* appeared often: *C1000* or, sometimes, *12:00C, 7:30C.* It could, of course, be a private way of
noting an erratic menstrual cycle. If the letter were a person,
however, Yvonne had been in almost monthly contact with C for
as long as she had kept this journal. Sheila made a note to ask
Walt for possible names, then tossed the journal aside and
reached for Nan's notes.

Written in a personal speedwriting, they were easier to decipher than she had expected, especially with the aid of a map
numbering the houses. Sheila translated and reduced them to a
timetable of her own.

Monday morning at seven, Walt and Forbes had driven out. In
the next hour Dee's girls went to school, Rilla's maid was
dropped off, and Slade Robinson left in a maroon Jaguar. His
wave to Nan rated two exclamation points, but Sheila was more
interested in what happened next at Walt's:

> 8:00   *Man w/ red hair from #2 rang bell #3,*
>   *pounded on door with fist. No answer.*
>   *Rang again. No answer. Went home.*
> 8:10   *Same man left #2 in black BMW.*
> 8:30   *Woman #3 left in a small cream Mercedes.*
>   *Why didn't answer earlier?*

Why indeed? Sheila starred that fact and read on.

The rest of Nan's morning must have been dull. Jaqui and her
son left about nine, Dee shortly afterward, Richard arrived at
the Marriots' at ten. At ten-thirty a white van pulled up to
Yvonne's and four women went inside, carrying cleaning imple-
ments. They left an hour later. Sheila put a star by that. How

many Dunwoody wives used a maid service? Most, Sheila suspected, would have a regular maid–cum–baby-sitter. But regular
maids tended to learn a good deal about their employers. Had
Yvonne used a service and a day care center to preserve her
precious privacy?

While the maids were at Yvonne's, a *"scruffy black man in
gray truck"* arrived at the Robinsons' to mow. Paula Divesty
left, and a male jogger—*"large, blond hair, twentyish"*—entered
the subdivision. Perhaps out of sheer boredom Nan had meticu-
lously recorded his strange behavior. *"Jogged down street three
times. Last time sat on curb of #3, seemed to study house. Asked
maid in house #4 for water, drank it, tied shoe, left. Gave me
dirty look on his way out."*

At that point, according to Nan's list, the only people on the
street were the Robinsons' yard man and four people at the Marriots'. Sheila jotted a question in the margin: *Does jogger Ivy
girls saw later match this description?*

There wasn't much more. Nan offered Slade's yard man some
tea and learned he was filling in for the regular service. *"Just my
luck,"* Nan's notes mourned. He left at noon just as Richard
drove Mac and Rilla out. Shortly afterward Yvonne returned and
parked in her garage, leaving the door up. At twelve-fifteen Walt
came home, parked in the drive, carried his golf clubs to the
garage, closed its door. He left forty-five minutes later.

At that point Nan left, too. Too bad. She might have seen the
murderer. Or had she? Sheila stared at the final entry until her
eyes burned:

> *1:00   Man left #3 in suit and tie. Ran down
> steps and backed out in hurry. At road
> turned left, burning rubber.*

The rain drummed against the windows. Sheila poured herself
yet another mug of coffee and flung herself on the couch to con-

sider the possibilities. Lady padded over and jumped up beside
her. Delighted not to be pushed back down to the carpet, she
nuzzled herself snugly under Sheila's left arm and sighed contentedly.

Sheila patted her absently. She was considering—and rejecting—scenarios. She rejected immediately any idea that some
stranger happened on that house in the only hour that Running
Ridge Road was empty, and committed an unpremeditated murder. Why would anyone committing a senseless crime arrange
the body so carefully—or leave the house without stealing a single thing?

Someone *could* have gone to Yvonne's after Walt left and before Forbes returned, but there were a lot of ifs: if the person
knew Yvonne would be alone; if the person knew the neighbors
were all gone and when Forbes was coming back; if the person
was someone Yvonne knew, had invited, or could be persuaded
to admit.

As Sheila turned all those ifs over in her mind, she found herself trembling. The one person most likely to fit any of those
categories was Yvonne's husband, Walter Delacourt.

She knew Nan's notes would have to be turned over to Jake
Drake, and they were just what he needed. They showed that
the time between Walt's departure and Forbes's arrival was
much shorter than Walt had admitted. They also showed he had
left in inordinate haste. Given that, and his prints on the letter
opener, why shouldn't a jury convict him of killing his wife?

She was still on the couch when Amory returned. While Lady
greeted him with yips of pleasure, he stood in the doorway,
brushing raindrops from his shoulders. "Boy, what a frog stran-
gler! Are all the windows down?"

Sheila stared at him, appalled. His words had reminded her of
something the rain itself had not. She had left two windows wide
open in Yvonne Delacourt's lovely guest room.

It was as good a reason as any to do what she dreaded doing: call Walt.

Running Ridge Road was certainly running now. Sheila, who had been dozing while Amory drove, opened her eyes to see water streaming down both sides of the street while Amory steered slowly down the center. As lightning flashed, huge trees seemed to leap forward, then recede into darkness. The lights were veiled by the downpour, leaving the street dim except for Amory's headlights, several lights at Walt's, and a glow from deep within the Divestys'.

"Make him come here," Amory had insisted when she'd told him she needed to see Walt. But Sheila wanted to talk to Walt in his own home. She wanted to visualize as much as she could of what might have happened. More important, if Jake Drake were tailing Walt, she didn't want him led to her apartment.

Walt was so calm as he opened the door and took Sheila's damp raincoat and glistening umbrella that she felt certain he was maintaining his rigid control only by stupendous effort. His face was as pale as if he had lived underground for weeks. His hair fell into his face. His glasses were askew and he made no attempt to push them back in place.

Seeing that he was fully dressed and slightly rumpled, she asked, "You weren't in bed when I called?"

He shook his head. "I h-h-had some w-w-work I needed to do." Like the terrified Forbes earlier, he stammered slightly when he spoke. He gestured vaguely toward his study door. She could just see his desktop, littered with papers.

She pulled a stack of mail from beneath her raincoat. "We parked by the mailbox, and I checked inside."

Without even looking through them, he went to his desk, opened his bottom drawer, and dropped the envelopes in. "Thanks." She hoped he'd remember them again before Georgia Power cut off his lights.

"Did you eat dinner?" she asked.

He gave a curious little shrug, half disclaimer and half embarrassment. "I w-w-wasn't very h-hungry."

"You've got to eat, man." Amory's voice was muffled, for he had entered the powder room under the stairs. "Okay if I leave my raincoat in here? Better than ruining the carpet."

Walt murmured a polite agreement. Amory returned, smoothing his hair with one hand and extending the other. "I'm Amory Travis." He sounded, Sheila thought, exactly as if they were meeting at a Suwannee alumni club.

Walt shook limply, then turned back to Sheila. "I closed the windows. The carpet got a little wet, but nothing serious."

At that point Amory endeared himself to Sheila for days to come. "How about if I rustle you up something to eat? I'm a mean cook." It was, she knew, no idle boast. Amory had been winning cooking competitions since high school. Without waiting for Walt's response, he headed for the kitchen. In a few minutes Sheila heard the homely rattle of pots and pans and a familiar rumble that she knew from experience was Amory's hummed rendition of "She'll Be Coming 'Round the Mountain." It was not, perhaps, the best song for the situation, but Walt probably wouldn't notice. She steered her old friend back into his study and without preamble told him of his father's request that she help with the murder investigation. He raised a hand in mild protest, but did not seem to care whether she got involved or not. She described Nan's notes, providing an eyewitness account of the exact minute when he left the house.

He sat at his desk, hands fidgeting with a brass cardinal paperweight and his gaze roving around the room, seldom meeting Sheila's. He answered her questions with single words or grunts.

Worry made her impatient with him.

"Walt!" she finally exclaimed. "*I* presume you are innocent, but no jury is going to believe it unless we can show that someone else could have been here. Do you hear me? Now tell me what happened while you were home!"

He shrugged. "Nothing. Look, Sheila, drop it. I've got a lawyer."

"I can't drop it, Walt. I promised Rip. When you got home that day you saw Yvonne?"

"Yeah."

"Did you have a fight?"

That roused him a bit. "Of course not!" Then he sank into lethargy again, his hands roving over papers spread untidily across the desk.

Sheila pressed him. "Where was she? What was she doing?"

He looked at the ceiling for inspiration. "Upstairs. Dressing. Then in the kitchen, fixing lunch."

"Dressing for what? Was she going out?"

He reached for a pencil and began to doodle as he used to do in especially boring classes. *This isn't school,* she longed to scream at him. *You may be on trial for your life!*

Instead, she slammed her palm down on the fat arm of the leather chair. "Was she going out, Walt? Was she?"

Her urgency shocked him. He put down the pencil. "I don't know, Sheila. She'd been playing tennis. She always showered after tennis. She may have had to show a house later. I don't know, okay? After dressing, she came down to fix lunch while I showered. But as I told you, my lawyer's handling this."

She refused to be put off. He sounded too much like the old Walt when he didn't want to study for a math exam. "What did she put on—do you remember?"

He made an effort to remember, shook his head. "Maybe something purple? She l-l-liked p-p-purple." Tears welled into his bloodshot eyes. Sheila remembered the lavender panties Yvonne had been wearing when he found her. Was that what he was remembering, too?

She stood. Maybe a walk-through would jog his memory. "Let's go upstairs, Walt, and look through Yvonne's clothes. See if you can remember what she put on."

"What difference does it make?"

She couldn't tell him she wanted to learn if Yvonne could have been dressing to meet a lover. "Probably none, but it might give a clue to whether Yvonne had an appointment." She put out her hand. "Come."

Upstairs, she crossed the master bedroom and opened Yvonne's walk-in closet. "Any of these things?"

He was in there so long, she thought he'd smothered. When she went in after him, he was standing with his head bent over the hangers. Tears streamed down his cheeks, ruining a blue satin evening dress. She touched his shoulder. "I can't bear it, Sheila," he whispered. "Her smell, her clothes—I keep waiting for her to come in a door, run down the stairs, call me to dinner. She can't be gone. She can't!" He crumpled to the closet floor and knelt there, racked by sobs.

Rejecting comfort as useless, Sheila filled a bathroom glass with cold water, returned to the closet, and poured it over him. Walt gasped, sat up, tugged off his glasses, and vainly tried to dry them on his drenched shirt.

"Get on some dry clothes," Sheila said firmly, helping him up and shoving him toward his own closet.

He went into the bathroom a few minutes later with his wet clothes and emerged triumphant, bearing the purple skirt Sheila had seen earlier in the hamper. "This is what she put on! I found it when I threw my shirt in the hamper." This was no time to remind him what happened to wet shirts in hampers. He returned to the bathroom and brought out the coordinating shirt and lacy lavender bra. "I think she had these on, too." The bra was manufactured by his own company, but he still avoided Sheila's eyes as he handed it over.

Sheila examined the rumpled clothes, trying to think coherently if not furiously. The skirt and blouse were stylish but casual, what a woman might put on if she planned to be home all afternoon—not what she'd put on to welcome her lover. Yet, unless Yvonne had taken them off for a lover, why would she put

them in the hamper only a short while later? A careful examina-
tion revealed no stains, spills, or even visible signs of wear.

Walt returned, took his wife's clothes and went to sit on the
room's only chair, stroking the skirt and staring at a spot somewhere beyond his long bare feet. Gently Sheila took back the
clothes from him, returned them to the hamper, and hung his
wet clothes over the side of the tub. He did not notice she had
gone or returned until she sat on the side of the bed and asked
gravely, "Do you have any idea who could have killed her, Walt?"

"I can't begin to imagine." His voice was hoarse from tears
and pain. "She was the sweetest, gentlest, kindest—" Tears rose
again. Silently he gripped the chair arms and fought for control.

Sheila realized what an enormous commitment she had made
to Rip. Walt had no intention of helping himself. He was fixated
on Yvonne's death as his own loss. That she had been brutally
murdered was incidental. That he might be suspected of killing
her was wholly unimportant. All he could feel or understand was
that Yvonne was gone and he was bereft.

For several minutes neither spoke. At last he pulled out his
handkerchief and blew his nose. "Sorry, Sheila. I—you lost your
husband, didn't you? You know what it's like."

She did. She had no longer adored Travis as Walt adored
Yvonne, but even now she sometimes found herself thinking, "I
must remember to tell Tyler that." Afterward there was always
a jolt of surprise and loss. Just now, for Walt, the pain must be a
thousand times worse. She said softly, "Yes, I know. And I want
to help you, Walt. But you must answer some questions. Did you
ever see Yvonne writing in a small green book?"

He shook his head, stopped, reconsidered. "No, but I came in
here one day and she was sitting in this chair"—his voice wob-
bled—"reading one. She shoved it down beside her and I didn't
ask what it was. I didn't like to pry. And I don't know where it is
now." He fumbled between the cushion and seat of the chair,
found nothing. "How did you know about it?"

His interest was unexpected and heartening.

"Amory found it this afternoon. But I can't make anything of it. It's all letters and numbers. I hoped maybe you could tell me about it. It looked like some sort of diary of appointments, and I think she'd been keeping it for years. It might help if we knew anything about her past—where she came from, who her people were."

He sniffed, wiped his nose on his sleeve. "I never knew much. We met at a party at the club and I . . . I never knew before what people meant by being swept off your feet, but—" His face softened with the memory. Then a more recent memory swept it with pain. "She didn't talk much about herself. She'd lived in Memphis, I think, and Florida. After Forbes's bath one night she started telling me how white the Florida sand is—like bath powder. She said when she was a little girl she used to put it all over her and pretend it was Chanel. I thought maybe she grew up there."

Florida was a big state, especially since Sheila didn't know Yvonne's maiden name. Neither did Walt. "She was a Hardwick when I married her. A widow. Her first husband was older, and died of heart problems—I do know that much." He shook his head gloomily. "She'd had a tough life, I think. All I wanted to do was protect her, Sheila. I wanted to take care of her!" He crumpled forward, arms on his knees and face on his arms, and wept again. At last he raised his head, glasses streaming, and begged, "Bring me back her journal, Sheila. Don't pry into her private affairs!"

She didn't have the heart to tell him that before she could do that she would have to turn it over to Jake Drake.

"Walt, did Yvonne ever mention a friend whose name starts with a C? Someone she'd known a long time?"

Again he started to shake his head, again reconsidered—as if he had to draw the little bits and pieces of what he knew from some deep reservoir of memory. "She had an old friend who called her sometimes. I never met him, or spoke with him, but she mentioned him occasionally. He had a funny name. Chip? Chipper? No, it was nicer than that, but it always reminded me of potato chips. Forbes might know. He talked to him once or twice, I think."

Sheila hated asking a child about his dead mother's friends, but better for her to ask than Jake Drake. Forbes had been terrified that she was kidnapping him. What might he fear from Drake?

"Finish telling me exactly what happened while you were home Monday," she urged.

"I already told you, Sheila. Nothing!"

"Try to remember everything, Walt. You came up here and she was done showering. She dressed, you showered. What did she do then?"

"Fixed lunch. Nothing happened. Look, Sheila, my lawyer . . ."

Sheila sighed in pure exasperation. "Something *must* have happened, Walt. The witness said you came out the door in a hurry and burned rubber at the corner."

He listened without expression, tried to remember. She knew the exact moment his mind connected with the memory. He spoke in a rush, as if glad to go back to that safe, untroubled time. "That's right, I was late! I had an appointment that I thought was at two-thirty, but I checked my book and saw it was at two. I ran down the stairs, got halfway out the front door, called back to Yvonne that I was gone, and left. I did not burn rubber," he added with dignity. "I just drove very fast. After all, it's over thirty miles to the office from here. As it was, I arrived ten minutes late."

"What was Yvonne doing when you left?"

Again he seemed to try to picture it. "Phoning."

Could this finally be a lead? "Phoning whom?"

He shrugged. "I don't know. She was on the kitchen phone."

"Could it have been a friend? Who were her friends?"

"Women from the club. Dee Ivy across the street."

"How about people from her office?"

"She doesn't have an office, except across the hall. She used to work for Alex's company, but Alex got nasty, so she quit. She could have been making an appointment to show a house, I suppose."

Something he'd said intrigued her. "What made Alex get nasty?"

"Oh, it was silly. Yvonne sold a few houses right after his contract on them expired. That meant she got the whole commission instead of splitting it with him. But it wasn't her fault. The buyers just didn't make up their minds before that." He raised his hands to show it didn't matter.

Yet Alex got nasty. Nasty enough to kill her? Was *A200m* Alex Divesty? Could *m* stand for "mad"? Did Yvonne rate how angry she made other people on some scale of her own devising? Could she possibly have angered that many people on April 23?

"What happened April 23?" she asked.

He stared as if she'd gone crazy. "I can't remember last Friday, much less April 23. Oh, wait! That was Yvonne's birthday! How did you know?"

"I didn't. She had a lot of entries on that date in her book, but they are all in code."

For the first time since the day of his wife's death, she saw Walt's gentle, shy smile. "Probably a list of her presents. Vonnie loved getting presents."

"What did you give her?"

"A car. She wanted a little Mercedes, so I got it for her. She loved it, Sheila, just loved it!"

And had entered it carefully into her journal: *Wmb*. Walt, Mercedes-Benz! Could *200m* be two hundred Mercurys? Two hundred Miatas? Two hundred—

She remembered another entry. "Did your dad give her anything for her birthday?"

He ran his hand through his rumpled hair. "He doesn't get to shop anymore, so he just gave her a card and a check. She was thrilled." *R100!* A surprise gift. But the other days' entries couldn't be presents. Nobody got that many. Besides, what about *D no dice?* Sheila knew one possible *D.* She must try to find out if anything happened between Dee Ivy and Yvonne Delacourt on May 28.

Meanwhile, Walt had remembered something. "She could have been calling Forbes's day care when I was leaving. I—" He hesitated and flushed. "When I let him off, I forgot to tell them to bring him home at two-thirty. She was pretty annoyed. Not really mad, though!" Was he convincing Sheila, or himself? "She'd promised Jaqui Robinson that Forbes would go play with Cornelius, and Vonnie hated letting people down."

He spoke with the earnestness of a lawyer defending his client's basic goodness. Sheila had to admit he was convincing. Walt had lived with the woman for over a year and found her loving, kind, helpful—a real Girl Scout. So why had Paula and Alex Divesty glared at her? Why had the mysterious gardener kept an eye on her? Why had Dee Ivy been so hostile to her? And why had one of them—or someone else—hated her enough to kill her?

"Dinner's served." Amory's voice floated up from downstairs. Sheila hoped he had cooked enough for at least two. Her sandwich at seven had not been intended to see her through a busy night.

Over supper they did not discuss the murder, but as they were leaving, Walt leaned close and spoke urgently. "Look, Sheila, the police will take care of all this. And if they make a mistake and arrest me, my lawyer will deal with that. You don't have to get involved."

"Your dad asked me to," she reminded him. "Rip's worried sick. And so far, Walt, you are by far everyone's best suspect. Don't you realize that?"

He shrugged and reached up with his left hand to adjust his glasses. For an instant he looked like the old Walt. "I didn't kill her, Sheila. I loved her. And I've got a good lawyer. You don't have to worry about me. To tell the truth, though, I don't care what happens to me anymore. It just doesn't matter."

"It matters to me," she assured him, giving him a quick hug. For an instant she felt his shoulders relax, then stiffen to their customary rigidity.

As he held her umbrella and escorted her with courtesy toward the waiting car, Sheila yearned to reassure him that one day this nightmare would end. But would it?

Amory was drooping with weariness. "I'll drive," Sheila told him. "I want to do some thinking anyway."

She had scarcely started the engine, however, when he suddenly grunted, "What's that?"

She slammed on brakes. "What?"

He craned his neck to peer through the rear window, which was blurred by rain. "Nothing, I guess. I was looking in the side mirror, and thought I saw a light in that empty house. Must have been the reflection of your backing lights."

"See if you see it again." She eased down the drive.

"No," he finally grunted in disappointment.

She turned off her lights and drove around the cul-de-sac, parked, and waited for several minutes. The rain thrummed on the roof. Finally Amory shrugged. "Guess I've started seeing—"

"Wait!" She waved him to silence. "Was that a flicker?" If so, it did not reappear.

"Must be a trick of reflected light," he muttered.

Amory was probably right. Reluctantly she started the engine.

"Fixing a steak for Walt was inspired," she told him as they turned onto Mount Vernon Road, "and your pilaf was delicious.

I'd bet that was the only real food Walt has eaten for two days."

"I'll say this for Yvonne." Amory spoke as if the dead woman had been a personal friend. "She kept a good freezer." He slid lower in his seat and rested his head against the headrest.

"Do you feel up to telling me about your time with Forbes? Was it fun? And did he say anything helpful?"

Amory gave a grunt that meant he'd rather be sleeping. "Said he got born in Memphis. Said his daddy was named Daddy, and that he'd already seen the Cyclorama with Crispin, whoever— hey! Keep this car on the road!"

Dunwoody prides itself on resisting efforts to widen its roads. Sheila's sudden swerve had taken them nearly into a ditch.

"Sorry!" She pulled back onto the pavement. "You startled me. I've been looking for someone Yvonne knew with the initial C, and Crispin fits. C appears regularly in that little book you found."

"The book is helpful?" Amory sounded pleased.

"It may be. I asked Walt who C might be, and he said Yvonne had a friend whose name reminded him of a potato chip. That could be Crispin."

"Yeah—chips are crisp. Might be a mnemonic, I guess." Amory sounded dubious.

"No, Walt studied at the London School of Economics. Britishers call chips 'crisps.' I wonder how we could find this man?"

"Forbes might know," he murmured drowsily. "I'll ask him Friday. We're going out to see the museum at Stone Mountain."

Sheila gave him a quick, sharp look. "I thought you were going home Friday morning!"

Amory made a sound somewhere between a *humph* and a *humm*. "I thought maybe I'd stick around a few more days. Help, if I can."

Now she understood his offer to cook Walt dinner and to take Forbes to Stone Mountain. Amory was getting detective fever.

"Is it okay if I stay longer?" he asked, obviously anxious.

"Sure, if the bank can spare you."

"It's *my* bank," he reminded her smugly.

They rode in silence while Sheila digested these new revelations—and wondered how long Amory planned to stay. She didn't really care, she realized. She was almost getting used to having him around. "You're awfully nice to take Forbes again," she told him. "Mildred will be glad for another breather."

He gave another grunt. "He's not bad company." He tarnished some of the stars in his heavenly crown, however, by adding, "Mildred promised me her pecan-peach cobbler recipe if I'd let her go see her auntie Friday."

"Friday?" Sheila remembered something. "But that's the day of Yvonne's funeral. Surely Forbes ought to be there. Can you go to Stone Mountain another day?"

"Could, I guess," Amory agreed, "but Walt and I discussed the funeral this evening while you went to powder your nose, and he doesn't think Forbes ought to go."

What Amory really meant was, Walt didn't want to be bothered with the child. Sheila herself thought Forbes needed a chance to say good-bye to his mother—but her unsolved homicide could turn the funeral into a media circus. They rode in silence, listening to the rain, until Sheila said with a sigh, "Like Scarlett O'Hara, we'll think about that tomorrow. Aunt Mary may have something to suggest. Did you finish telling me about your time with Forbes today?"

Amory considered. "Well, he did ask when it was going to be Friday. I thought that was because of the funeral, but he said he has to go see Momsy on Friday."

"Who is Momsy?"

He shrugged. "I asked, but Forbes didn't seem to know who she is or where she lives. Said his mama was supposed to take him Friday. Then he got sort of teary, so I dropped it for the time being. Later I asked if his momsy was his mama's mama or his daddy's mama. He went into a fit of the giggles and said 'Mamas and daddies don't have mamas, they have babies.' Smart little cookie."

"Did he sound like they were going on a trip? Walt doesn't have a mother, so it would have to be Yvonne's. Plane reservations might help us find where she lives."

Amory was nonplussed. "I didn't think of that. I'll ask when we go to Stone Mountain."

"There's something else you might check out another time," Sheila told him. "An entry in that little green book—'D no dice.' That could be your friend Dee Ivy. She and Yvonne seem to have quarreled about something. If you're going to see Dee again, ask as tactfully as you know how if anything happened between them on May 28—and what."

Amory turned his head and opened his eyes. "Now, don't start thinking Dee's a suspect, Sheila," he growled. "She knows more about the Civil War than any woman I ever met. At dinner tonight she argued me down about the Battle of Mobile, and when we stopped by the library afterward to check, she was right!" Amory was the only man Sheila knew who would take a date by the library to try and win an argument. He was also, she had to admit, the only man she knew who took genuine pleasure in losing a good argument. It was gaining knowledge, not winning, that he relished.

"Being a good historian doesn't necessarily exclude Dee from being a suspect," she felt compelled to point out.

He shook his head stubbornly. "The only person she might kill would be her ex-husband. That bum played around, then left her for a younger woman. He's always flying to the Bahamas or taking girlfriends to Europe while Dee struggles just to keep food on the table." His voice was gruff with righteous indignation.

Considering the house Dee lived in and the car she drove, Sheila was inclined to be less sympathetic. "She could move to a cheaper part of town."

Amory's eyes were closed again. "I asked about that. In the divorce settlement she gets the house and a leased car until the girls are grown—unless she marries again."

"Thinking about asking her?" Sheila teased.

His final grunt was noncommittal. Aunts don't get told everything.

*What does a Dunwoody matron wear
to a funeral?
Her black tennis dress.*

The next morning Sheila telephoned Frank McGehee to thank him for the smuggled documents and to tell him to expect Nan Quentin's notes by courier. He could tell Jake Drake what he pleased about where they came from. She also asked him to look for someone named Crispin. Frank made a note and promised he'd look into it.

"There are a couple of other things, too," Sheila continued. "The night of the murder, I heard that Dee Ivy's children had seen a jogger on the street earlier in the day. In the papers I'm sending, you'll see that Nan saw a jogger that morning, and she got a good look at him. He got a drink of water from the Marriots' maid, who might also be able to describe him, although she seems a bit simple to me. He could be the same person that the Ivy girls saw later."

"Could have been casing the place," he agreed. "I'll look into it. Drake wants us questioning the neighbors about Walt Delacourt. I might as well ask a few other questions, too. Is that all?"

"Not quite. Did you see that lily Yvonne was holding when she was found? Was it really white, or maybe creamy yellow?"

"No, it was pure white. Like those they put in church for Easter. Is that important?"

"Could be. There aren't any white flowers in Yvonne's house. You might ask Dee Ivy about that. She decorated the house, and probably would remember if there was a white lily in an arrangement. If not, somebody had to bring that flower into the house."

"Good point. But I don't think Jake's gonna let me spend too much time chasing lilies. He's closing in on Walt, Sheila, and he's getting pretty close."

There didn't seem to be much she could do about that. Just before lunch, however, she thought of something she *could* do.

Alex Divesty answered the phone himself. From background noises, she guessed he was talking from his car. Since she hated driving behind people talking on the phone, she reminded him who she was and came right to the point. "Last Monday night I was supposed to view the house across from Walt's with Yvonne. Would it be possible for you to show it to me instead?"

He was instantly all charm. "Of course! It's a great house! Lots of room, good neighborhood—" He broke off with a short laugh. "Usually, anyway. You've met most of the neighbors, I think. It's a friendly street, but people let you do your own thing, if you know what I mean."

She didn't, but she set up an appointment for five-thirty. They should be finished before visiting hours began at the funeral home.

She had scarcely hung up when Nan Quentin called. Her voice was high with excitement. "I've been at the library all morning, reading old papers, and I found a couple of articles that mentioned Yvonne. The longest was an account of her wedding last year, and guess what? It mentioned a hotel in Hawaii where they spent their honeymoon, and I remember it from when I was stationed over there. They give folks letter openers as souvenirs, brass ones with Hawaiian honeycatchers on them. That's the hotel's trademark—they put little birds on everything. Do you reckon it's possible the letter opener that killed Yvonne Delacourt came from there? It could have been her own! Should we call the police and tell them?"

"Go ahead," Sheila told her. "Ask for Captain Jake Drake."

Since Walt had already admitted the letter opener came from his desk and a Hawaiian hotel, surely Nan couldn't do any harm. And maybe she and Drake could form an alliance that would keep her out of Sheila's hair for a day or two.

Thelma Hardwick was having a hard time making herself understood over the telephone, but she had no intention of taking an arduous trip downtown unless it was absolutely necessary.

"No, I do not want custody of the child. I am not capable of taking care of a four-year-old. I just want to find out where he is. Do you understand? I want to know that he's *safe.*"

She listened to the legal jargon flowing from the other end, then interrupted impatiently: "No, I do *not* want my connection with the child made known at this time. I merely want to know his whereabouts."

She had to insist four more times before she got assent from the other end. When she hung up she leaned back against the couch and closed her eyes. "Your mills, oh, God, grind slowly," she murmured, "but they grind exceedingly fine."

Nan had carefully chosen her clothes that morning to look like her own impression of a professional reporter. Sheila, who had been interviewed by women reporters wearing everything from flowing flowered dresses to jeans, could have told her that the beige cotton suit would get terribly hot outdoors on a June afternoon, and would impress Dunwoody only as inexpensive, not professional, but Sheila was at work when Nan steered her Toyota to the curb of Running Ridge Road, gathered up her notebook and pen.

At Slade Robinson's she was glad no one answered. She did

not have the courage to interview him yet. She went up the curving walk next door to the big house that looked like an English castle, and took a deep, nervous breath before she rang. Scented by roses and boxwood, the air in this neighborhood even *smelled* rich.

"I am a reporter working on a story about the Delacourt murder," she told the tall, plain woman who answered the door. "I'm trying to get a little background on Mrs. Delacourt. Do you happen to know where she came from, or how long she had lived here?"

"Sorry. I scarcely knew her, and I'm on my way to play tennis." The woman closed the door in her face.

Nan gathered what dignity she had left and headed for the house at the bottom of the cul-de-sac. It was a longer walk than it looked, for the lots were large. She was getting sticky under her jacket, but she didn't mind the walk. It was like strolling through a park. Dunwoody might have the same azaleas, dogwoods, day lilies, and roses as the rest of Atlanta, but no Dunwoody plant would dare straggle or droop. Like their owners, they knew what was expected of them, and did it.

Nan didn't know why someone had left that funny gully there, though—a deep cut full of woods and underbrush. The big cedar-and-stone house beside it was hidden by an arm of the woods. Nan would have cut those trees down if she'd bought the house. Why have an elegant modern house if nobody could see it?

She preferred the brick colonial house next door, with flamboyant beds of flame-red hibiscus and crotons brightening the soft lawn, and begonias lining the walk. Nan was once again awed at what it must cost each spring to replant this yard.

She climbed the steps to the large front door, admiring the etched glass panes, dark green shutters, creamy columns, and brass light fixture hanging from a single chain. How, Nan wondered, did they ever clean that light? The maid who answered the door must climb a ladder pretty regularly to keep it that shiny. Unfortunately, however, the couple who lived there was away for the day and the maid had not known Mrs. Delacourt.

Hotter but not yet discouraged, Nan trudged back up the hill. House six was also a brick colonial, but prim, with black shutters and white trim. Its lawn—landscaped with boxwoods, azaleas, and red-tips—would require a minimum of care. Nan remembered seeing a woman leave for work from this house the morning she'd watched the street. Maybe this family didn't have time to plant flowers.

They had money, though. Nan had seen a teenager drive to school in the red Miata convertible now parked in the driveway. She had wondered what it would be like to have a gorgeous new car when you were so young. Nan had never had a new car in her life.

Nor had Nan looked as good in her teens as the girl who opened the door—the girl who had driven the Miata. She was of medium height, a bit stocky, and not even particularly pretty, but her brown hair was beautifully cut and conditioned, her teeth were straight, her shorts and sandals expensive, and her makeup flawless. Money, Nan reflected ruefully, might not be everything, but it sure could do a lot with what you started with.

It was not money, however, that had given the girl those huge brown eyes and long, curling lashes, and they were her best feature.

Her eyes widened, impressed, when Nan explained her errand. "I'm Lori," she said. "Mother's not in right now, but I can talk. I got home early because 1 only had a math exam at school today—1 probably flunked." She made a moue of mock despair and tugged the bottom of her black T-shirt, stretching a wolf's head across her chest. "I don't have to go anywhere until I pick up my sister at middle school in an hour. Come on in. Would you like a Coke?"

Through the open door Nan could hear a soap opera continuing its snail's pace through the day's script. "If I'm not interrupting anything . . ." She let the sentence trail into a question. If *she* had just had a murder in her neighborhood, she would be slow to invite in a stranger.

Lori, however, seemed to feel no threat. Soft brown hair flicked her cheeks, and she stood back from the door. "No, really, come in. I'd like to talk about it—you know, the murder. I still can't believe it happened right down the street!"

Nan was delighted to go inside. She took deep breaths of the crisp cold air and accepted Lori's offer of a drink.

Lori poured them both a Coke (adding what she thought was a surreptitious shot of bourbon to her own), then led the way to a cluttered den. Nan was wondering what questions to ask, but she needn't have bothered. Lori had started talking before she turned off the television.

"I knew Mrs. Delacourt real well. She even asked me to call her Yvonne, so I did—when Mom wasn't around. Yvonne was the sweetest *thing*. And she wore the darlingest clothes. She had a real good figure." Lori contemplated her own slightly dumpy one and tugged her shirt again, as if to conceal it. "Are you into saving wildlife?" she asked, pulling out the shirt's front so Nan could see the wolf better. "I am. Whales, wolves, it doesn't seem right that they should become extinct. Mr. Delacourt is into birds—I mean, *really!* Gets up at dawn and goes out to look for them."

Nan dragged the conversation back to its original subject. "Did his wife also like birds?"

Lori shook her head. "I don't think so. She liked tennis, and flowers, and clothes, of course. She looked great in anything she wore, and she bought the most beautiful *things!* I used to baby-sit for her little boy, Forbes, sometimes, and after he was asleep I'd, you know, look at her closet." Nan hid a smile. "Try on her clothes" was what Lori probably meant.

The teenager chattered on. "When she was short of cash she'd give me a scarf or something. She was the *sweetest thing.*"

Without warning, Lori jumped up. "I wanna show you something." She left, returned in a minute carrying a silver whale dangling from a thin silver chain. "Yvonne gave me this last Christmas. It's a blue whale. She ordered it for me special because she knew I'm really into saving endangered species." The girl fastened the chain around her neck and fiddled with the tiny whale.

"Yvonne used to talk to me a lot about when she was a teenager," Lori continued, her voice carefully casual, clearly proud of being Yvonne's confidante. "She went to boarding school in Switzerland, then she took a cooking course in France afterward—lucky her. I asked my mom if I could go to Europe this summer with my friends and she said positively not. 'We can't afford it.' " The words were her mother's, but the mocking tone was entirely Lori's own. "I'll probably have to hang out at the club pool with Megan and the other babies."

"Did Mrs. Delacourt tell you anything about her son's father or where she lived before—things like that?"

"No." Lori shook her head with obvious regret. "She may have told my mom, but she never told me anything about that. Except she was married to a doctor before Walt. My dad's a doctor, too." Lori bent forward earnestly. "I just hate that she got killed, you know? She was so sweet."

She had been steadily sipping her drink between sentences. Now her voice was getting slurred, and she swayed a little. Nan stood to end the interview. At the door, however, she turned and blurted out: "Look, if you're planning on driving anywhere this afternoon, lay off the bourbon."

Lori backed up a step, held the glass close to her chest. "It's my business," she muttered.

"It's my business, too. I'm a nurse as well as a writer, and car accidents mess up people real bad. I get the fun of helping sew them back together—when we can. You've got a pretty face. Isn't it—and maybe your life—worth more than a few drinks?"

Nan hurried away, wondering if she'd done more harm than good. Why did blunt truth sound so prudish? But Lori watched her go, then walked slowly to the sink and poured the rest of her drink down the drain.

Sheila arrived at the vacant house by five-twenty, but Alex was there before her, sitting in his black BMW like a real estate agent rather than a neighbor. He hurried to open her car door, took her elbow at one rough spot in the sidewalk, and opened the front door of the vacant house with a flourish. It felt cool and spacious after the steamy afternoon.

He led her through enormous rooms, praising cathedral ceilings, vast windows, the deck off the master bedroom (did one have a master bedroom in a house where there was no master?), and the family-size Jacuzzi. She should never have looked at this house so late in the day, Sheila realized. She would almost sign on the dotted line just to spend an hour in that Jacuzzi.

She wandered around the large open rooms, trying to keep a thoughtful look on her face and hoping Alex would think she was trying to mentally fit her possessions into proper nooks and crannies. She was actually searching for the exact spot someone would have had to stand to cast a light down Walt's drive. There! She could see the drive through only one front upstairs window.

It was in a small room Alex had called the "bonus room" and declared was perfect for a nursery. Sheila had no need for a nursery, and doubted it had been an infant up there the night before. Whoever it was had left no sign.

"I've seen enough." She turned and went back down the carpeted stairs.

"Just see the backyard." He led the way.

It was lovely, surrounded by a high privacy fence and shaded by towering poplars and sweet gums. Sheila immediately saw why Mac Marriot discouraged potential buyers: a paved patio with built-in barbecue abutted the fence between this yard and his. Fires built in that pit would almost certainly smoke his deck.

"What's the price?" she asked as Alex led her around the side and let them out a gate. When he told her, she could not hide her astonishment. "Isn't that high, even for this neighborhood?"

"Well," he hedged, "a house is worth what you sell it for. The owners were very fond of this one, and don't want to let it go too cheaply. They might negotiate a bit . . ."

"I'll have to let you know. It's bigger than I really need."

"If you'd like to see something a bit smaller—"

She interrupted him with a smile. "Let me think about this one first. I appreciate your showing it to me on such short notice. Did Walt mention that you and Yvonne used to work together?"

Alex's face grew a bit pinker, but maybe it was the heat. "She worked for me when she first started out."

"But she wasn't working for you when she died?"

"No, she'd gone out on her own. I helped her get started, that's all." He gave a genial little chuckle.

Sheila took a deep breath of June air, considered a graceful willow, and asked casually, "Did Walt say you came to her birthday party in April, too?"

Divesty looked blank. "No, I didn't know her birthday was in April."

"Yes, April 23. Didn't you give her two hundred—"

The change in Alex's expression was astonishing. His face went from pink to a dull, mottled red. "I didn't *give* her anything!" Veins stood out in his neck. "I *lent* her that money, and she damn well knew it! If she told Walt anything different, she *lied!*"

"Two hundred . . . ?" She paused, raising her voice in an unasked question.

But he rampaged on. "Said she had old debts to pay, didn't want to tell Walt so soon after they'd gotten married. I made her a business loan. That's *all* it was! Then when I needed it back, she started that song and dance about thinking it was a gift. You can tell Walt I'm talking to my lawyer about it tomorrow. There ought to be some way to get it back!"

He started quickly down the walk. Halfway down he turned

back, his face twisted with fury. "If you *are* serious about a house," he said in a voice heavy with sarcasm, "you know where to find me." He got into his BMW without a backward glance.

Again Sheila had failed to consider rush-hour traffic. It took her well over an hour to drive from Dunwoody to her apartment to pick up Amory, then he insisted on eating before they went to the funeral home for Yvonne's viewing. By the time they arrived, designated visiting hours were almost over.

Walt greeted them at the door of the viewing parlor, dignified and solemn in a dark blue suit and conservative tie. But then, Walt was dignified and solemn in whatever he wore.

"Thank you for coming," he murmured, clasping each of their hands. Sheila doubted that he even knew who they were. He looked and sounded like a man on automatic pilot for the duration.

Inside, people stood in hushed circles, carrying on stilted conversations. The men wore the same dark suits they had worn to work and so many women were in black that the gathering had the air of a somber cocktail party—with a sprinkling of reporters.

Sheila was glad Aunt Mary had decided to bring Forbes early this evening for a private leave-taking rather than subject him to tonight's dreary ritual or tomorrow's funeral.

Sheila herself had planned to chat briefly with Walt, then find a corner to watch who else came and how they behaved. Amory, however, had not been raised socially correct for nothing. Before she could protest, he had steered her toward the coffin and remarked on how natural and lovely Yvonne looked.

Since he had met the murdered woman once, at Rilla's party, Sheila thought he might be overdoing it just a bit, but now was not the place or time to tell him so. She was getting, she reflected, rather a long list of things to tell or do to Amory at some unspecified future date.

He was right about one thing, though. Yvonne did look natural and lovely. Walt had chosen a lavender dress that would have looked fussy on most women, but it made Yvonne look eerily like Snow White awaiting her prince.

"Damned shame," Amory muttered.

"Oh, yes!" Dee Ivy came up behind them, dabbing a handkerchief to her eyes and batting her lashes to keep back the tears. Tonight she had pinned a small organdy rose to the neckline of her black polka-dot dress. She looked feminine and helpless, and Amory was already hovering solicitously. In case Dee fainted? Needed a shoulder to weep on? Wanted to tell him why she'd stabbed her best friend?

Deciding Amory could handle any of that better than she could, Sheila moved around the room, reading cards on floral arrangements. A pretty wreath of lilies and pink roses was signed, *Paula, Alex, Dee, and the girls. Rest in Peace.* The red carnations were from Rip, the white roses from Mac and Rilla, and the white gladiola with yellow iris from—herself! She stooped to examine the signature. It was almost perfect. Had Aunt Mary signed Sheila's name to the charge slip as well?

"I love your flowers," cooed a voice at her shoulder. Rilla Marriot stood behind her, chic in a simple black dress with a narrow cascade of lace at the throat. "Wasn't this just terrible?" She dabbed a handkerchief to her nose and shuddered. "Since it happened, I just hate to be at home without Mac."

"So it's a good thing she doesn't have to." Mac, natty in a black suit and pearl-gray tie, joined them and gave his wife a fond squeeze. "The time this woman spends alone can be counted in minutes per week. What's retirement for, if not to spend with the person you love?"

As a person who had no one around to spend retirement with, Sheila had no immediate reply.

Rilla's eyes widened and she fluttered her scarlet nails. "Oh, there's Alex! I want to tell him about tomorrow night!" Flustered, she turned back to Sheila. "I hope you'll come, too. We're not having our usual crush, but just a few friends over about nine for drinks. Come and bring your lovely friend from Alabama. We'd love to have you."

She had most of the facts wrong, but her heart was in the right place. Sheila murmured her thanks and started back toward her unlovely nephew from Mississippi, who was hovering over Dee like a tall, plump vulture over a golden kitten.

This kitten, however, was spitting with indignation. "If they had increased their fortifications before Sherman arrived—"

Sheila backed away. The Battle of Atlanta had been successfully fought for a hundred and thirty years without her assistance. She planned to keep it that way.

As she moved toward the front of the room, a wreath of purple orchids caught her eye. They were by far the loveliest flowers in the room—as delicate as the woman they honored. She stooped to read the card, then caught her breath. It contained one word, written in bold black ink: *Crispin!* Tomorrow it should be easy to trace this wreath to its donor.

Feeling like something was finally going right in this investigation, she made her way to Tom and Ava Settis, who were chatting with another couple. Ten minutes later she had gotten herself invited to play tennis with Ava at the Dunwoody Country Club on Saturday morning at ten. If anybody knew what the quarrel was between Dee Ivy and Yvonne Delacourt, it would be someone at that club.

When Sheila got back to Amory, he and Dee were still fighting the Battle of Atlanta. "Time for the Confederacy to fold its tents and steal away home," she murmured in his ear.

He turned to her with the look of someone who could recall meeting her but couldn't quite remember when or where. "Aunt Sheila," she prompted him. "The woman you came with and get to leave with—*if* you leave pretty soon."

"I've got to—" Dee began, then gasped.

The room fell silent. Walt was still standing at the door, pale and trembling. In front of him stood Jake Drake and two uniformed officers. In the hush, Drake's voice was soft and pleasant.

"Walter Delacourt, you have the right to remain silent. Anything you say—"

Walter wasn't going to say anything. He had fainted dead away.

*A Dunwoody nanny went away for the
weekend. "Didn't you ever change this
baby?" she asked when she returned.
"I didn't need to," the child's mother assured
her. "The diaper box says they are good for
eighteen to twenty-four pounds."*

FRIDAY

DELACOURT ARRESTED FOR MURDER OF WIFE!
The front page of Friday morning's *Constitution* pictured
Walt being led to a waiting squad car, head bowed, shoulders
slumped. How had the reporters known to wait outside the funeral home?

"Drake alerted them," Frank told Sheila when she called him
at half past eight to ask. "He's good at using the media to tell the
story he wants told."

"They can't convict Walt on what you've got," Sheila protested.

"What we've got was enough for the magistrate," Frank replied grimly. "Delacourt was the last person to see her alive, and
he lied about when he left. His fingerprints were on the weapon,
and no one else seems to have a motive for killing her."

"He didn't lie, he just didn't remember when he left," she insisted. "And what's *his* motive? He adored her, Frank."

He sighed. "I hate to do this, Sheila, but I'm going to give it to
you straight. Until his father dies, Walter Delacourt doesn't have
a lot of loose change to spend. It's all tied up in the business."

"So?"

"So he's been spending a lot of money this past year, and his wife had nearly five hundred thousand dollars in her business account—money her husband swears he had no idea she had. You tell me what that looks like."

Sheila's heart sank. "It looks bad," she admitted. "But I still don't believe he did it, Frank."

"Well, you've got two weeks to find another suspect before your friend comes before the grand jury. But I warn you, Drake is strutting like a peacock. He's sure he can get what he needs for a conviction. If it makes you feel better, though, the big cheese around here isn't exactly happy with Drake's making an arrest during the visitation hours. 'Gauche,' 'publicity-hound,' and 'stupid fool' are the mildest terms he's used this morning."

"But Walt's still in jail, Frank."

"No, he's not," Frank told her. "He's probably getting dressed for his wife's funeral. The magistrate came down, his lawyer showed up, they shoveled out the required dollars, and Mr. D. slept in his own bed. We couldn't have *Walter Delacourt* spend a night in jail."

Sheila could understand his bitterness. Frank saw too many indigent men and women awaiting trial in jail while wealthy ones went home—even after conviction—to await a leisurely appeal.

She thanked him for his help—wondering miserably, *What help?*—and hung up. She tried Walt at home. Not even the answering machine came on the line. Next she tried his office.

"Mr. Delacourt cannot be reached. His wife's funeral will be held at two o'clock." The secretary sounded more mechanical than human.

"Tell him Sheila Travis is on the line, and I don't blame him for hiding out, but ask if he'll speak to me for just a minute."

The secretary returned in less than a minute. "I am sorry. Mr. Delacourt thanks you for calling, but he cannot be disturbed."

At least a trace of humanity had crept into her voice, Sheila thought. She sounded smug.

———

Paula Divesty took another Advil before nine. It wasn't time yet since the last one, but her headache showed no signs of diminishing. She carried coffee to her favorite chair in the den and sat cradling it, brooding. She was going to have to do something soon. But what?

"You okay?" Alex had filled his mug too full, as usual. He carried it to the sofa, adding a few drops of coffee to the trail already dotting the carpet. When she got more energy, Paula would shampoo it, but what difference did it make? They never entertained anymore, and she had bigger things to worry about than spotted carpets.

Alex stretched out on the sofa, resting his mug on his chest. Why should *he* be so tired? He hadn't been up almost all night. "Something bothering you?" he asked, his eyes meeting hers. She knew that look. He suspected something. He also had something to hide.

On the table beside her, a women's magazine advertised its lead article: "Trust—Glue for a Lasting Marriage." Paula's lip curled at the editor's naïveté. When it came to holding two people together, mutual suspicion was best. She and Alex would never dare leave one another until each knew what secrets the other did and did not know.

When she didn't reply, he persisted. "You had to work very late again last night, didn't you? When did you get in?"

She sighed. "After two, and this morning my head's pounding and my stomach feels like somebody's been trampolining on it. I can't keep this up, Alex, I just can't."

"Then quit, or find another job. A daytime one. Stop pretending you are volunteering and admit you need to work. Or haul good old Steven into court and demand that he support Craig for a while. He ought— Okay, don't get that expression on your face. I won't say it again. You already know what I think."

"The same thing my daddy thinks," she said bitterly. "Why knock yourself out for a kid who doesn't even know who you are?

Because he's mine, Alex! Mine!" Her breath came in short gasps which became sobs as her fury increased. "I love him, even if he doesn't know who I am! When I see Jaqui hugging Cornelius . . . why, Alex? Why? Why is her son whole and beautiful, while mine . . . ?" She wept, then raised her head to say, "And Yvonne—"

"Now, Paula." He held a hand up to check her, but the words tumbled from her mouth. They had been dammed too long.

"She *beat* Forbes, Alex! The day before she died. I saw her! From our window! Then, when she saw me, she just gave him a big hug and took him inside, pretending nothing had happened! But remember when he had all those bruises on his legs and told us he'd fallen off his bike? I'm sure she did that, too. Oh, God! Why should *she* have a beautiful, bright son while mine . . ." She rocked back and forth in agony.

Alex crossed the room in three steps, sat on the arm of her chair and held her in an awkward embrace. "It's okay, Paulie. It's gonna be okay." When her storm of tears had subsided, he muttered, "I'll try to help you a little, really I will. But business isn't that good, and there are other reasons . . ."

She pulled away. "I know your reasons," she said bitterly.

"You don't know a damn thing!" He stood and paced, flinging his arms around. "What do you care that—"

"I don't know that I do care," she said wearily. "Not anymore."

He averted his face, but not before she had seen the pain in his eyes. She felt a rush of liquid warmth, as if some chunk of ice deep within had met a spring thaw. Why had she said that? She didn't want to hurt Alex! No matter what he'd done, she loved that compact man with his square, ruddy face. She even loved the blazing temper that matched his hair. His affection used to flame as strongly as his temper. Could it again? She wasn't often able to say so, but he made her feel alive. She needed that. Usually she felt so dead.

She reached for him, pulled him back to sit beside her. Holding his hand with its short, blunt fingers and sprinkling of red hairs firmly in her big, strong one, she asked, "What are we going to do?"

"We?" He sounded surprised.

She nodded and fumbled in her pocket for a tissue. "It's a mess. We're both in a hell of a mess. But maybe it won't be so bad if we're in it together." She laid her head against his shoulder. For the first time in months, she felt content.

Later Friday morning Sheila called the funeral home and got the name of the florist who had delivered the orchid wreath. When she called the florist, however—explaining that she was helping Walter Delacourt with his thank-yous but could not find an address for Mr. Crispin—she drew a blank.

"I'm real sorry," said a voice that sounded like it might belong to a fourteen-year-old chewing gum, "but I don't have an address or nothing for nobody named Mr. Crispin."

"Do you have a record of a wreath of orchids delivered to the funeral home yesterday?" Sheila persisted.

A long silence followed. Sheila wondered if she should have spelled "orchid."

The child finally came back on the line. "I ast out back, and they said the man come in hisself, and paid cash. Dotty took his money, said he was real nice, but didn't leave no address nor nothin'."

"Thank you very much." Sheila managed not to sigh until after she hung up.

Amory had not spent much time among children, but of children he had known, he liked this one best. Last Wednesday at the Cyclorama, Forbes hadn't thrown tantrums when told "no," hadn't asked for everything he saw, and seemed quite happy to putter about while Amory read every placard and examined every display. When they set out Friday morning for Stone Mountain, therefore, they were both in good spirits.

"Do we get to ride the train?" Forbes asked when he was tucked into his seat belt. "Can we climb the mountain? I can walk almost all the way up by myself."

"That's great!" Amory was trying to decide between the expressway and a route through town. Later he would rue that he had answered the child so absently.

He decided they would drive along Ponce de Leon Avenue, lined with enormous old houses, stately trees, and strips of lush park. It might take longer, but would be much prettier. Amory's normal life did not permit much time to enjoy nature. Today he would.

He turned off Peachtree at Fourteenth and took Juniper south. Lost in thought, he almost didn't hear Forbes say in a quiet little voice, "There's Momsy's house."

"Where?" Turning to look, Amory nearly swerved into an ancient Ford in the next lane. The driver, whose long brown hair was pulled into a ponytail to show off his earring and whose shirt was sleeveless to show off his tattoo, made an inelegant gesture and roared away. Amory brought his own car under control and tried to control his voice, too. "Which house was your momsy's?"

"Back there." Forbes sat formally, legs straight out and hands clasped in his lap. For the first time Amory wondered if a small boy was supposed to sit quite so still or be quite so good.

"We're going to go around the block and drive real slow," he told Forbes, turning the corner. "You show me which house, all right?"

But when they got back to Juniper, Forbes was strangely reluctant. "I don't want to," he said in a whisper. His skin had gone so white that his eyes looked huge in his narrow face.

Puzzled, Amory drove on. "Okay, fellow, but if you want to

show me on the way home, just say so." Forbes must be mistaken anyway. The block was all tall buildings and businesses.

Thirty minutes later they got their first glimpse of the enormous hump of granite rising from the Georgia plain. Amory, as always, felt a twinge of awe, but Forbes bounced in his seat with unconstrained delight. "There's the mountain! There's the mountain!" It was the first emotion he had shown since he'd refused to point out Momsy's house. "Let's ride the train, an' see the animals, and swim in the water hole, and swing on the swings, and go to the laser show, and . . ."

"You sound like you've spent your life at Stone Mountain," Amory said, paying the entry fee and trying to conceal his disappointment.

"I go there all the time," Forbes boasted. "Me and Crispin."

Amory kept his voice carefully casual. "Who's Crispin?"

Forbes gave him a sideways glance. "My friend. Look! The lake! Can we ride the paddleboats?"

"No. We came to see the museum, remember?"

For Amory, Stone Mountain had only two attractions: lying in the grassy meadow beneath the carving that dominates the mountain's face, trying to picture ten people dining on the shoulder of Robert E. Lee or a six-foot carver sheltering from rain in the mouth of Lee's horse Traveller, or puttering around Confederate Hall, reading historical plaques and imagining Sherman's march through Georgia as tiny bulbs lit up the route across a huge plaster model of the state. He had dedicated this day to puttering, and Forbes had agreed.

"Oh, yeah." Forbes gave a satisfied sigh. Perhaps, Amory decided, they could ride the train later. He gave the little boy beside him a sunny smile. What could go wrong on a day like this?

The museum was a success for both of them. Amory prowled contentedly while Forbes played secret games around life-size statues of six Confederate generals. Since neither paid the other any attention whatsoever, they were both supremely happy.

Baby-sitting, Amory decided, was far simpler than most women led him to believe.

"Ready for lunch?" he asked when they came out into the bright summer sunlight. "The Stone Mountain Inn serves a great lunch."

"Swings first," Forbes announced with unusual firmness, "then the Whistle Stop Barbecue!" He pointed to a small restaurant perched by the railroad track that circles the granite hill.

Amory was feeling cooperative, so he pulled out his map. It had been years since he'd been a boy. He had forgotten that boys need pushing on swings, watching on slides, and admiring on monkey bars. He was weary and relieved when Forbes at last announced, "Now for that lunch."

It was past noon, and far too hot to eat outdoors. Amory headed for a blue-and-white-checked table in air-conditioned comfort. Forbes balked. "Let's eat under the trees."

"It's blistering hot out there," Amory reasoned, "and there are flies."

"Flies don't bite," Forbes said scornfully, heading for the door. With a heavy sigh Amory picked up their tray and followed him.

"Here's a good spot. Where's my hot dog?" Forbes climbed onto a picnic table bench beneath a pine. Amory shooed away a crow, but it merely flapped a few feet to a garbage can and kept a greedy eye on their food. The air was humid, thick enough to swallow. Amory was sticky all over, his fingers smeared with sauce. He was wishing he could find a sink with soap and water, when Forbes made a rude sound with his straw and announced, "This is the *bestest* day."

Suddenly Amory felt the shade instead of the heat, heard the birds, and smelled the pines. He grinned and made a sound with his own straw. "It is, isn't it?"

Forbes peered up at him without raising his head from his drink. "My mother doesn't let me play with straws."

"Mothers are like that," Amory told him. "Men don't have to be so polite when their mothers aren't around."

"Did you have a mother?" Forbes asked in unflattering surprise. He rubbed at a spot of mustard on his blue shorts, doing neither any good. When Amory grunted assent, he demanded, "Did she make you drink from a glass and stay clean?"

"You bet your boots. She still does."

Forbes gave a delighted chortle. "I don't have any boots. I'll bet Corny's instead." Then he asked, looking down into his drink, "What did your mother do if you didn't be good?"

"She switched me," Amory told him, "and I had to cut my own switches. If I didn't cut a good one, I had to cut another."

"My mother hits me," Forbes volunteered, still careful not to look up, "or locks me in the closet. I—I don't like the closet. It's dark. But if I fall asleep, it isn't *too* bad."

Amory didn't know how to evaluate or answer that, so he lay down on the long wooden seat, making his clasped hands into a pillow. "It's not dark out here. Why don't you play quietly for just a minute and let me take a little nap?"

"Okay." Forbes climbed down and began to gather small stones.

Amory was dozing when he heard Forbes give a shout of delight. "Crispin! Wait a minute!"

Amory's eyes flew open. Forbes was speeding toward the base of the mountain. Amory hauled himself dazedly to his feet. "Hold on there!" He didn't reach the child until they were both stumbling across the railroad tracks. "Not so fast, fellow." He grabbed a fistful of yellow shirt. "Where do you think you're going?"

"It's Crispin!" Forbes started to point, then stopped, bewildered. "He was over here, but now he's gone! Let's go see if we can find him." He was almost dancing with eagerness.

Amory peered in all directions. A young couple walked slowly toward their car and a family party of eight headed toward the path up the mountain. "I don't see anyone, Forbes."

"He didn't see me," Forbes mourned. "I was too slow."

"We have to clean up, ladies or no ladies," Amory decreed, hoping to distract him. They returned to where they had eaten, wadded up the remains of their picnic, and threw them in the garbage can. The crow squawked his thanks.

"Can we climb the mountain now, Mr. Amory? I can do it almost by myself."

Amory peered up the trail. It didn't look very steep, but he was feeling sluggish and his shirt was wet with sweat. Before he could speak, Forbes reminded him, "You *promised*. In the car you promised."

Had he? Amory couldn't remember. With a sigh he compromised. "We'll go until we get tired."

Forbes was as good as his word. For the first half of the climb, while Amory plodded along the narrow rocky trail, trying not to pant out loud, the boy darted ahead and then trotted back to Amory's side, covering at least three times the necessary distance.

Regretting how seldom he had used his health club membership, Amory glared at a woman carrying her poodle as she easily passed him. What kind of fool climbed a mountain with something that couldn't make it up under its own steam?

Less than a minute later he hauled himself over the next stretch of boulders to find Forbes sitting cross-legged in the middle of the path. The boy looked up wearily. "I need to be carried now," he announced.

They had come more than three-quarters of the way. "We can't quit now," Forbes protested when Amory suggested turning around. "We can take the cable car down." Amory peered up at the mountaintop, then reluctantly agreed.

It had been years since he last climbed Stone Mountain. He had forgotten that the last quarter is almost straight up.

When he staggered the final steps to the top, he had a blister on his left heel. His arms ached. He and Forbes were plastered together with sweat. Neither of them was interested in the film at the top of the mountain. Neither of them cared about the spectacular view. All they wanted was another Coke and lots of ice. When they had recovered a bit, Amory bought tickets to the cable cars, thanking the good Lord for an easy way down.

Just before they reached the bottom, a whistle sounded in the distance. Forbes was instantly revived. "The train!" He bounced in his seat. "Let's take the train! And when we get off we can put a dime on the tracks. It'll get real flat—honest!"

A train ride sounded like a great idea to Amory, too. They could sit down. He could doze while Forbes enjoyed the scenery. Maybe they could ride around the mountain for several hours. Exhausted, he took Forbes by the hand and limped across the meadow toward the station.

Amory was surprised the train wasn't crammed with parents of small children taking advantage of this unique baby-sitting service. He took a seat to the right of the aisle and agreed to let Forbes sit in one on the other side. As soon as the engine started, Amory slid down in his seat, laid his cheek against the window, and fell fast asleep.

"Sir? Sir! You'll have to get off now!"

Amory awoke slowly. Where was he? And why? Then, remembering, he sat up quickly.

He was sitting at the train station with a young man shaking his shoulder. One last family was leaving the railroad car.

Forbes was nowhere to be seen.

Amory pushed the young man aside and climbed out, looking up and down the empty train in bewilderment. "Did a small boy already get off? About this high, with black hair?"

The young man shook his head. The mother of the departing family, however, turned back. "He got off back at the Whistle Stop, with his daddy."

"His daddy?"

Something in Amory's frantic tone made her reconsider. "Well," she said uncertainly, "a man who was on the train. He sat up there"—she pointed—"and the child went up and sat with him. You were sleeping." Her eyes accused him before she added, "I didn't know he belonged to you."

Amory looked from her to the youthful conductor. "Does another train go back that way?"

"No, sir," the conductor told him. "You can go inside and buy another ticket and ride all the way around, but that'll take over half an hour. If you walk, it's not more than a mile."

Now Amory knew what they meant by having your heart in your throat. He would stop and throw it up if he'd had the time. Instead, he sped along the tracks. The conductor yelled something at him, but he was already galloping in the opposite direction. For a regular jogger, it would have been a short run. For an overweight banker with terror in his throat, it seemed the width of Siberia.

Hot, out of breath, frantic with worry, he tried to think clearly. Where would someone take the child? Why had he lured him away? What did he intend to do with him? What would Sheila think?

To care what Sheila thought was new for Amory. It surprised him. Formerly, he had always seen Sheila as part of Uncle Tyler, and since childhood Amory had viewed his uncle Tyler as only slightly less than God. It had seemed fitting, therefore, for Sheila to give up her own life—and submerge her thoughts—to serve Tyler and his important career. Now, for the first time, pounding down a railroad track through a muggy June afternoon, Amory began to question whether that had indeed been such a good way for any woman to spend all those years. Halfway to the Whistle Stop he was grudgingly admitting that Sheila might not have had the best deal in marriage. By the time he could see the barbecue stand in the distance, he was certain she was better off now. Not until many years later would he know that this hot

June run had made him a better husband than his uncle Tyler had ever been.

At last, when he was beginning to get blue spots in front of his eyes and his blistered heel felt like it was on fire, he reached the barbecue stand. Under a pine on the large picnic table perched a small figure in yellow shirt and blue shorts, dejected and alone.

"Forbes!" Amory cried, feeling a spurt of energy and an amazing surge of love. "Forbes!"

Forbes looked up, shaded his eyes, and jumped down. "Mr. Amory! Here I am! Here I am!"

They met in the middle of the tracks. Amory swooped the child up and hugged him fiercely, then held him out at arm's length. "Are you all right?"

Forbes wriggled to get down. "I'm fine. Can we go home, now?"

Amory set him on the ground, but did not release his shoulders. "Why did you get off the train? What happened to the man you got off with?"

Forbes wriggled some more to get free. "I want to go home *now*. I'm very tired." He turned his back and trudged toward the car.

"*You're* tired?" Amory spluttered, following him at a weary limp. It seemed like a hundred years since lunch. "Why did you get off that train without me?"

Forbes's small shoulders hunched up, then down. "I just did."

He fell asleep in the car without saying another word. Relaxed, his fist fell open and something shiny fell out. Amory knew what it was, from his own childhood. A dime, flattened by a train.

Sheila returned from Yvonne's funeral hot and disgruntled. Perhaps it was foolish to have expected Walt to have spoken to her after the service, but he had been curt even with his father. As soon as the Episcopal priest had pronounced the final amen by the graveside, Walt had wheeled Rip to his waiting limousine. Then he drove off in his own car.

For two cents, Sheila thought fiercely, I'd let him go to jail.

She reached for a large brown envelope that had not been on her desk when she left. "Masako," she asked her assistant, who was carrying in a hot cup of coffee, "where did this come from?"

"Nan Quentin left it while you were out. She couldn't stay."

Sheila sipped her coffee and read with interest Nan's report on her Thursday interviews, particularly Lori Ivy's story of Yvonne's past. Now, that was intriguing. Why had Yvonne confided more fully in an adolescent than in her own husband?

Nan had also included the text of a short article she had written, and three black and white photographs of the Delacourts' house. "What do you think?" she had scribbled on page one. Sheila read the uninspired prose and one cutline: *Instead of black, the wreath is pink, blue, and mauve, but this is a house of mourning.* Then she shoved Nan's story aside and reached for her full In box.

Downtown, two journalists considered a very different story. One's face was worried as he confronted his friend across a desk at the *Atlanta Journal & Constitution.* "I tell you, Todd, I wouldn't touch that with a ten-foot pole until I knew where it came from—and why."

"Who cares where it came from?" Todd retorted. "I've checked it out, Jim. It's all true—and a hell of a story!"

"What about slander? You may find yourself hauled into court faster than you can slide down a greased pole."

"It's not slander if it's the truth. I'm not going to print one thing I can't back up with dates, places, and times."

Jim shrugged. "It's your funeral, fellah."

"You're getting conservative, man. Must have something to do with expecting a baby."

Jim stuck out his chest in pride. "Twins. We did an ultrasound yesterday, and there's two of them in there! But about this story. Keep in mind that the old man takes a dim view of smut."

"It's not smut, it's truth," Todd reasserted with dignity. "The people have a right to know."

Jim chuckled. "So Congress keeps telling the President. He doesn't believe it any more than I do." He picked up a sheaf of clippings and handed them to his colleague. "Do what you want with them. It's your funeral," he repeated. "But I'd be careful of anything that came to *my* desk in a plain brown wrapper."

"You're just jealous," Todd told him, returning to his own desk. But he couldn't help wondering. Who *had* sent the envelope full of clippings? And why had it been sent to him?

What's the latest in Dunwoody
household appliances?
Riding vacuum cleaners.

By the time the clock on Sheila's desk said five-thirty, she was fuming. Where was Amory? Probably lying on her couch, reading another Civil War history, oblivious to the fact that he had his aunt's car. Sheila dialed her own number, prepared to growl.

She had plenty to growl about. A major evening's entertainment on the senators' Japanese itinerary had fallen through that afternoon. She was still furious at Walt for the way he had ignored both friends and family at the funeral. She had no idea whatsoever who had killed Yvonne Delacourt. Amory had not yet decided when to return to Tupelo, *and he had her car.* At the moment the last grievance was her greatest. When he did not answer her phone, she once again called a cab.

She stormed into her apartment to find Amory sitting on the couch, nursing his left foot.

"Why didn't you answer the phone?" she demanded.

"I just got here five minutes ago." With one forefinger he gingerly prodded a nasty blister.

Something in his expression made her put ice in two glasses and pour two drinks before she asked, "Did you and Forbes have fun?"

"Fun!" he spluttered, scarcely able to say the word. "Fun?"

He started giving her a minute-by-minute version of the day's events—until she doubled over with laughter.

"It wasn't funny," he insisted. "Have you ever carried forty pounds up a mountain?"

"He told you he could *almost* make it up all by himself," she pointed out reasonably.

"Keep laughing," he muttered darkly, "and I won't tell you about how the kid got kidnapped and returned."

"By the spirit of Stone Mountain?"

"No, by the mysterious Crispin—I think."

That sobered her. When Amory had finished, she asked, "But Forbes never admitted that he'd seen the man?"

He shook his head. "But where else could he have gotten that dime? He didn't have any money when we set out, and kids who put coins on tracks stick around to pick them up afterward."

She went to the phone. "Maybe when Mildred's putting him to bed tonight she can get the whole story. She's good at that." Sheila had good reason to know.

After dinner, in spite of his blistered heel, Amory was game for the Marriots' party. "I read something at Confederate Hall that supports my position." He gave his hair an extra swipe and his nose gave a couple of twitches. "Dee will have to admit I'm right."

This Friday, as last Friday, the Marriots' house was a blaze of lights, and from the walk Sheila could see no perceptible difference between these "few friends" and Rilla's "usual crush." A wall of chatter flowed like a glacier to greet newcomers.

Once again Norris manned the door. "Good evening, Mr. and Mrs. Travis," he greeted them gruffly.

"Why so gloomy, Norris?" Amory asked.

The big man shook his head and pursed his lips. "It's the Phillies, sir. They're not doing so well."

"You'd better switch to rooting for the Braves this year."

"Can't, sir. I've been a Phillies fan since I was a boy."

"Time for a change, then, Norris." Without waiting for an answer, Amory headed for the bar. When he had a drink, he joined Dee Ivy, who had once again claimed her chair by the fireplace. Sheila hoped Dee noted his priorities.

She herself filled a plate in the dining room, giving Richard a smile as he slid a slice of ham onto her plate, then she drifted around the room, surprised at how many people she knew. Some she knew from the neighborhood, some she had met at the funeral. Ava and Tom Settis introduced her to a couple who had just returned from Tokyo. They had news about people Sheila had known in the American business community there. In a few minutes Alex Divesty joined them and greeted Sheila with such bonhomie, he must have decided she was a potential home buyer after all. Paula was at the shelter, he said.

Eventually Sheila wandered back into the kitchen. The cook, her face damp with heat and hurry, was putting together hors d'oeuvres.

Sheila admired them, praised her chutney cheeseball, then asked, "Did a friend tell me you gave a jogger a drink the morning Mrs. Delacourt was killed?"

The woman nodded without looking up. "White boy, yellow hair. Real thirsty."

"Did you see him around later, too?"

She shook her head. "Didn't see nobody."

Sheila started toward the door to the deck. "I've been wanting to see Mrs. Marriot's roses."

The cook held up a hand to stop her. "Mr. Mac don't want nobody going out there unless he or Miss Rilla's with 'em. His dogs are loose."

"Dogs?" Sheila had heard no dogs from either adjoining yard.

"Two big black 'uns. He brings 'em home for parties. Keeps folks from crashing over the back fence."

Sheila tried to picture anyone dressed as the Marriots' guests were dressed, scaling an eight-foot fence. She failed. "What kind of dogs are they?" she asked.

"Big black 'uns," the cook repeated, her attention on her work. "Sump'un fierce. Great dames or something. Or the pinching kind."

"Dobermans?"

Sheila's guess was greeted with a broad, happy smile. "That's it! Dover men!" Sue Ella's gold tooth gleamed.

Sheila returned to the dining room and fortified herself with crab claws, picturing Mac's back fence guarded by pinching men from Dover.

In just a moment Rilla moved past with a tall, thin man. "You really must see my roses," she was telling him.

"Could I see them, too?" Sheila asked.

Rilla beamed. "Why, of course! In just a little while, sugar!"

Sheila waited until they went outside, saw that Mac was engaged with several friends in the den, and quickly mounted the stairs, seeking a room on the back of the house which overlooked the famous rose garden.

She found a masculine den and had just entered it when a husky voice rasped behind her: "Hands up, dear! The upstairs is off limits to guests, I'm afraid." She spun around guiltily to see a tiny round woman aiming an enormous bright blue and yellow water gun in her direction!

It was the old woman Sheila had seen from Walter's window. Her wispy white hair was as short and curly as Mac's, her eyes as blue. They were two unexpected sapphires in a fat, wrinkled face on a thick body bent almost double over the huge gun. Rubies and emeralds sparkled on her spotted hands.

She shook the gun at Sheila. "Don't make me shoot you, dear. This Super Soaker would just ruin your lovely dress. Please come into the hall."

"Of course." Sheila complied quickly. "I was just looking for— you know."

"Powder room's downstairs." She peered up at Sheila. "My, you are tall, aren't you? Are you the woman I saw next door earlier this week? She was tall and dark, too." When Sheila nodded, her face puckered in concern. "I didn't know you were a friend of Mac's, dear. I hope you didn't mind my calling the police." She added with typical southern genteel understatement, "We'd had a bit of trouble over there early in the week."

"I understand." Sheila considered her jewels, her cultured voice, and the whimsy of the Super Soaker, and gambled. "Do you happen to know my aunt, Mary Beaufort?" She held her breath and prayed that Atlanta's vast ol' girl network reached this far.

The sapphire eyes lit with delight. "Of course, my dear! Mary and I used to see each other regularly. I don't get out much these days, of course. Arthur keeps me so confined. Arthur-itis, you know. I'm a real burden to my son and his wife." The old woman heaved a sigh that cried out for reassurance.

Sheila touched her shoulder lightly. "I know they don't think that. I'll tell Aunt Mary I saw you, shall I, Mrs. Marriot?"

"Oh, I'm not Mrs. Marriot, dear, I'm Mrs. Harlow. Diane Harlow. Mac took my maiden name when—well, when he came back to Atlanta." She began the tedious process of turning her crippled body in the other direction. Halfway around, she paused. "Give Mary my love, dear. Tell her I think of her fondly." She pointed the Super Soaker toward the stairs. "Powder room's under the staircase. Richard will show you." She toddled off to a room down the hall.

When she turned, Sheila saw that Richard now stood at the head of the stairs, something that might pass for a smile curving his thick lips. One hand was in the pocket of his white dinner jacket. When he said, "Come on," and offered her his elbow, Sheila meekly took it and went with him down the stairs. She had seen too many television shows to want to find out what was in that pocket besides his hand.

"I came up to see Mrs. Harlow," she told him as they descended. "She's a friend of my aunt's." Something in the way he held her elbow made her doubt he believed her, and something in Norris's expression as he watched them both from the bottom of the stairs made her doubt he'd believe her, either. On the last step she halted. "I'd like a breath of fresh air."

"Take Mrs. Travis out for air, Richard," Norris growled, and turned to greet a couple just coming in the door. Richard escorted Sheila out onto the small front stoop—and stayed.

Up the hill, the half moon hung above the pines in the gully like the ear of God. The air was cool, humming with cicadas and flickering with lightning bugs. With the right companion it would have been a lovely evening. Through Sheila's mind flitted the picture of someone with a too-square chin and a pirate's smile. She turned to Richard, who was definitely *not* the right companion, and said crossly, "Go back inside. I'll just stay out a minute longer."

He considered, then gave her a curt nod and obeyed. She suspected, however, that he'd keep a close eye on her for the rest of the evening.

She was wondering what to do about that, when Slade hailed her from the top of the walk. "Are you the welcoming committee?"

He and Jaqui made their way down the long walk. Jaqui was elegant tonight in black and diamonds. They exchanged greetings, then Sheila mentioned, "By the way, on the day Yvonne was killed, did your yard man—"

Jaqui interrupted with an emphatic shake of her head. "We don't have a yard man right now. Ours had surgery a couple of weeks ago. I've been on Slade's case to get somebody for the interim, but he hasn't done it." She rolled her eyes at her negligent husband.

Baffled, Sheila looked from one to the other. "But someone came to mow your yard that day."

Slade and Jaqui shook their heads simultaneously. "We don't have a yard man right now," Slade assured her. "But I've got something I want to ask *you* about that day. As a friend of Walt's, maybe you can advise me. I'd like to help him get out of this mess, but I don't want to put anybody else in unless they belong in. Do you follow me?"

"I think so."

"Well, the day Yvonne died, Walt ran out into the street yelling, but he wasn't yelling bloody murder. He was just yelling that she was dead. You still following?"

Sheila nodded.

"Okay, Alex and I both got there at the same time. I started to go inside, but he grabbed my arm and said, 'Don't go inside there. This is a matter for the police.' Now, my question is this: How did he know? She could have died of a heart attack, or slipped in the shower, or choked on a piece of candy."

"I suppose he could have thought you ought to call the police in any of those cases," Sheila suggested.

Slade shook his head. "He didn't say, '*Maybe* we ought to call the police.' He said, 'This *is* a case for the police.' Now, how did he know?"

Sheila remembered the day after Yvonne's death, and Alex's strange behavior when he brought muffins to Walt. "I don't know. Tell the police and see what they think. It might help Walt. It certainly can't hurt him." She seemed to be thinking that a lot lately.

"I'll call them first thing tomorrow," Slade promised.

"Let me ask you a question," Sheila said as they started in. "Does Alex recycle glass for the Delacourts?"

"He might. It's such a pain to take it to collection sites, lots of people don't bother, but Alex and Paula are real issue-oriented people."

"Well I'm a mama-oriented person right now," Jaqui interjected, "and I found out something this afternoon that nearly made me sick. Cornelius told me that the day Yvonne was killed, he and Forbes went to that house about four o'clock to try to get some grape juice off the rug before Yvonne found it. Corny said the door was shut and locked, and Forbes said he must have pulled it hard when he left. Do you suppose that child was in the house with his dead mama and didn't know it? Or even, maybe, with the murderer?" Jaqui's eyes reflected the horror Sheila felt.

Sheila left them inside and cruised the crowded rooms. Mac and Rilla circulated so well among their guests that she could seldom keep an eye on both of them at the same time, but whenever she looked toward the food table, she met Richard's gaze.

It was close to midnight before she finally got a break. For a moment the scene looked like a repeat of the previous week: Norris was greeting latecomers; Richard was carving roast beef and ham at the buffet; Sheila was eating crab claws; Rilla passed through the room with a short, plump woman, murmuring "Let me show you my roses"; then Mac approached the buffet and said genially, "One of our guests needs assistance, Richard." He took the knife and began to carve. Richard said something nervously to him and looked in Sheila's direction before he went out the front door.

Sheila let Mac put a piece of beef on her plate and gave him her most charming embassy smile. "I'm in Richard's black book, Mac," she confided. "My aunt, Mary Beaufort, is a friend of your mother's, and I went up to say hello. Richard was *not* pleased to find me up there." She hoped her voice oozed enough *we upper classes need to stick together.*

It must have, for Mac's chuckle was as golden as his skin. "Poor Richard, he gets uptight sometimes. Don't let him worry you. Have fun."

"I am. It's a great party." She drifted into the living room, then into the foyer—which was blessedly empty. Norris must have accompanied a couple out onto the front stoop.

As quickly as she dared, Sheila climbed the stairs, hurried into the den, and was about to approach the window when she noticed a bathroom opening off the room. That would be better. She could lock the door.

Safely locked inside, she opened the blinds a crack. Her view was largely blocked by an enormous magnolia just outside the window, but she could just make out Rilla's bright head moving slowly around the rose garden. When she raised the window slightly she could even hear Rilla's voice. "This is my peace rose. It's my favorite, next to the Princess Elizabeth, over here. Don't you just adore pink?"

It was a perfectly ordinary scene of a woman showing her flower garden to a friend. Except there was no friend.

Rilla was alone.

Sheila pressed one slat down and through the larger crack peered into the backyard. Dark motion in a far corner she interpreted as dogs rooting around the base of a shrub. As Rilla continued to walk and talk, the dogs moved like lotion across the yard and joined her. She patted them and continued her monologue.

Then, without warning, the plump woman's dark head was beside Rilla's yellow one and Sheila could hear her voice, richly southern and ironic. "They certainly are the prettiest roses I've seen in a long time, honey." Her chuckle rolled through the night. Had the woman been there all along, in the shadows? If not, where had she come from?

A sound in the next room startled Sheila. If it was Richard, and he had a slender, sharp instrument, he could open the bathroom's simple push lock in a couple of seconds. He'd made it quite clear that guests were not supposed to use the upper floor. If he found her . . .

Quickly she scanned the room for a place to hide. Rejecting the shower and linen closet as obvious, she turned to the only other possible place: a closely woven wicker hamper.

It held a sheet and two damp towels. When she heard a gentle knock she jerked them out, folded her lanky limbs compactly inside, pulled the soiled linens over her head, and lowered the lid —feeling extremely foolish. The person on the other side merely wanted a bathroom. He or she would go away when no one answered.

Whoever it was did not go away.

She heard a faint scratch, a click, and a smooth gliding silence that meant the door was opening. Then, after a pause—as if someone were peering inside—it closed again. She would never have heard it if she hadn't been listening so intently. There was another click as the lock button was pushed, then silence. She could sense someone inside the door, moving just enough to scan the bathroom without taking a step.

She held her breath, feeling her heart begin to pound. After a moment, she more felt than heard footsteps on the thick carpet, heard the linen closet door open and shut almost silently, heard the fastener on the glass shower door released. Then, for what seemed like an eternity, she heard absolutely nothing.

Who was it, and what did he or she want? Was he still there? Could she have missed the sounds of leaving? She had almost decided to cautiously raise the hamper lid, when she heard an infinitesimal squeak. Someone sitting on the toilet lid had shifted position.

It was a man. He was heavy. He wore expensive aftershave. And he obviously had no intention of going anywhere for a while.

She would learn later that she was in the hamper for over two hours. It seemed like two weeks. To stay awake and alert, she tried to recall poems she had once memorized, all the verses to her favorite hymns. She named fruits in alphabetical order, then animals, then capitals of the world.

In all those hour-long minutes the intruder made scarcely a sound, but his presence was heavy in the darkness. Did he know she was there, too? Did he think he could out-wait her? What else could he be waiting for? What would he do to her if he found her?

Her only hope, she decided, was Amory. Drinking steadily below, he would eventually reach belligerent truculence and start shouting for her. Hopefully at that point people would begin to search for her, the intruder would leave, and she could come out of hiding with a modicum of grace and dignity.

A cramp shot like an electric current up her right leg. She abandoned her need for grace and dignity. *Come on, Amory,* she willed with all her being. If he would just come into the room next door, she would spring from the hamper, shout for his help, and run out—hopefully before the intruder shot or stabbed her.

Amory didn't come.

Below, party sounds diminished and died. Then, unexpectedly, she heard Mac's voice in the next room. "Everybody gone?"

"Yeah. Was it a good night?" Richard! Then who was in the bathroom with her? Norris? That was a chilling thought!

Mac was his usual genial self. "Not so good as usual, but that's to be expected until things settle down next door. Did you take care of that fellow from Mississippi who'd lost his date?"

"He left. Figured she must have left with somebody else."

Oh, Amory! How could he? What was she supposed to do now? Sheila wished she had not tried to see the backyard. She wished she had not eaten so many crab claws. She wished desperately she could use the toilet!

"Everything closed up tight?" Mac asked.

"Yep, and Sue Ella and Norris are ready to go. See you tomorrow afternoon." Richard's voice grew faint on the last words. He must be headed downstairs.

Norris was ready to go? Then who on earth *was* on that toilet?

The front door slammed and a car started, roared down the

drive. Mac moved about the next room for a few minutes, then went out. Sheila heard Rilla come up, the sound of conversation as she and Mac prepared for bed, then—at last—silence. Still the other person had not moved. She knew he was still there, though, waiting as she waited. For what?

Just when she thought her legs and arms were permanently dead, she felt a sudden movement toward the door. His going was not so much a sound as a wind, but so attuned was she to his slightest movement that she was certain that he had crept out of the room.

Cautiously, she raised the hamper lid, then her head. Struggled out of the sheet and towels. Stood, each limb shrieking. She had to hold on to the wall to keep from falling, and command as she would, she could not persuade either of her knees to flex so that she could step out of the hamper. If she did not, she was going to wet her pants.

By fierce concentration she pivoted on the balls of her prickling feet, reached down and placed one hand behind her thigh, and tugged. Miraculously her right knee shifted slightly, then bent. Clinging to a towel bar and hoping the person who tiled the bath had set it firmly, she climbed, slowly and in agony, out.

Dared she use the toilet? Not unless she closed the door. He might be just beyond it! She pushed it, quarter-inch by quarter-inch, and eased it shut. Then she hurried across the bathroom, lined the bowl with paper, and took a chance. If only she could get a drink of water, too! Her mouth felt like the floor of an abandoned stable—dry, foul, and full of straw. But she could not gamble on someone hearing the water run.

As she cast a regretful look in the direction of the lavatory, she caught a reflection in the large mirror over the counter. A flickering light was moving in a back upstairs room of the vacant house next door!

Had Yvonne seen a mysterious light, too? On a sleepless night had she stood at her front window and watched someone moving through the empty rooms? Did whoever it was know she had watched? Was that why she had died? Sheila shivered.

Aunt Mary's favorite fictional detectives would have crept next door, followed whoever it was, and solved the crime. Sheila had no intention of being that dumb. All she wanted was to get outside, limp to Walt's or Jaqui's, and call the police.

Slowly, silently, she hobbled across the bathroom and opened the door, wincing at the minute click. In the next room Mac snored lightly. Rilla sighed once and turned over. No other sound.

Where was the man? Probably burgling the house. Philosophically, Sheila might have agreed it was her duty to wake Mac and Rilla and tell them he was around. Pragmatically, she was terrified they would wake and ask what *she* was doing there. She had to will her legs to creep, not dash. The police could tell Mac about the burglar if she could get out, without meeting him, to call them.

She tiptoed out, tensed for self-defense.

He was swifter than she.

A hand covered her mouth, another immobilized her arms, turned her, and propelled her ruthlessly back into the bathroom.

"You!"

In the bathroom mirror Sheila could just make out the features of Yvonne's gardener. He looked as astonished as she felt.

Dropping his hands, he took a quick step backward, placed his back squarely against the door, and folded his arms.

They considered each other warily. All she could see was a shadowy face. He was dressed entirely in black—pants, long-sleeved shirt, and cotton gloves. He gestured around the small room. "Where the hell *were* you?" Even whispering, he was arrogant.

She pointed to the bulky shadow of the hamper. "In there."

"Never! A good-size child wouldn't fit."

"There's a trick to it. A magician taught me when I was fourteen, so I could help him in a show at our high school."

He raised one eyebrow. "Did you wear black silk and pearls for every performance?"

She rubbed her arms, which were still achingly numb. "Of course not. You surprised me. And I thought you'd never go!"

"I was waiting for something." Without saying what it was, he turned. "Come on. You can explain later."

She could explain? Before she could protest, he had silently opened the door and glided through it. She hesitated. Which would be worse: to follow him, or to make a noise to wake the Marriots? She didn't ask which was wiser. That was easy. Neither.

He was back. "Come on!" he spat out softly. "We can get out a back window."

"How about the front door?" she whispered back.

"Security system. I disabled one window in the breakfast room."

She dragged him back into the bathroom and motioned for him to close the door. When he had, she said softly, "Mac puts Dobermans in the backyard when he has a party. They may still be around."

He swore softly. "That's very bad."

They confronted each other across the room. The bathroom was as much a prison as ever.

"Who *are* you?" Sheila demanded suddenly.

He laughed softly, a very piratelike laugh. "A free spirit."

"A narcotics agent?"

In the dimness she could feel him tense. "Why do you say that?"

"Because there's something going on between this house and the one next door. I've seen lights, and Rilla keeps showing very ordinary roses to a stream of people at every party. The simplest answer is drugs. Are you on the case?"

He moved from the door. "Look, we've got to get out of here. You may get your jollies spending the night with strange men in bathrooms, but I've got places to go."

"Good luck getting there."

He went to the window and peered out. "*I* could climb down that magnolia. And it may be close enough to the fence to jump over."

"Aren't these windows wired, too?"

"Not the upstairs ones. Last Friday night, while you were charming people in green, I made the rounds. None of the upstairs windows are wired." He opened the blind and pushed up the window. "Can you climb a tree?"

She sighed. "Why do I suspect we're about to find out?"

The moon was high in the sky, and bright. A breeze stirred the curtains, rippled their hair, and carried up the scent of blooming magnolias and roses. In the darkness Sheila smiled ruefully. Had she inadvertently prayed to stand in the moonlight with this particular pirate? If so, what quirk of divine humor had added those two prowling shapes beneath?

So far the dogs had not looked up.

The screen was light and slid up easily. "Ladies first?" He bowed.

She stepped back. "Not at all. Be my guest."

"Okay." He straddled the windowsill. "Here goes."

He climbed to his knees, reached for the branch, and swung out. It swayed and bent with his weight, but did not break. She watched him go, hand over hand for only a short distance, and then there was another branch below to stand on. In just a few seconds he had reached the trunk. "Come!" He said it with one peremptory motion of his hand.

While he was inching hand over hand, she had stripped off her panty hose and tossed them into Rilla's hamper. They'd reach Rilla's armpits, but maybe the maid could use them. She amused herself for one instant with a picture of that awkward woman in black stockings. Then she strung her black sandals together and threaded them over her belt.

She ought to take off her dress, too. It had not been designed with tree climbing in mind. But there were limits to what she was willing to do for any stranger. At least the dress had a long, full skirt.

Poised on the windowsill with almost certainly vicious Dobermans below, she was strongly tempted to go back inside, look for a vacant bed or couch, and attempt a colossal bluff the next morning.

"Come!" This time he breathed it. As she stood and reached for the nearest bough, four points perked, two noses rose, and frantic barks sliced the silence of sleeping Dunwoody.

Sheila leapt, dangled, willed her arms to forget their recent punishments and carry her. Hand over painful hand she inched along the branch, found a foothold, and raced toward the bole of the tree as fast as her bare feet could carry her. When she reached the bole, the man snatched her waist and drew her around to the other side to balance beside him where two large limbs met. "Up!" he ordered, giving her a shove. She climbed up several feet, then stopped, trying not to pant. The trunk was thick, the leaves thick and glossy. Hopefully they would not be visible from either the house or below, but the dogs still raged at the base of the tree.

He joined her and pinned her body to the trunk with his own. She felt his breath on her neck, his heartbeat on her shoulders, and the toe of his shoe pressed painfully against her bare left heel. She pushed, and he moved back slightly, then pressed even closer as light streamed around the edges of the trunk. They heard Mac's "What the devil?" and Rilla's sleepy "What is it?"

Mac's next words were louder as he reached the bathroom. "Hey! This screen's up! Somebody's gotten in or out this way!" The dogs, meanwhile, were frantically trying to climb the tree.

"Do the dogs have him?" Old Mrs. Harlow joined the others.

"Sounds like it. I'll go down and turn on the floodlights. He won't get down without our seeing him." Mac slammed the window shut.

"What now, Sherlock?" Sheila murmured.

He took her chin, twisted her head around, and kissed her full on the lips. "Just in case."

She remembered she did not know his name. This did not seem like the time to ask. For one thing, she was a bit breathless.

Light flooded the yard. Sheila prayed it did not reach this high. They heard Mac walk onto the deck, and Sheila could see the glint of his bright hair below. She hoped he could not see an equal glint of her bare white legs. She shoved them closer to the trunk and willed them invisible.

Mac came to the base of the tree, and she knew he was looking up. "If you're barking at squirrels, I'll have you put down," he snapped at the circling dogs, "but if there's a burglar up there, you can eat him for dinner."

"See anything?" she heard Rilla call.

"The light makes the tree darker," Mac called back. "But I'll just sit out here awhile and wait. He's got to come down sometime." They heard him drag a chair close to the edge of the deck; the dogs whined. Suddenly Sheila felt her companion stoop. The branch beneath her shook, and she heard a distant thud.

The dogs whirled, dashed to the back fence next to Walt's yard. In an instant their growls turned to doggy sounds of satisfaction. Mac joined them. "A shoe? Damn, he must have gone across the roof, down the walnut, and over the fence. Rilla," he bellowed, "call Walt! Tell him to turn on his lights! Damn fellow went over the fence. We've got to cut some limbs out here." In a quieter tone; "Good fellows. Come on in, let's get you a treat."

The dogs pranced in after him, strung tight as wires.

In another minute Mac's voice floated lightly from inside. "Yeah, down my tree and into your yard. See if he's still there, will you? I'll call to get some limbs cut in the morning."

Lights filled Walt's backyard, deepening the shadows high in the magnolia.

Sheila and her companion exhaled identical breaths of relief, then he drew back and she could feel him straining to see in the dark. "This tree doesn't quite reach the fence. Got a helicopter?"

"No."

"Then when we get there, jump like hell."

"What if I can't jump like hell?"

"Dobermans are marvelous incentives to learn."

They climbed quickly down the tree, landing just beside the fence. Without conscious thought Sheila stepped into his offered palms and hoisted herself over. She heard her skirt rip. A camellia broke her fall—and tore her bodice. Clutching the shredded dress, she pushed herself from the bush's embrace and turned—straight into the muzzle of a waiting gun.

Behind the gun, Richard's square face gleamed from sweat and moonlight. "Hands up!" he growled softly. "Who's got the cash?"

He should have been terrifying, but he wasn't. Perhaps it was the nervous looks he kept darting at the moonlight-dappled fence, as if himself terrified that Mac would find him there, too, and ask why.

"Cash?" Sheila asked blankly.

He waved the revolver. "Don't pretend you don't know what I'm talking about, Mrs. Travis. I practically caught you at the boss's safe!"

"I told you," she said with a dignity she wasn't quite feeling, "I was visiting Mac's mother, a friend of my aunt's. If anybody's got the money, it's him. I found him near the safe when I went back up to tell Mac's mother good night." She indicated her startled companion. "Try his left front pants pocket. Just keep your trigger finger steady."

As Richard dug for the money, Sheila moved. After years of karate, her movements were swift and automatic, and the man crumpled at their feet—but as he fell his gun exploded. Sheila heard her companion grunt suddenly as the suburban silence shattered.

"Are you hurt?"

Before he could answer, the dogs erupted into the backyard next door. "We'll get him, babies!" Mac shouted, pounding across his yard toward the fence.

Forgetting the unconscious Richard, Sheila grabbed the other man's hand and tugged. "Come *on!*" The basement door was ajar. He stumbled after her down the two steps and through the door. She slammed it shut behind them and led the way through the darkness to the first floor. Stopping only to lock the door at the top of the stairs, she hurried, breathless, toward the front door, dragging her stunned companion. She could already hear Mac and the dogs in the backyard—proof of a hidden gate between the two houses. Dobermans might leap that fence, but Mac couldn't.

From the angry shouts that interspersed their frenzied barks, she deduced Mac had found Richard and Richard had regained consciousness.

The front door was locked and dead-bolted. Her eyes and memory frantically sought another exit, for Yvonne's yard man was groaning with pain. She touched his sleeve. It was sticky and damp.

"Ow!" he protested.

"Come on!" she said again, pulling him by his good elbow toward the dining room. It had large windows that should be outside the fenced yard. As she raised open the center window she heard Mac bellow, "They must be in the house!" The baying dogs raced with him toward the basement door.

Sheila's companion swayed at the open window. They were

cornered. "Out," she ordered, giving him a shove. He tumbled over the sill and she leapt after him, flattening him and what had been a perfectly good azalea.

He groaned and muttered beneath her. She hauled herself to her feet and offered him a hand. He took it, still muttering, and climbed off the bush, then stood, shaking his head to clear it.

"Don't stop yet," she pleaded, grabbing his hand. "We've got to get to Walt's."

Quickly but gingerly they made their way through the woods in front of the vacant house. Wincing as pine cones and sweet gum burrs pricked her bare feet, Sheila remembered her companion had only one shoe.

At the edge of the street he dropped her hand. "Go . . . De-lacourts. I'll go . . ." He jerked his head to finish the sentence. "Confuse the . . . dogs."

"You're hurt," she argued.

He shook his head. "Flesh wound . . . okay." He leaned forward and kissed her so quickly it could have been her imagination. "Go!" He pushed her shoulder. Sheila paused just long enough to see his silhouette disappear into the woods of the gully.

She felt strangely desolate.

But only for an instant. She could hear the dogs baying inside the house. She raced, barefoot, tattered, and breathless, across Running Ridge Road. Thank God Walt's bedroom light was still on.

He answered the bell with a book in his hand, his hair on end, his pajama top open. "It's three o'clock," he greeted her as if she didn't know. "What are you doing here?" He grabbed his glasses firmly in his left hand and peered down at her. "You've got twigs in your hair, and just look at your dress!"

"I'd rather look at a glass of water." She pushed past him into the hall. She was shaking all over, and could scarcely walk. "Close that door before you get more visitors. The next ones might not be so friendly!"

"What do you mean?" A wary look came into his eyes. "You didn't have anything to do with that hullabaloo over at Mac's, did you?"

She went into the kitchen, drew herself some water, and drained the glass. Then she sagged wearily against the counter. "Let me tell you the story of my evening."

"Let me get you a robe first." He hurried upstairs.

Outside, the dogs began to bray in the cul-de-sac. She froze, waiting for them to fling themselves against Walt's front door. Instead, she heard their barks grow faint as they climbed the hill. One part of her slumped with relief. Another tensed with terror. Could the gardener—in one shoe and wounded—escape them? Her knees wouldn't hold her any longer. She stumbled to the kitchen table and collapsed into a chair. When Walt appeared, a gold silk robe over one arm, she urged him, "Whatever happens, don't let those dogs in!"

"Of course not," he replied in the tone of one stating the obvious. "You know I'm allergic to dogs. Now, go put this on, then come back and tell me what's going on."

She told him everything—almost. She didn't tell him why she'd gone upstairs at the Marriots' in the first place, because she didn't think Walt needed to think Mac and Rilla were dealing drugs unless it was a proven fact. She also made certain omissions about what had transpired in the magnolia tree, for reasons of her own.

Long before she'd finished, they were both drinking coffee. She'd made it. It would never have occurred to Walt. But she had chosen the wrong time and the wrong audience for her tale. Walter Winwood Delacourt could not understand why she had hidden in the hamper instead of simply telling the person at the door the bathroom was occupied. He wondered at length why

she'd left by a window and down a tree instead of waking the
Marriots. By now Sheila was wondering herself. But Walt's tedious moralizing was more than she could bear. After all, he'd
been safely reading while she'd been traveling hand-over-hand
above raving Dobermans!

"Never mind," she snapped. "Sometimes we do things when
we're panicked that we'd never do if we stopped to think."

Hearing a voice outside, she padded nervously to a front window, clutching the robe around her. She peered out, saw Mac in
the moonlight jogging back down the hill with two black shapes
milling anxiously around him. They were alone. Did that mean
they had not found their quarry—or that they had handed him
over to the police? Would they now come for her? She drew a
ragged breath of relief as the trio passed Walt's and entered the
Marriot house. In a couple of minutes Mac's outside lights, front
and back, went dark.

"He'll call the police now," said Walt at her shoulder. Sheila
jumped. When had he joined her? He added gloomily, "I don't
know what you're going to tell them."

"Nothing," she replied severely, "because you're not going to
let them know I'm here."

She returned to the kitchen. "Now, this man you were with,"
Walt said, following her. "What's his name?"

"I don't know. He's *your* gardener."

He shrugged. "Vonnie hired the help. I don't even know who
cleans the place. Some service, I think."

"In a white van." She nodded. "A woman saw them the day
Yvonne died."

"Did she also see the killer?" he asked eagerly.

"Unfortunately, she left right after you did. I'm afraid it was
her notes, though, that convinced Jake Drake you murdered
your wife."

"Well, I didn't." He said it as he might deny having left the
garden hose uncoiled overnight.

Sheila wanted to shake him until his teeth rattled. What would it take for him to get passionate in his own defense?

To keep from shaking him, she stood up and headed for the refrigerator. "I'm starved. What do you have to eat?"

"You're always starved," he chided her, pushing back his chair and following her. "You should weigh a ton by now."

"I burn it up eating," she said tartly. "Let's see now. There's a bit of chicken salad left. Is it still good?"

"I don't know." He reached into the refrigerator and took out a package of corned beef. "I don't eat chicken salad."

She turned, puzzled. "Didn't you have it for lunch the day Yvonne died?"

"I don't eat lunch, either. Ever."

"Sure you did," she argued. "You came home for lunch and then went to the office."

"Nope." On a slice of rye bread he was spreading a layer of mayonnaise that would make a heart specialist see dollar signs. He layered corned beef, lathered hot mustard over the whole thing, and clapped on a top. "Here." He put it on a plate, handed it to her, and went back to his chair. "I came home, showered, and left. Vonnie was fixing her own lunch, but I didn't eat."

"Somebody did," Sheila insisted, pointing to the dishwasher. "There were two plates, two goblets, and two sets of silverware."

He shrugged. "All *I* ate here that day was breakfast with Forbes. Cereal. Is Forbes okay, by the way?"

She had wondered if he'd ever ask. "Yeah, he's doing well. He got separated from Amory at Stone Mountain this afternoon"— she stopped and sighed. Was it only *this* afternoon?— and Amory thought somebody had kidnapped him. Somebody named Crispin. But—"

Walt snapped his fingers. "*That's* the name I was trying to remember! Crispin! But why should he kidnap Forbes?"

"I don't know. Have you met him?" She spoke around an enormous bite of sandwich.

"No. I don't think he ever came here. Vonnie"—his voice trembled—"Vonnie just talked to him on the phone."

As he said the word, his phone rang. Sheila nearly jumped out of her skin. "If it's Mac, don't you dare—" she began.

Walt was already answering. "Oh, hi, Mac. Did you ever find the fellow? . . . No, he didn't come through my backyard. Any" —he cleared his throat and threw Sheila a reproachful glance— "any idea who he was? . . . Well, I'll turn out my lights, then. It's okay, you didn't wake me. I wasn't sleeping anyway."

He hung up. "Mac says the fellow got away, but he's got one of his shoes. Must have been a burglar, he *says*." Walt yawned.

Sheila stood, discovered her legs had almost stopped shaking. "I'd like to go now, but Amory took my car. Can you run me home, or shall I call him?"

"You could stay the night."

They both knew that was no invitation to passion. Picturing the rust-colored stain in the center of the guest room mattress, Sheila repressed a shudder. "Thanks, but no thanks. I'm supposed to play tennis at ten. I can't do that in shredded silk and bare feet."

"Maybe Vonnie—" He stopped, and they both shook their heads.

"Giraffes don't wear doll clothes," Sheila told him. They both managed a pallid smile.

"I'll just go dress, then," he said. She'd known he would. Walt would never be caught in a road emergency wearing pajamas and slippers.

While she waited, Sheila prowled from one window to the other, hoping—what? That a barefoot man with a bleeding shoulder would limp down Running Ridge Road to assure her he was all right? That Mac *would* call the police to report an anonymous burglar?

Finally Walt descended. "You can wear the robe home, but bring it back sometime. It . . . Vonnie gave it to me last Christmas."

Sheila nodded gravely. "Thanks, Walt—for everything." Not just for sheltering her, but for letting her take from the house a precious piece of his wife. "I'll get it back soon," she promised.

As Walt backed down his own drive, Sheila pulled the robe tightly around her and slid as far down in the front scat of Walt's blue Riviera as her long legs would permit. The Marriot house was now completely dark. Apparently Mac hadn't called the police. Sheila had not really expected that he would. But the house's dark silence was more terrifying. Richard, after all, knew who she was. If he spoke, Mac could find her.

*DOCTOR: John, it's bad news. You have only
six months to live.
JOHN: Is there anything I can do?
DOCTOR: You could marry a woman from
Dunwoody and move her to Philadelphia.
JOHN: Will that help me live longer?
DOCTOR: No, but it will make six months
seem like a lifetime.*

S A T U R D A Y

Seven hours after Sheila got home, she was back in
Dunwoody in tennis whites, racquet in hand. For years she'd
played tennis almost daily. Today she'd had to dust her racquet
when she took it off the shelf. She hoped she wouldn't disgrace
herself.

She made a decent showing, but lost the match. "Winner buys
drinks," Ava told her gaily. The air-conditioning inside the club-
house felt wonderful, and Sheila would have liked just to relax
and enjoy the company of this pleasant woman. Instead, after
they'd chatted about this and that, she brought up the subject
she'd come for.

"My nephew has been dating Dee Ivy," she said casually. "But
Walt and I are friends, and I understand that Dee and Yvonne
had some sort of disagreement. I wondered . . ."

"They didn't disagree, Dee was just plain tacky." Ava wrinkled her long nose and bent over her drink so that sun-streaked
hair swung down to hide her gaunt cheeks. "Yvonne let Dee
decorate her house and sent a lot of business her way, then she
asked Dee to decorate a house she had sold. Dee turned her
down—can you believe it?" She looked up, tawny eyes inviting

Sheila to share her incredulity. "After Yvonne had been so sweet!" Ava shook her head. "We just can't understand it." Sheila took the "we" to mean Dunwoody matrons who had exhaustively discussed the matter—probably from a single point of view.

"Do you remember when that was?"

"No. The end of May sometime, I think." She twisted the diamond bracelet on her wrist.

May 28: D no dice. One mystery solved?

Ava sighed and continued. "Of course Yvonne didn't hold a grudge or anything. She was one of the sweetest women I ever knew. But the rest of us don't understand what made Dee act that way. She probably feels terrible now that Yvonne's . . ." Her voice wavered. "I just can't get over it. Can you?"

What Sheila wanted to get over right now was this conversation. She needed to find out if Dee Ivy had eaten chicken salad with Yvonne Delacourt the day Yvonne died.

Maybe, she thought, angling onto Mount Vernon Road for yet another trip to Dunwoody after lunch, I ought to buy that vacant house just to save wear and tear on my car. What she said was "Let me do the talking."

She hadn't planned to bring Amory along, but he had fed her homemade gazpacho and fresh zucchini bread and called Dee to set up a talk with Sheila at three. How could she refuse his request?

Now he slouched in his seat, drumming his fingers on one thick thigh. "I just want to see if she'll go with me to the ball game tonight, since you won't."

"Not *won't*, Amory, *can't*. I am beat."

"I still think you ought to tell me where you disappeared to last night. If you'd said something before you left, I wouldn't have worried."

"If I could have said something, I would've," she assured him.

"I promise you it won't happen again. When we get to Dee's, I'm going to ask where she was the afternoon Yvonne was murdered. You keep quiet until I get an answer. Got that?"

"Of course," he rumbled, aggrieved.

When they turned onto Running Ridge Road, Sheila eyed Mac and Rilla's house anxiously. It stood placid and cheerful in the afternoon sunlight. Nevertheless, she shivered. Had Richard identified the intruders? If so, what would Mac do? And if not, for heaven's sake, *why* not?

Dee was not at home. "She's got a flat tire," her younger daughter, Megan, informed them. She was a miniature Dee, complete with flyaway blond curls and a short, pert nose. Her older sister, Lori, must resemble their father, Sheila decided, for she was tall, stocky, and darker.

"Where?" demanded Amory the chivalrous.

Megan looked at him as if he were an idiot. "On the car, of course." She looked meaningfully over her shoulder at the den, where a television movie was moving loudly to its conclusion without her presence.

He glared. "I mean, where is she?"

"Oh. Up at the grocery store. She said she'd try to change it, if you could wait."

Five minutes later Sheila let him out in a Kroger parking lot. Dee stood beside her silver BMW, hot and close to tears. Her pale yellow dress was smudged. "I've tried and tried, but I can't get the bolts off."

To Sheila's utter surprise, Amory the fastidious neatly folded his coat over the passenger seat of her car and rolled up his sleeves. "Let me see what I can do."

They bickered amicably about whether she could permit him to soil his hands, she acquiesced, as Sheila had known she would, and together they bent to the task.

"I'll run into Kroger's and pick up some things," Sheila told them. She doubted that they even heard.

When she got back, they had gone! "Of all the ingrates," she fumed. "I ought to leave him up here and let him make his own way home." Only a desire to know if Dee had shared lunch with Yvonne made her drive back to Running Ridge Road.

But Dee was not yet home. Her daughters had neither seen nor heard from her, and were far more concerned about the outcome of the TV movie than about the whereabouts of their mother.

"Tell Mr. Travis I've gone on home. He can take a cab," Sheila snarled. Back in her car, she pressed her foot so hard on the accelerator, she nearly collided with Paula Divesty's passing station wagon.

Sheila would never know whether she followed Paula out of temper, frustration, or curiosity. She did know that she got a kick out of keeping the blue Mercedes wagon in view without being seen.

Paula took the expressway and headed south in the fast lane. In the afternoon haze the sky was almost white, the city hidden by tree-covered hills that rolled in successive shades of green and blue toward the piedmont. The speed lulled Sheila's spirit. She was sorry when Paula turned off into the city.

As she recognized the part of town to which they were heading, Sheila was surprised. Once these streets had been lined with stately homes and, later, prosperous businesses. Now large buildings stood like big teeth gapped with littered parking lots. Sheila knew battered women's shelters had to be put in secret locations where neighbors would not complain, but surely battered women's children deserved better than this?

When Paula slowed and turned, Sheila was puzzled. Why was Paula parking her gleaming Mercedes in the lot of a club called the Little Red Rooster? And why was she hurrying inside?

At this early hour on a beautiful summer Saturday afternoon the lot was nearly empty. If it had been fuller, or Sheila had not been dimwitted with lack of sleep, she would have backed out immediately and gone home. Instead, she pulled into a spot near Paula's, locked her car carefully, and strolled inside.

She met the curious eyes of the man at the register and paid the cover charge without a word. Then she strolled down a dim hall to the dimmer bar within.

Sheila gritted her teeth, prepared for pruience and sleaze. Instead, as her eyes adjusted, she saw a tastefully decorated lounge with thick carpeting and subdued lighting. Low chairs were grouped around three platforms where perhaps twenty men watched three tanned women lazily removing costumes in time to music. The women looked a lot healthier than the men, none of whom appeared to have seen the light of day for years. The pallor of their skin made Sheila think of maggots, as did the way they slumped, boneless, in their chairs. They scarcely noticed as she made her way to the bar.

"What can I do for you?" The Latin American bartender spoke in the cynical tone of one who expected to get nothing from the exchange except a chance to show off his green card.

"Give me a gin and tonic."

He paused, as if it took a while for his brain to accept that she had actually ordered, then reached for the bottles. Sheila leaned her back against the gleaming oak bar and looked around. The walls were decorated with life-size pictures of women in various stages of disrobing. If she hadn't seen Paula enter the back door, Sheila would never have recognized the woman pictured in a brief cowgirl skirt trimmed in emerald sequins, a cowboy hat, and bright green boots, bare breasts almost covered by a waterfall of soft chestnut-brown hair, eyes heavily lined and painted violet, lips painted a vivid, luscious red.

A man in a black suit and alligator shoes came from a back room and headed directly for her. "May I help you?" he asked.

He was so short that she could have rested her chin on his head. Instead, she took a step back to reduce the angle at which she was looking down. "No, I'm just stopping for a drink."

Someone should tell him, she thought, that narrowing his eyes did not improve his appearance.

He looked her up and down. "You dance?"

She shrugged. "Maybe. What're you paying?"

"We don't pay, sugar, *they* do." He jerked one thumb at the customers. As he spoke, Sheila saw one man reach toward a woman with a bill. The dancer modestly covered her not quite private parts with one arm to hold her garter open for him to slip it under. "The good ones make good money. Some take home—" He named a figure that might have tempted half the employed women in Atlanta. Then he shook his head. "But sorry, honey. I don't want to insult you or anything, but you're a bit old."

She shrugged again. "It's your loss." She pointed to Paula's poster. "She looks like she's no spring chicken, either."

He grinned. "Ah, but that's Polly. She's been with me for years, and has a real class act. And she can still give you ten years." He reached up and patted her arm. Sheila managed not to jerk it away. "She's on in half an hour. Stick around and catch her. You'll see what I mean. She's got class!"

He squeezed her arm, crossed the room in a glide, nodding to the customers as if they were old friends, and disappeared into what she presumed was his office.

She carried her gin and tonic to a vacant couch in the corner and set it on a low table that she suspected was supposed to be a private stage. She hoped putting the drink down was not a subtle form of invitation. What must the men in the place already be thinking?

And who were they—these men who had nothing better to do on Saturday afternoon than sit in a darkened room, watching naked women dance alone? Watching was all they could do. The room was liberally posted with signs warning THIS CLUB HAS A STRICT TOUCH AND GO POLICY. YOU TOUCH AND YOU GO. So what brought them? Did that stout one have a wife and three pudgy children at home? Did he fantasize that he was an Eastern potentate for whose sole pleasure these slender women performed? That short, wiry one in the corner who glared at anyone who looked his way—did he really want to beat up every woman he saw, or could he just not help the way he looked? Of course it was possible, she told herself as she sipped her gin, that these men were merely lonely with nowhere to go.

There are lonely men, her self argued back, who make friends, volunteer to help others, and find healthy places to spend their time.

She was glad she didn't know any of them, decided if someone she recognized came in, she would embarrass him before he could embarrass her. As the dance ended, she leaned back in her chair. She wanted to see Paula without Paula seeing her.

In a few minutes new music swelled. Sheila had not expected Ravel's "Bolero." A spotlight wavered, then found the center stage. Paula glided on, draped in multicolored scarves, one pale hand above her head, the other provocatively on one hip. There were dancers on the other stages, too, but most eyes in the room were on Paula as—slowly, hypnotically—she began to dance. Her movements were beautiful, those of a professionally trained dancer, not a professional tease. Sheila looked again at the leering men. Did any of them appreciate that they were seeing art? No, they were waiting for the music to get louder, for Paula to stamp and whirl, discarding scarves as she turned. When the "Bolero" reached its crescendo, she stood, naked except for a garter, her body sleek with sweat and as lovely as any Sheila had ever seen.

The men were frenzied, eagerly extending paper money. One hand shielding her groin, Paula held her garter with the other and helped slide bills underneath. Then, with an enigmatic smile, she turned to leave the stage. Her eyes met Sheila's across the room. She hesitated, then lifted her chin, and strode toward the dressing room.

Sheila waited ten minutes, then approached the bar. "Would it be possible for me to talk with Polly?"

The bartender shrugged. "Sure. Go on back. We don't let men in, but I don't think the girls'd mind a lady."

The back hall was well lit, carpeted, and smelled of sweat, showers, shampoo, and perfume. The dressing room looked like a feminine locker room, with a long counter, big mirror, and pink lockers. Showers opened off one end.

Sheila knocked on the door frame. "Paula?"

At the mirror, Paula turned. She was damp from a shower, wrapped in a blue kimono. Her eyes flickered, then she jerked her head in invitation. "Come in." Six new dancers were putting on costumes that were very elaborate—especially since they would soon be taking them off again. The girls welcomed Sheila like a flock of bright parakeets, then returned to their own chatter.

Paula seated herself at the far end of the counter, where the mirror had a butterfly pasted whimsically near its top. She invited Sheila to sit in a nearby pink wicker chair with a flowered chintz cover, and began to brush her chestnut hair. Loosened, it flowed almost to her waist.

Dragging it back into its familiar drab style, she asked, "What're you doing in a place like this?"

"Looking for you. I saw your car parked in the lot, and thought maybe that women's shelter you mentioned was somewhere around. Then I saw you come in."

Paula rose, opened a locker, took out her street clothes with an air of defeat. Sheila reached out to stop her. "Are you through so early?"

Paula nodded. "I always promised myself that the first time anybody I knew came in and recognized me, I'd quit." She turned her back to dress, then looked over one shoulder and asked in a wistful voice, "Was it that easy?"

Sheila shook her head. "If I hadn't known you were here, I'd never have made the connection."

Paula looked relieved, but she slipped on street shoes and reached for her purse just the same. "What are you going to do now that you know?"

"Treat you to dinner," Sheila replied promptly.

Two hours later Paula Divesty set down her coffee cup and
sighed. "That was delicious—the first real dinner I've eaten in
two weeks. My nights off, Alex had to show houses, so I micro-
waved TV dinners." She blotted her lips on her napkin, looked
wryly at a speck of lipstick that came off. "I forgot to finish
cleaning my face."

"Do you never use cosmetics except at work?"

"No. I've gone without them for so long that people who've
known me for years have forgotten I ever wore them. I thought
people were less likely to make the connection that way." Her
long body was now clad in a prim white blouse, black slacks, and
black pumps. Her hair was tied at her nape with a large black
bow. She pushed away her plate. "And now that you've fed me,
you want to know how I got started in all this, don't you?"

"If you want to tell me," Sheila admitted. "From the way you
danced, you must have trained in ballet."

"I did. Jazz, too. I'm the Cinderella story in reverse. I grew up
in a more than comfortable home, took dancing from the time I
was four. By high school I was pretty good."

"Very good," Sheila amended.

Paula shrugged, then nodded. "Yeah, I was. I got a scholarship
to a New York studio. Then," she sighed and started to fiddle
with her teaspoon, "I got pregnant the end of senior year. The
guy came from a family that went to our church, and he had a
football scholarship to Georgia Tech. My dad insisted we get
married." When she looked up, there were tears in her eyes.
"Guess who got to go to college and who got to go to work."

"Dancing in bars?" Sheila didn't believe it.

"Heavens no! We were *Baptists!* I was a waitress, file clerk,
anything I could find."

"And the baby?"

Paula was silent for so long that Sheila wondered if the child
had died. Then she whispered, head bent over her plate, "He's

brain damaged. He's in a real good school, and nobody but his dad, my family, and Alex even knows he's still alive—or cares. Steven, his dad, adored him when he was born, but when he found Craig wasn't normal, he couldn't handle it. The year he graduated from Tech—"

Sheila knew what was coming.

"—Steven asked for a divorce. He told me to put Craig in a state institution and forget him. My father backed him up on that. I . . . I couldn't abandon my baby. But I couldn't afford to pay his doctors' bills and for day care while I worked, either, and the little bit Steven gave me didn't go very far. The child support laws weren't as good then as they are now. I was desperate! So when a friend told me they were looking for dancers at the Red Rooster . . ." She began to trace elaborate designs on the tablecloth.

At another table a man finished speaking and the woman with him laughed—probably louder than the joke deserved. She reached over and drew his fat hand to her lips, smiling into his eyes. She was young, pretty, and obviously not his wife. Paula looked in their direction and shuddered. "I could never do that— go out with a man and make up to him for what he'd give me. I didn't even think I could take off my clothes. But it's not too bad. You don't have to relate to the customers, or even see them, really. I just pretend they're not there. And the boss, Bud—"

"A short guy in a black pinstripe suit?"

Paula nodded. "He's really insecure about being so short, but he's a fine man. Really. He lets me write my own routines and choose my own music, and he keeps my secret. Before Craig went to school, Bud even let me bring him down and put him to sleep in his office some nights when my sitter couldn't come."

A kind man running a stripper club. A well-to-do, respectable church member refusing to pay child support for a brain-damaged child. Was no man what he seemed? A face flashed into Sheila's thoughts: dark, with a taunting grin, and a curl that fell onto his forehead. She stuck to the subject at hand. "And you make enough dancing to pay all Craig's bills?"

"I did." Paula's voice was somber, and for the first time Sheila realized how much Paula had given up that evening when she quit.

"But after you married Alex . . ." She let the sentence trail into whatever Paula chose to let it mean.

"I don't ask him to help much with Craig. It takes most of his income to pay our bills."

"Yet he insists on living in Dunwoody?"

"Heavens no!" Paula's face lit with humor at the idea. "Alex wouldn't care where we lived. It's me. I couldn't imagine living anywhere else. It's a wonderful, stable community. Our friends are there, our church—I do go to church again. God and I have worked things out. Everybody else thinks I work at a shelter— even Alex." Her eyes met Sheila's with a silent plea.

Sheila smiled. "Don't you?"

Paula's eyes twinkled. "As a matter of fact, yes. One day a week. I couldn't just lie, you see."

It was time to put that veracity to the test. Sheila leaned forward and said, "Paula, one day at Walt's I heard you and Alex arguing. You were afraid the police would find out about something. What was it?"

Paula picked up her cup of ice-cold coffee and drank it as if it were delicious. She set down the cup, took her time about blotting her lips, then shook her head. "You must have heard the television. I'm addicted to soap operas when I'm home."

It was a lie, but Sheila was suddenly too weary to argue. Her eyes felt as if she had a handful of sand in them.

"You're falling asleep on your feet!" Paula exclaimed.

Sheila swallowed a yawn. "I was up late at one of Mac and Rilla's parties."

Paula smiled. "I've been to only one, the one where I met you. I'm not around much on Friday nights, you know. Alex likes to go. Says he meets some good prospects there. Mac and Rilla invite the world."

"It seemed like a strange conglomeration of people last night." Sheila's brain was getting fuzzy, but a warning signal deep in the back was nagging that she ought to ask one more question before she left. What could it be?

Yvonne. Did Paula kill Yvonne? No, she couldn't ask that point-blank. Even at this stage of exhaustion she knew that. Ah!

"Did Yvonne know about Craig? And that you danced?"

Paula had been rearranging her silverware. Now she grew quite still. "Why would you think that?"

Why had she? Sheila struggled to remember.

"Because of what she said at that party. About you being the little red rooster of the neighborhood. And not having a child at home. She did know, didn't she?"

Paula gave a high, artificial laugh. "Oh, those were lucky shots —or unfortunate ones. I scarcely knew Yvonne. We had nothing in common." She slid from the booth and reached for her purse. "Thanks for dinner." In an instant, she was gone.

MAN TO DUNWOODY PAPERBOY: "Son, I'd like to give you a tip. Got change for a dollar?" *PAPERBOY:* "Sir, in Dunwoody, a dollar is change."

S U N D A Y   M O R N I N G

"**A**ll you had to do was say where you were going." Amory's voice was shrill with righteous indignation. "I didn't mind asking Dee to bring me back here, but it's damned inconsiderate for you to keep disappearing every time we go somewhere together." He forked a crisp waffle off the iron with such force, Sheila suspected he'd rather fork her.

"I didn't disappear. You did," she pointed out reasonably. "When I got to where I'd left you, you weren't there." She accepted the waffle, smeared it with butter, and smothered it in blueberry syrup. She resisted an impulse to hurl it into Amory's face.

"We'd only gone to the tire store a block away, and it only took ten minutes to buy it." He poured his own waffle onto the iron. "Any fool could have figured she'd need a new tire."

"Since I'm *not* a fool, I figured you'd gone back to Dee's. When you weren't there . . ."

"We *were* there, five minutes after you left. If you'd stuck around, instead of dashing off God knows where . . ."

"God knows and I know," she told him, taking down an enormous mug from the top shelf. "And as I've already said, I am not going to tell you." She filled the mug to the brim with black coffee.

The way she felt this morning, she was going to need a lot of coffee. She had barely made it home last night before she fell asleep, but Amory had stomped into her room about one o'clock to growl, "So *there* you are!" as if he'd been looking all over the city for her. When she ignored him and buried her face in her pillow, he had stomped out and made enough noise getting ready for bed to thoroughly awaken her. She had lain awake until three, puzzling the case over in her mind.

Yvonne had to have known about Paula. Her stinging remarks about the "little red rooster" and Paula not having children at home were too accurate to be coincidental. How she had discovered Paula's fiercely guarded secrets was a mystery. As Walt had said, Yvonne liked to know things about people.

Who would be most dangerous to know something about, Mac Marriot or Paula Divesty? Or, perhaps, a gardener who wasn't really a gardener?

Sheila had tossed and turned until her sheets wound about her like a shroud. Finally she fell into a shallow, restless sleep only to be wakened a few hours later by Lady, whining softly to be taken out.

Returning from their walk, Sheila had met Amory's wrath. It still smoldered between them in her galley kitchen, so she carried her waffle, coffee, and the morning newspaper out onto the deck. The air outside was cool enough to compare favorably with air-conditioning–plus–Amory.

Lady, as usual, flopped down on one side of her chair. Sheila dropped the paper to the deck on the other side while she ate. Anger certainly didn't impair Amory's culinary skills. She considered asking for a second waffle, then told herself she wasn't too proud to ask—just too comfortable in the wicker chair.

She cast a surreptitious look over her shoulder. Through the glass doors she saw him seated at the table, wolfing down a waffle. Sticking out her tongue at his broad, bathrobed back, she wiped up the last blueberry syrup with one finger and licked it greedily. Amory made her feel childish sometimes.

"Two only children, both spoiled rotten," Mildred had told her once. This morning, wondering how to make up without apologizing (after all, he *had* left the parking lot first), Sheila had an uncomfortable suspicion Mildred might be right.

She bent down to give Lady a scratch, then reached for the Sunday *Journal and Constitution.* It should occupy her until time to dress for church. She unfolded section one—and froze.

MERRY WIDOW'S TRAIL OF DEATH ENDS IN MURDER

Yvonne Delacourt, gentle and lovely, smiled from the center of the page. But who was the man holding her hand? *Rodney Sanders, the second husband to fall for this lovely widow's deadly spell.*

The article began with a recap of recent facts: how Yvonne had been found murdered last Monday by her husband, Walter Winwood Delacourt, in their Dunwoody guest room, stabbed by a brass letter opener from a Hawaiian hotel. *But this was no ordinary Dunwoody housewife,* the article continued. *In her thirty-one years, Yvonne Gates Jones Sanders Hardwick Delacourt left a trail of dead husbands and friends.*

Sheila found it hard to believe. Yvonne—who looked and dressed like a direct descendent of the first Junior Leaguer— raised in a tiny house in Pensacola, the daughter of an elementary-school cafeteria cook and an unknown father? Married four times and widowed three, each time in suspicious circumstances?

Appalled, she read quickly. . . . *At nineteen married sailor Henry Jones . . . doctor's receptionist . . . soft June evening ten years ago this month . . . vacant lot . . . bullet through his head . . . no suspects . . . home with a migraine . . . verified by a friend . . . one-hundred-thousand-dollar insurance policy.*

A brief editorial note followed that paragraph: *The friend who verified Mrs. Jones's story died of accidental salmonella poisoning one year after Jones's murder.*

Sheila sipped her coffee, but it was cold. She felt cold, too, and numb. Her fingers would scarcely turn pages to find the rest of the story.

*Five months later Yvonne Jones married Rodney Sanders, a
pharmaceutical salesman she met at work.* Again Sheila scanned
for vital words. *. . . had lunched together when Jones at sea
. . . gave up custody of his son . . . moved to Memphis—*

Her concentration was broken by the sound of the glass door
sliding open. "You want another waffle?" Amory held up the
bowl. Lady trotted over and licked his ankle, making peace between them.

Sheila found she was no longer hungry. "Not yet, but save me
some batter. I'll be in in a few minutes."

"May I have sports and the comics?"

She gave up the sections with a small smile. It was the best
either could do by way of an apology. She appreciated his making
the first move. She would not, however, tell him about what she
was reading. Not yet. He'd want to grab the paper or read over
her shoulder.

As he padded out with the coffeepot and refilled her mug, she
concealed the story from him. When he went back in to hunch
over the latest baseball scores and Lady elected to follow him,
Sheila was too engrossed to feel slighted.

Yvonne and her second husband had moved to Memphis and
traveled in wealthy circles. Rodney Sanders told friends he was
worried about money—his wife was spending more than he
made. He even talked of divorce. Then one day Yvonne returned
from shopping to find her husband shot dead in his den. His son,
sixteen, had threatened his dad and stepmother a few weeks
before. When the boy's mother was questioned, however, she
swore he'd been at home with her in Macon, Georgia. A friend
verified that Yvonne had been shopping with her all day. The
widow received one million dollars in life insurance.

The writer noted: *The friend who verified Mrs. Sanders's story
committed suicide a month after Sanders's death. Her husband
assured this reporter that her death had nothing to do with the
Sanders case.*

In less than a year Yvonne wed Dr. Martin Hardwick, one of

Sanders's customers. Hardwick, fifty-eight, was a childless widower. They had a son the following year, and Hardwick suffered a severe heart attack six months later. Their friends were surprised when Yvonne, who was having the house redecorated, placed the ailing doctor in an apartment with a personal attendant "to save him having to deal with the smell of paint." However, all swore that she seemed a devoted wife in all other respects.

One afternoon while his attendant was picking up a prescription, Dr. Martin Hardwick had decided to take a bath. He drowned in the tub. His estate was valued at three million dollars. The doctor's mother—Sheila paused and read that again. How old would his mother have been? Not too old, apparently, to file suit to prevent Yvonne from inheriting, accusing her of being responsible for Hardwick's death. Later she dropped all charges and refused to talk with the press.

Where had Yvonne been when the doctor drowned? Sheila searched. There it was, a couple of paragraphs down: Yvonne Hardwick's decorator, Wilson Braswell, affirmed that they had been together at the house, discussing fabrics. The reporter had tried to reach Braswell, but he, too, had drowned—in a Caribbean sailing accident two years ago.

An incredible story. But was it true?

Sheila dropped the paper beside her chair and tried to be fair. Yvonne could have been spectacularly unlucky. Some people, she told herself, attract disaster the way others attract good fortune.

"But why," she murmured, "would a widow who'd inherited more than four million dollars in the past decade need a free decorator for her Dunwoody home? Why would she borrow from a neighbor and her father-in-law to pay old debts?"

Down the hill, the ducks on the pond were busily pursuing the day's feast of water bugs. Sheila scarcely saw them. Instead, she saw a delicate heart-shaped face with a tall, bony one beside it, lit with loving pride. Had Walt seen this story yet?

She rose and went to the phone.

It rang before she reached it.

As soon as she said hello, a familiar deep voice commanded, "Sheila, come immediately. This changes everything."

It was natural for Aunt Mary to assume Sheila was up and had already read the paper. Aunt Mary, however, was not an early riser. "What got you up so bright and early?"

"Mildred. She thought I ought to know. She was quite right. Don't bother to dress. Just come right away."

Aunt Mary did not mean "Come in your bathrobe." She meant "Don't take time to get ready for church." If Aunt Mary planned to dispense with church, she must be as worried as Sheila was. The only difference was that Sheila was worried about Walt, while Aunt Mary was worried about his father.

"I was just about to call Walt. Shall I ask him to come, too?"

"If he will." Aunt Mary hung up without saying good-bye.

Forbes was overjoyed to see Amory and dragged him off to see a set of "real Confedrit sodjurs" Mildred had unearthed. "There's Lee, and Forrest, and . . ."

Sheila raised one eyebrow at her aunt, exquisite in a lavender lace robe, sitting in her sunny dining room primly spreading Mildred's excellent peach jam on one of her equally excellent pecan muffins. "Great-granddaddy's lead soldiers? The ones you always said were too valuable for me to play with?"

Aunt Mary waved one hand, amethysts twinkling in the sunlight. "Forbes is a careful child. Besides, as I get older, people are becoming more valuable than things."

"Not all people, just that one small person," Mildred amended, setting a plate and cup of black coffee before Sheila. "She makes like she doesn't care a thing about having him here, but when you come to take him away, be prepared for a fit. Have a muffin," she added.

"Nonsense!" Aunt Mary raised her chin. "I merely permitted the child to play with some of the few old toys we have around the place. Now, Sheila, we have far more serious matters to discuss. Serious enough even to talk about at the table. Is Walter coming?"

Sheila would have liked to discuss the soldiers—and the number of times she'd been denied permission to play with them. But if Aunt Mary was willing to bend her code to discuss unpleasantness at the table, they'd better discuss it. "Walt didn't answer his phone. Maybe he went up to their place on Lake Burton for the weekend. If so, maybe he won't see the paper."

"He'll have to know sometime, Sheila. It's all true," Aunt Mary assured her gravely. "I spoke with the editor before I called you."

"But they've publicly convicted her of three murders without a trial!"

"There have been six deaths," Aunt Mary replied crisply. "Even though the deaths of those who provided alibis were all considered accidental, taken together they form a pattern we cannot ignore."

Sheila had not planned to add muffins to her previous waffle, but now she buttered one and took a bite without thinking. "Yet no one got suspicious before—except one poor old woman?"

"Mrs. Hardwick may not be a poor old woman at all, Sheila," said a very wealthy one. "I have asked Charlie to try to trace her, and to ask whether the insurance company investigated her accusations. Sometimes they are more thorough than the police. They do so hate to part with their money."

"Like somebody else we know," Sheila murmured. Aunt Mary gave that remark the attention it deserved: none. She continued to eat silently until Sheila remarked, "Even Charlie will find it hard to learn anything on a Sunday."

She did not doubt, however, that Charles Davidson would do everything in his power, Sunday or not. What *was* it that made one of Atlanta's leading financiers move heaven and earth for Aunt Mary, caused him to give her the privilege of calling him Charlie when even his wife called him, reverently, Charles? No one knew—except Charlie and Aunt Mary.

"He has his methods," Aunt Mary murmured absently. She was consulting a list beside her. "Now, let me see. Have you found out anything more about Yvonne's neighbors? Did anyone see anything on the day she was killed?"

"I've found out a lot about the neighbors. But apparently nobody saw anything or anybody on the day she was killed. Here's what I've learned so far. . . ."

"So," Aunt Mary mused when Sheila finished, "we have several possible suspects besides Walt. The Marriots, Paula Divesty, Alex Divesty, Dee Ivy—" She lowered her voice. "You don't think Amory is serious about that woman, do you? It would be dreadfully awkward if Amory married her and then discovered she had murdered Mrs. Delacourt. I don't know how Hetty would ever forgive you."

"It would be more awkward for Amory than for his mother," Sheila pointed out. "I think we'd better stick to discussing this case, Aunt Mary, and let Amory take care of himself."

"Of course, dear." Aunt Mary sounded like that had been her suggestion all along. "Now, about that couple next door . . ."

Mildred peered around the kitchen door. "I'm sorry, Miss Mary, but it's Mr. Rip on the phone. He says it's urgent."

Aunt Mary trotted into the hall—she never would permit a telephone to invade her living or dining rooms—and returned almost immediately. "Sheila, please come to the phone. Walter is about to do something very foolish. Rip needs your help."

Rip Delacourt's words were harder than ever to decipher over the line. Excitement made him try to speak more rapidly, and his

paralyzed throat refused to comply. It took several tries before
she realized what he was telling her.

"But he *can't* leave town, Rip! Not without permission of the
court. Where does he want to go?"

She listened again, trying to translate, finding herself repeat-
ing his words to make sure she had them right.

"Florida? Pensacola? If he tries to get on an airplane, he could
get arrested. What? The company plane?"

Winsome Brassieres had been one of the first in Atlanta to get
a corporate plane—not for the financial advantage, but for the
fun Rip got out of it. In addition to the bird-watching party, he'd
twice flown Walt's classmates to Destin for a Saturday afternoon
beach party. Sheila was willing to bet this was the first time Walt
had ever used it for anything personal.

Gradually she understood what Rip wanted. Walt was already
on his way to the airport. Rip had called the pilot and told him
not to leave the ground until Mrs. Travis got there.

"Talk him out of it, Sheila. You gotta!" he urged. "I can't keep
him from taking off, but you can."

She doubted it, but she promised to try.

Walt stood beside the plane, arguing with the pilot, when
Sheila and Amory arrived. Amory had come because "You may
need to use force to keep Walt here." She hadn't argued. Telling
Amory she had idled away her time while married to Tyler by
earning her black belt would only further complicate her life. But
she did insist that he wait by the hangar while she talked to
Walter.

It was hot and gusty on the tarmac. The sultry wind whipped
Walt's hair into his face, but he didn't seem to notice. "I'm glad
you finally got here," he said peevishly by way of greeting. "This
fool said he was under orders not to take off until you arrived.
Let's go."

"I didn't come to go with you, Walt. I came to tell you that you can't go, either. The police won't let you leave Atlanta without their permission."

His face was haggard and sullen. "I won't be gone long—probably just for the afternoon."

"Where do you want to go, and why?"

He hesitated, shuffled his feet, and looked over his shoulder at a bank of snowy cumulus clouds building in the west. Then he looked down to where his toe was mutilating an old cigarette butt. "Did you see today's paper?"

"Yes."

He didn't speak again until the cigarette was no longer visible on the tarmac. Then his eyes met hers, and his were wild. "They're lying, Sheila! *Lying!* And I'm going to prove it!"

"How, Walt?"

"Ask questions, talk with the police, things like that."

"You think you can just barge into a town and ask the police to open their files? It's not done, Walt—even if you weren't already under arrest. Which, let me point out, you are."

He turned his back. On a nearby runway a small jet raced toward liftoff. When it was aloft, he turned back, pounding a fist into his palm. "I've *got* to go, Sheila. I just have to! Those things they're saying about Vonnie—they aren't true! I know they aren't! And I'm going to prove it, one way or another. If they won't let me look at the records, I'll find people who knew her. I can't just sit here and let everybody in Dunwoody think these things about my wife!"

"They'll read the paper, Walt."

"I bought them all," he said with a smug smile. "My paper boy comes early, and I was already up. When I read what they were saying, I went out and emptied every single paper box in Dunwoody. Then I picked up all I saw lying in people's yards."

She stared at him in astonishment. Those were not the acts of a staid, conservative businessman. She knew desperation when she saw it. She was wondering what to say next, when he grabbed her arm. "I'll tell you what! You come with me!"

His fingers bit into her arm. Tomorrow she'd have fresh bruises on top of the ones the gardener had left. "You told Dad you'd help me? So help me! Come to Pensacola. Help me prove Yvonne never killed anybody. She was the sweetest, kindest, gentlest, dearest—"

Sheila waved at Amory and boarded the plane. It was the only way to shut Walt up.

WOMAN TO ST. PETER: "*I don't understand. This isn't Dunwoody! I thought when I died I was going to Dunwoody.*"

The jet circled over a flat landscape bristling with pines. Far to the south, beyond two ribbonlike islands, the gulf lay like a carelessly thrown sapphire scarf with a border of dazzling white. A little girl might easily pretend that soft sand was powder.

"Plane on our right!" Amory leapt from his seat and gripped the pilot's shoulder.

The pilot shrugged him off. "Keep your shirt on. He's heading for Navy Pensacola Airport, we're going in to International. You can see his landing strip just off our right wing. You'll see ours in a minute."

Sheila sipped a Coke and watched while houses that seemed stolen from a Monopoly set grew into ones large enough for a child to play in. She was no longer worried about leaving town with Walt. She had worried while the plane droned south over the pinelands of Georgia. What if Jake Drake found out they had gone? What if this evening Walt refused to return? What if they found nothing to rouse him from his mounting despair? By now, after an hour in the air, she was worried out. Besides, Amory was worrying enough for everybody.

"This is illegal," he muttered for the fiftieth time. He took his seat and fastened his seat belt as the pilot nosed toward the ground. "We are abetting a felon."

"Walt's not a felon," Sheila told him mildly. "He hasn't been tried. Now, hush. I need to think about what to do when we land."

"If my dad knew . . ."

"If you mention your dad once more, I am going to personally put you on a plane for Tupelo as soon as we touch down."

"You don't have to get huffy." He turned his body so one large shoulder was aimed in her direction. "You've been a bitch ever since you got up this morning."

Sheila sighed. "Why did you come, Amory? Tell me that. If you are so dead set against being here . . ."

"Somebody's got to look after you. Besides, I've never been a detective before. Now, don't talk to me anymore. I always pray during landings."

"Good." She closed her own eyes. "Keep praying until we're safely back home."

Walt had hunched silently in his seat for most of the trip, pale face pressed to the window as if he could speed the plane by pushing it with his nose. Only once had he roused himself, when Amory had asked if he had anything to drink on board. He'd brought Cokes for each of them, then slumped back into his seat without a word.

Sheila had asked, "Do you have a phone aboard?"

"Sure." He pointed one thumb to show her where.

She had consulted her memory and dialed Frank McGehee at home.

When the young officer learned where she was—and with whom—his voice went from a baritone to a squeak. "If Drake finds out, he'll have all your hides!"—but at least he knew an Officer Brakestone in the Pensacola P.D. He had called Brakestone and called Sheila back to say they had an appointment for one o'clock.

"He won't arrest Walt and send him right back to you, will he?" she had asked anxiously.

"No. He should, but he won't. But if you aren't back here by midnight, I'll call him and issue an all-points bulletin."

Atlanta had been hot. Pensacola bypassed hotter and went straight for hottest. Sheila expected her hair to start frizzing as soon as the airplane door opened, but the wind that met her face was dry. "We haven't had a bit of rain all month," the Avis agent told them. Sheila knew better than to be publicly grateful, but at least she wouldn't arrive at the Pensacola Police Department looking like one big kink.

To her pleasant surprise, Amory insisted on signing for the rental car. "I'm on vacation," he explained with a grand wave in Walt's direction, "in case anybody checks up." She would tell him later how touched she was. Right now she was writing down directions to the police station.

The station was located one block down a one-way street, going the wrong way. After two unsuccessful attempts, they finally reached the parking lot, their tempers hotter than the temperature outside.

To make matters worse, Frank's friend Brakestone was not at all sure he wanted to help a man accused of one murder to investigate another. The more reluctant he got, the more desperate and irate Walt became. When Sheila attempted to explain the situation, the officer was polite, but made it very clear this was no proper concern for a lady.

That was when Amory earned his trip.

"Young man," he said to a man who could not have been more than two years his junior, "we have flown down here in a private plane to seek the Truth." As he paced and presented their case, Sheila watched in amazement. Amory might have his mother's ugly face, but when he needed it, he unquestionably had his father's silver tongue. "We will seek Truth with or without your assistance," he finally thundered, "but I believe you would rather be praised for helping Justice than censured for standing in its way. Am I correct?"

Dazed, Brakestone nodded.

"Very well." Amory sat down, hitched his chair closer to the desk, and put out one hand commandingly. "Let's just see what you have on that case." Without demur, Brakestone pushed the file in his direction.

Amory opened it, took up the top sheet, and began to read. He completed the page at a snail's pace, passed it on to Walt, and slowly perused another. Third in line and fuming, Sheila wondered if an all-female jury would acquit her if she strangled both men and pleaded extenuating circumstances.

Eventually, in a trickle, she got the documents and tried to piece together the ten-year-old crime.

Some of the facts were stark and clear. Late Saturday evening, June 18, a teenage couple had found Naval Petty Officer Second Class Henry Jones slumped in the front seat of his white 1963 Chevrolet Impala, which was parked on a vacant lot in Pensacola, near the railroad tracks. Jones had been shot in the head at close range, and had been dead approximately twenty-four hours.

"Those poor kids who found him," Sheila murmured, hoping she could inspire Brakestone to expand on the bare facts. "Looks like someone would have seen him before."

To her delight, the officer complied. "Almost nobody goes up there in the daytime. It's at the end of a dead-end street, on a bluff above the main road, and shielded by trees. Those kids went up to neck after a movie, and got the shock of their lives."

"Why'd they look inside the other car?" Amory demanded. "Bad taste, if you ask me."

Sheila regarded him quizzically. How much experience had her ugly nephew had with desolate parking places?

"They wouldn't have looked in," Brakestone replied, "but they'd seen the same car in the identical spot the night before, and both times it looked empty. It was in mint condition, and the boy was a real Impala buff, so that second night he decided to take a closer look. When he peered in—" Brakestone shook his head. "Both kids were in pretty bad shape when the officers got there."

"Did you ever find a weapon?" Sheila asked, impatient to know that before Amory and Walt plodded through the reports.

"Never did. Probably got thrown into the bay, which is just down the bluff and across the street."

"See?" Walt interrupted, handing Sheila another page with an air of triumph. "Vonnie was home all night with a terrible headache. She gets—got"—he amended miserably—"migraines."

Migraine, or a well-planned alibi? Who could tell? The report oozed sympathy for the lovely widow whose husband had been brutally murdered. How helpless Yvonne would have looked at twenty-one, giving her statement! Sheila could picture the soft dark hair curling on her shoulders, violet eyes wide with grief. Could hear that soft drawl thick with tears.

"My car was in the shop and my head didn't start to ache until after Henry left. I don't know where he was going—he didn't tell me. He's been worried about something lately, moody, almost like he was afraid of somebody."

"I don't know who," she had replied when pressed, "but he snapped at me these past two weeks, and went out a lot by himself in the evenings. I finally called his family about noon today, because I thought he might have gone up there, but his sister Nancy said they hadn't seen him since we drove up last weekend for Sunday dinner. I didn't like to pester them, but I'd hoped he'd be there."

Sheila could imagine the investigating officer murmuring soothingly, "Tell us what happened last night, ma'am."

Yvonne's statement continued. "I was out of Tylenol, and the pain was getting terrible, so I called my mother about seven . . . yes, Mary Jo Gates. But she was going to choir practice and I didn't like to ask her to miss it. Then I called Edna Warton, a friend. She was so sweet, offered to go buy me some Tylenol. I didn't like to bother her, either, but I let her do it, my head ached so bad."

Edna Warton (white female twenty-two) said she had gone to

a suburban K Mart for the Tylenol, where she got an employee
discount, and arrived at Yvonne's about eight-thirty. She found
her friend lying on the sofa with an ice pack on her head. "She'd
been throwing up and everything," Warton stated, "and she just
plumb begged me to stay. I helped her to bed and watched television, wondering where Henry was. At midnight I woke her up
and told her I needed to get home, because I had to work today
and needed to get to bed. Vonnie cried, told me she and Henry
had had a fight, and begged me to stay all night. She said he was
probably at his mother's, and she was scared to be in the house
by herself."

Sheila scanned Edna's statement for an earlier sentence.
"Henry and Vonnie were so sweet. He'd give her anything she
wanted—that he could afford, of course. They didn't have much
money, but they were very happy."

So happy, Sheila mused, that he had stormed out and never
called all night to tell his wife where he was? What could the
quarrel have been about?

The investigating officer had asked that same question, but
Yvonne had insisted, "It was personal, and had nothing to do
with him getting killed." She added that she had called Henry's
superior officer on Saturday afternoon, frantic, and spoken with
his wife.

The wife had been more forthcoming. "Yvonne Jones told me
she was worried sick about Henry, that for two weeks he had
acted like he was afraid of somebody. She said they'd had a big
fight because he wouldn't tell her what he was afraid of."

Walt leaned toward Sheila to point out that statement with a
trembling finger. "See," he cried, face flushed, "isn't that exactly
like Yvonne? Always concerned for other people. How could they
believe she ever killed anybody?"

"Apparently they didn't," Amory said, finishing the last sheet
in the file folder on his ample lap. "Nobody ever accused her. Did
you all ever find out who Henry Jones was afraid of, Officer?"

Brakestone shook his head. "On that, as on every other lead, we ran into a dead end."

Sheila finished the last report and stood. "Thank you very much." She meant it. Brakestone had been merciful. He should have locked up the visitors and called the DeKalb County police to come fetch them.

"Where now?" Amory asked when they were back in the car. Walt answered immediately. "I want to see where she lived."

It was not far from the police station to the Joneses' former duplex. Sheila stood on a hot root-buckled sidewalk and tried to picture Yvonne Delacourt living in this cream stucco box with a rust-red roof, built a scant fifteen feet from the sidewalk. Ten years ago, the lone magnolia might have provided a bit of grace and beauty. Today the magnolia, like Yvonne, was dead—or close to it. The grassless plot of sand between house and sidewalk was littered with thick brown leaves.

A drive—two strips of concrete with sand between—ran between the duplex and an identical one next door. Sheila walked warily down it, hoping she would not get shot at by a resident who did not take kindly to trespassers. All she saw was a sandy lot large enough for two cars to park behind each building. One duplex had a pink and yellow plastic tricycle at the back door. Somewhere inside, she heard a child shriek.

Walt insisted on knocking on both doors. He spoke with two women in shorts, then returned to the car, dejected. Sheila could have told him nobody would stay in this place for a decade.

Back at the car, Amory—who had been checking his map—suggested lunch. "We don't have time to eat," Walt protested.

"We certainly do," Amory told him. "There's a place here called McGuire's Irish Pub. It brews its own beer, and it's only a few blocks away."

It was, complete with copper brewing vats and oak barrels in a plate-glass-front room. The ceiling was covered with thousands of dollar bills, which Sheila was astonished to find were real.

Amory's day was made when a smiling waitress in a long green skirt brought him a foaming mug. "Real home-brewed Irish stout," he told Sheila, "and my own mug!"

He had just bought the mug in McGuire's Gift Shop, and had his name put on it, planned to leave it as a part of McGuire's Mug Club, which already had over fifteen thousand members. "We'll hang it up with the others," the waitress told him, "and anytime you come in, it will be here for you. On Wednesdays, Mug Club members pay half price."

Sheila wondered how many times Amory would be back here in Florida on a Wednesday. She also wondered, as she sipped her home-brewed root beer, how McGuire had gotten the idea for the dollar bills. The waitress explained. "When McGuire and Molly first started the pub, Molly stapled up her first dollar tip. A friend added another, and there's more than sixty-five thousand of them by now." She added, "If you want to put one up, we'll ring the bell for you."

Amory reached for his wallet, but Sheila put out a restraining hand. "We're ready to order," she said firmly.

As the two men added their choices to her own baked shrimp stuffed with more shrimp, she couldn't help admiring the clever McGuire. Who but an Irishman could convince patrons they were privileged to purchase fifteen thousand mugs and leave them with him, honored to be permitted to staple thousands of dollar bills to his own ceiling?

If he fed his customers blarney, McGuire also fed them well. The food was delicious. Even on a lazy summer Sunday afternoon, with a spectacular beach only a few miles away, the place was comfortably full. The chocolate brownie pie would be worth flying down from Atlanta for.

Amory, at the waitress's insistence, tried the bread pudding. "Not enough raisins and cinnamon," he announced. For Amory, there could never be enough raisins and cinnamon.

Walt, meanwhile, had consumed a beautiful steak with the

same attention he would have given to a plate of Styrofoam. Most of the time he had fiddled with the gray aluminum blind by their booth and urged the others, "Hurry!"

Finally Sheila took pity on him. "Okay, Walt, what do you want to do next?"

"Go see Vonnie's friend"—he consulted a scrap of paper from his pocket—"Edna Warton. I took down her address."

"But she's dead," Sheila said, bewildered.

He looked at her blankly. "Dead?"

So he hadn't read the morning paper thoroughly. It was just as well. If he had, he might have wanted to visit Memphis next. Pensacola plus Memphis would be too much for Frank McGehee. Too much for Sheila, too.

"Edna Warton died of salmonella poisoning nine years ago," she told him gently. "A year after Yvonne's first husband died."

Walt crushed the paper in a shaking fist, then slammed his fist on the table and turned his face back toward the blinds.

"We could drive by the house she used to live in," Amory offered, expansive after good food and ale. "Maybe somebody there used to know her." He signaled for the check.

As they left, Sheila put a tiny green "Erin Go Bragh" flag from her dessert in her pocket as a souvenir for McGehee—knowing he'd rather have a pint of ale.

Edna Warton's former address turned out to be another tiny cream dwelling with a rust-red roof, but it was shingled, not stucco, a single-family house with fresh green paint around the windows and blue hydrangeas blooming by the front door. Liriope lined both sides of the front walk, which inexplicably ended twenty feet from the street.

Amory parked across the street, near an enormous live oak with branches reaching toward the ground like an octopus's arms—arms hairy with resurrection ferns along their tops.

Sheila, Walt, and Amory crossed the street and stood at the edge of the lawn, pressed down by the hot air, considering the situation. "Must have thought the street would be widened one day," Amory told Sheila and Walt. He jerked one hand toward an elderly dogwood which intermingled its boughs with a cedar. "Looks like they'd have cut one or the other."

Sheila, whose knowledge of trees was almost nil, was annoyed to find herself reminded of someone else who seemed to know a lot about gardens. "If you're done with the commentary, shall we go in?" she asked acidly. They picked their way across the lawn. It flourished near the street, where there was no walk, then grew bald and sandy as it neared the house.

The woman who answered the door wiped wet hands on the sides of pink double-knit bermuda shorts and peered up at them suspiciously. "What you all want?"

She was nearer fifty than forty, and so short that Sheila found herself looking down into brown hair with gray roots. The woman was plump, her waist as thick as her hips and bust, making her look like a cylinder with a round head and short, stubby arms.

"Edna Warton," Walt blurted out, pushing past Sheila. "Did you know her?"

He was so distraught, he'd forgotten a cardinal rule of southern communication: You have to give information—preferably wrong information, that can be corrected—before you get any. The woman stepped backward, started to close the door.

Amory put out a hand to stop her and spoke persuasively. "What he meant was, we're looking for anyone who used to know Edna Warton. We were told she used to live here, but that her family moved away."

The woman peered up at Amory, then at Walt, and finally at Sheila. Then she gave Walt a second look and decided she would be better talking on her small front stoop than inside. Sheila didn't blame her. Walt's hair was still windblown, and he had a wild look in his eyes.

"Edna was mine." The woman pulled the front door closed behind her. "My oldest. She's been gone nearly ten years now. What did you want to know?"

"About Yvonne. Yvonne *Jones.*" It was so hard for Walt to say the last word that he gave it too much emphasis. He also moved closer in his eagerness. The woman backed until her shoulders pressed the screen door. Sheila tugged Walt back a couple of steps.

"He's Yvonne's husband," she explained. "Yvonne died last week, and he wants to find out about her past. Edna was Yvonne's friend, wasn't she?"

Southerners are raised from their cradles to be courteous to the grieving. "I'm sorry to hear that about Vonnie," the woman said grudgingly. "If you want to know anything recent, I don't know who might help you. Maybe Henry's mama or sister, but I don't know how to find them. . . ." She trailed off into helplessness.

"But you knew her?" he pressed hoarsely. "Yvonne? You knew her?"

She nodded. "Since she was three. She and my Edna went to school together." She turned. "Wait a minute."

She went inside and was gone nearly five minutes. She brought back a high-school yearbook and wiped it against her pink shorts. "Sorry I was gone so long. I'm canning beans. Had to turn the stove down. Now." She handed Walt the annual. His hands shook so, he could scarcely turn the pages. Sheila took the leather-bound volume and turned them for him. A teenaged Yvonne appeared frequently: Best-Looking, Homecoming Queen, assistant editor of the yearbook, member of the French Club and Glee Club.

"That's my Edna." A plump finger pointed to a dot only a mother could recognize in the middle of the chorus.

Sheila could tell nothing from the tiny image except that Edna had her mother's round chin. "Do you have a larger picture, Mrs. Warton?" she asked.

Edna's mother hesitated, then went back into the house. When she returned, she handed Sheila an ornate brass frame that held what must have been her daughter's senior picture. A black drape and expert retouching had added some glamour to that dumpy face, but nothing could add intelligence to the expression.

"She and Yvonne were very close?" Sheila suggested.

Mrs. Warton shook her head. "Not since they left grade school. After she was eleven, Vonnie started giving herself airs—begging your pardon, sir." She nodded toward Walt. He didn't respond, but the stocky woman continued unperturbed. "She seemed to have come into a bit of money about then, and started running with what you might call a richer crowd. After sixth grade we scarcely saw Vonnie until her wedding. Now, *that* was a posh affair! Must have cost Mary Jo a pretty penny, but she never let on how much."

"Mary Jo?" Walt asked hoarsely. Sheila knew he was hoping to find someone else who had known his wife.

"Yvonne's mother." The hope in Walt's eyes faded as she added, "She died in March. Cancer." Mrs. Warton buffed her palms on her shorts as if rubbing off cancer germs.

Walt regarded her in disbelief. "March of *this* year? Are you sure?"

"Of course I'm sure. She lived right over there for nearly thirty years, beyond the friendship oak." She pointed to the huge tree across the street. "They're called friendship oaks when their branches grow down," Mrs. Warton explained. "They reach out, like, to welcome you."

The tree looked as if it had lived three hundred years and could stand several hundred more. The small gray house beyond it would not. Dwarfed by the massive oak, it was a house a child might draw: one window, a door, a peaked roof, one round bush beside a small porch. The child probably would not show how badly the asbestos shingles were chipped and the paint peeling, but might draw the porch with just that much sag. From that little house to a Dunwoody neocolonial was no mean feat.

Walt took off his glasses, wiped them on his sleeve, and peered down at the woman. She peered back up at him, like a gnome. "She died just this year?" Walt repeated. "Her mother, I mean. Yvonne never—"

"Oh, Vonnie didn't come. She never got back after she moved up north—Nashville, I think, or somewheres like that. You from Nashville?"

He shook his head. "Atlanta."

"Maybe that was it. Anyway, after Vonnie went up there, Mary Jo kept saying she was too busy to come. You'd know more about that than I would, but it seemed to me like she ought to get a vacation sometimes." She waited for him to answer. When he merely continued to stare at her, uncomprehending, she bent and pulled a dead flower from the hydrangea with one angry snap. "Maybe not. She was ambitious, Vonnie was. She maybe didn't take vacations. She did send money sometimes, but not much. Mary Jo had it rough toward the end. Our Sunday school took turns taking in meals, and the church took up a collection to bury her."

Walt gave a strangled cry.

Sheila spoke quickly. "You said Edna went to Yvonne's first wedding. Did they become better friends after that?"

Mrs. Warton shook her head vigorously. "Edna's friends were mostly her own sort—clerks at the K Mart, people she knew from church, single people. Single girls and married ones don't have a lot in common. I don't think Edna saw Yvonne five times after she got married."

"Yet Yvonne called Edna the night her husband died?"

The woman nodded, put a hand where one hip must be. "I asked my Edgar, 'What's she bothering Edna for?' Edgar said Vonnie'd bother the Pope if she needed help. She would, too." With a deep sigh she added, "Edgar's passed now, too. A year after Edna. Deaths always come in threes, they say. We had Henry, Edna, then Edgar."

Sheila wasn't certain why Henry Jones got counted in the

Warton family toll. Perhaps to convince the angel of death that the family debt was paid?

Amory edged closer. "Why did Edna think Yvonne phoned her that night?"

Edna's mother shook her head, but not because she didn't know the answer. "Because she couldn't think of anybody closer. Most of her friends lived clear across town, but Henry couldn't afford that rent and he was too proud to let his wife pay. That night Yvonne just wanted somebody who would run get her some pills. But Edna didn't care. She'd got herself a new car a week or so before, and took every excuse she got to use it. She'd been showing it off to Vonnie and Henry that very week. Her first car—and she didn't get to drive it a year." She pressed her fingers to her lips and turned her head, overwhelmed by sudden grief.

Amory patted her with one heavy hand. "I'm sure she enjoyed it while she had it."

Mrs. Warton nodded and sniffed. "She sure did. Before that she just had a bike. Used to bike everywhere, her and Vonnie, when they was little. Mary Jo and I found them all the way down at the railroad tracks one day when they were just eight. Might near scared us to death! And then poor Henry got himself killed down at the very same place. Don't that beat all?" She shook her head at the capriciousness of fate.

Walter turned toward the steps and said woodenly, "Well, thank you for telling us what you know."

Sheila, however, was not ready to leave. She'd had an idea. Fate might not be all that capricious after all. "Did Yvonne still use her bike after she was married?"

"Oh, my, yes. She and Henry liked to bike. Cheap entertainment, I remember he called it. They were riding by here that time Edna showed them her car. That was the last time I ever saw Henry Jones alive." She gave that memory the solemn sniff it deserved.

"Why didn't Yvonne bike for her headache medicine, then?" Sheila asked.

"Her bike tire was busted, that's why, so don't go thinking Yvonne biked over and killed Henry while Edna was fetching the medicine!" Mrs. Warton put her hands on her hips and regarded her uninvited guests belligerently. "The police asked Edna all about that. Edna told them Vonnie was sick as a dog when she arrived. Threw up several times. And her bike tire had a big hole in it. Edna saw it when she got there with the medicine. They kept the bikes in a little hall at the back, and she had to push them out of her way. Vonnie had her faults, but she wouldn't have killed Henry Jones. They were devoted to each other!" Her eyes snapped.

While Amory soothed her, Sheila mulled things over. Yvonne could have damaged the tire just before Edna arrived, and induced the vomiting. But who could prove now what Yvonne had or had not done ten years before? She did have one more question, though. "Mrs. Warton, how did your daughter die?"

Edna's mother wiped sweat from her jowl and fanned herself with one hand. Sheila could feel beads of moisture running down inside her own blouse and could smell Amory and Walt growing steadily hotter behind her. If they stayed out there much longer, they would none of them be fit to share a small plane!

Just as she decided Mrs. Warton was not going to answer, the short woman said in a faraway voice, "I don't guess we'll any of us know what happened. They went out to dinner—Edna, Vonnie, and several of the girls they went to high school with. They'd got in the habit of going out sometimes. Yvonne started those little parties after Henry died—to cheer herself up, she said. Three of them ate the same thing. The other two were awfully sick, but Edna . . . Edna died. Just weak, I guess."

"Do the other two still live in Pensacola?" Sheila asked.

Edna's mother took a step back toward her door, an expression in her eyes that Sheila had seen before. "I think I've done told you enough. Anything else you want to know, you ask the police."

Sheila knew that expression. It was the look someone gets when it first occurs to them that someone they loved may not have died accidentally.

What does a Dunwoody matron make
for dinner?
Reservations.
How does she call the children to a meal?
"Get in the car, kids."

SUNDAY NIGHT

"Maybe we'll get home in time for *Murder, She Wrote*," Amory said at the airport, checking his watch.

Instead, they got home in time for a consultation. Sheila had called Aunt Mary en route and was told, "Come straight here, dear. We have many things to discuss."

When they arrived, Mildred was just carrying out plates from a light supper for two. She paused by the kitchen door to say in a low voice, "That writer woman called—Quincy or something? She talked so fast I couldn't keep up with her. Asked if you'd seen the paper, and I told her you had, then she said she'd found out where the second husband's son, Harley, is—right here at Georgia Tech! She was so full of herself, I didn't like to tell her we already knew it."

Sheila looked at her blankly. "We did?"

For an answer, Mildred nodded to the living room.

"Come in, Sheila, Amory," Aunt Mary greeted them. "I want you to meet a new friend of mine, Harley Sanders. Harley, this is my niece, Sheila Travis, and her husband's nephew, Amory."

A blond young man rose quickly from Sheila's favorite ivory chair, thrust out his hand at Sheila and Amory in turn, and gave his hostess a charming smile. "I really ought to be going, Miss

Mary. But thanks very much for inviting me over. It's great to meet a friend of Grandmother Sanders."

While Aunt Mary bade her guest farewell, Sheila retired to brush her hair and repair her face. She returned to find Amory and Aunt Mary at the dining room table, discussing McGuire's pub.

"You could have brought some of their beer back," Aunt Mary was saying reproachfully. "It's sold in local grocery stores."

"How do you know?" Sheila demanded, taking her chair and nodding to Mildred that she would love some of whatever the others had eaten.

Instead of answering, Aunt Mary frowned at the cup of coffee Mildred was placing before Sheila.

"Don't say it!" Sheila ordered, holding up one hand. "Just tell us what's so important it can't wait until tomorrow."

Aunt Mary looked from Sheila to Amory. "Where's Walter?"

"He went home. He's had a rough day. We all did, actually. We would have liked to go home, too."

"Don't be ridiculous, dear." Aunt Mary waited for Mildred to serve them each a generous serving of homemade chicken pot-pie and a crisp green salad, then ordered, "Now, tell me everything."

When they had finished, she sat nodding like a tiny sparrow with silver plumage. "So you think Yvonne called Edna to give herself an alibi, went to the railroad tracks, shot her husband, bicycled home, and punctured her tire for Edna to see?"

"Well . . ." Amory the banker was reluctant to commit himself.

"That's exactly what *I* think," said Sheila. "Don't you?"

Aunt Mary drummed her fingertips on the polished tabletop and considered. "I think it's very likely."

"How would she know he was going to be there?" Amory objected.

"She could have ridden with him," Aunt Mary suggested,

"having hidden her bicycle nearby previously. This was no spur-of-the-moment murder. She had to put her car in the shop, get rid of all her Tylenol, arrange an alibi with Edna and her mother. She would surely have figured out a way to get to the deserted spot and home after disposing of the gun."

"Poor devil." Amory chased the last crumbs of flaky crust from his plate with his fork, ate them before he added, "But why would he go to that place with her? You can't just say to your husband 'Come drive me up to a vacant lot.' No man's that dumb."

"She would have used a lot of charm," said one who had used charm with excellent results for over seventy years. "Perhaps she told him she had something special to tell him. Or, if they really had quarreled, as she told Edna, she could have suggested they go somewhere with more privacy than a duplex. In any case, she must have planned it carefully beforehand—just as later she planned carefully how to murder Edna."

"She couldn't have killed Edna, Miss Mary," Amory argued. "Two other girls got sick on that meal, too."

"I know." Aunt Mary reached for a stack of papers beside her. "I have discovered the name of the doctor for whom Yvonne was working at the time of her husband's death."

Sheila raised her brows. "And how did you do that?"

"Oh"—Aunt Mary waved her hand to show it was of no account—"I simply called the Pensacola newspaper and asked them to read me the accounts from their morgue."

"And they did it—on a Sunday?"

"I may have *implied* I was Celestine Sibley meeting a tight deadline," the old woman said shamelessly, "but I certainly never said so." She held up a sheet she had chosen. "This doctor was engaged in research. He has since gone into full-time study of gonogenesis." Meeting Amory's blank stare, she explained. "The maturation of germ cells. A doctor at the Center for Disease Control tells me several different germ cultures can give the effects of salmonella poisoning. The size of the dosage would determine whether it was fatal. We could never prove it—thank God we won't need to—but I believe that woman obtained germ samples from her doctor's lab to kill her friend."

"Why?" Amory demanded. "Poor Edna didn't suspect anything."

"Not then," Sheila agreed, "but could Yvonne be sure she wouldn't at a later date? And Yvonne was about to marry Rodney Sanders and leave town. She didn't want any dangling ends."

"You don't kill off all your friends when you move," Amory said with Travis tenacity.

"How would you know?" Sheila asked him. "You've never moved. Now, Aunt Mary, since we've told you about Henry Jones, I assume you are going to tell us all about Harley Sanders —who happens," she added for Amory's benefit, "to be Rodney Sanders's son, the one originally suspected of killing his dad."

Amory looked from one woman to the other, stupefied.

"I am certain he had nothing to do with that." Aunt Mary nodded thanks to Mildred for a glass of sherry and sipped it before she continued. "If you could hear him tell how much he missed his father after the divorce, and how much he loved his grandmother . . ."

Amory accepted more coffee. "It's amazing that you know her!"

"It would be if she had." Sheila held her cup up for a refill. "I assume you made sure his grandmother was dead before you called him, Aunt Mary?"

"Of course, dear."

"You lied—told that boy you knew his dead grandmother?" Amory was so scandalized, he nearly forgot to eat the piece of chocolate cake Mildred had just set before him.

"Of course not!" Now it was Aunt Mary who was shocked. "When I called to invite him to supper, I told him his grandmother was a wonderful woman and I was certain she would want me to give him a call. Neither of those was a lie."

"And what did you do when he expected you to share a few touching reminiscences?" Sheila wondered.

"Young people don't want reminiscences, Sheila. It's the middle-aged and old who like to remember the past. Harley Sanders was far more interested in talking about Tech's recent football season. He's going to be a linebacker on the varsity team next year."

"And, of course, you had all last year's statistics at your fingertips, Aunt Mary?"

The little woman's brown eyes twinkled. "No man ever cares what a woman knows, dear, if she'll let him tell her what *he* knows."

"What if he *had* wanted you to talk about his grandmother, Miss Mary?" Amory was no longer scandalized. Now he was intrigued.

Aunt Mary assumed a self-righteous expression. "Simply the truth, Amory! That I never got to Macon as often as I would have liked to while his grandmother was alive—I've been there only once—and that her azaleas were lovely."

"Had you ever seen her azaleas, ma'am?"

Aunt Mary primmed her mouth. "*All* azaleas are lovely in Macon, Amory. Anyone knows that."

"Not as lovely as Tupelo's," he replied. "If you could see Mama's Pride of Mobiles . . ."

Sheila had no intention of getting sidetracked by an argument about relative flora. "If you don't think Harley killed his father, does he think Yvonne did? Did he kill *her?*"

"Sheila!" Amory had not been shocked so thoroughly in his thirty-five years. "You can't just ask a guest in your home if he committed murder."

"Sure you can," she assured him, "but I doubt that Aunt Mary did. What *did* you ask him, Aunt Mary?"

"Oh, when he first learned Yvonne was in town, dear, and whether the police have spoken with him yet about jogging on Yvonne's street the day she was killed. The boy got a bit pale, but he's been well raised. He didn't deny it. He said he saw her picture in Friday's paper and decided to go see where she lived. He did not say whether he killed her or not, of course. He certainly hated her for luring his father into divorce and marriage. According to Harley, his parents were perfectly happy before Yvonne."

"Rodney was grazing over the fence before that," Sheila pointed out. "He took Yvonne out to lunch while she was married to Henry."

"Yes, dear." Aunt Mary sighed. "Men are so prone to that."

"Hey!"

Before Amory could complete his protest, she stood. "Why don't you all go into the living room? I'll be right back." She trotted to her bedroom and brought back a large brown envelope.

"Dear Charlie," Sheila murmured. "He came through once again, I see."

"Yes, dear." Aunt Mary's lips curved in a fond smile. She sat on the couch, tiny feet tucked beneath her, and pulled a sheet of yellow paper from the envelope. "Insurance companies investigated each death. All were satisfied that Yvonne had nothing to do with any of them. She did, after all, have someone ready to swear in each case where she had been, and none of them were people who would be expected to lie for her. Edna, as you said, had seen her only occasionally since her marriage, and was summoned merely because she lived nearby and had a car. The woman with whom Yvonne went shopping the day Rodney was shot was the wife of one of his customers, a woman who was very flattered, apparently, to be asked to spend a day with Yvonne. She had a history of depression on which her husband blamed her suicide."

Sheila let her head drop against the soft back of the over-stuffed chair. She was so close to sleep that she scarcely heard Amory ask, "What about that decorator chap who drowned?"

Sheila drowsily wondered when he'd learned so much. She hadn't known he'd even read the article in that morning's paper.

Aunt Mary sighed. "Yes, in Nassau, it says here."

Sheila was immediately awake again. "Nassau? Yvonne had a glass from a Nassau hotel on her desk. I jotted down the name."

"Good work, Sheila!" Aunt Mary actually clapped her hands. "They probably went there together, went sailing, and she drowned him."

"Then sailed the boat back to port single-handed?" Sheila asked, skeptical.

"We'll have to ask what kind of boat it was." Aunt Mary jotted herself a note. "First we must call and see if the decorator ever stayed at that hotel, and if he had a companion. I'll ask Charlie to fax Yvonne's picture to them tomorrow. Call me first thing, dear, please, with the name of the hotel."

Sheila hunched deeper into her chair and stretched her legs full-length on its fat ottoman. "Aunt Mary, we can trace all these crimes and prove Yvonne killed a hundred people, but that's not our problem. Our problem is, who killed Yvonne? There are plenty of people in her neighborhood who were angry enough to have done so. We need to find out about Alex Divesty, and Mac Marriot, and Dee Ivy—"

"Hey! Dee's all right!"

"She's wonderful, Amory," Sheila agreed, "but don't forget that Yvonne had started hurting her business. Badly, if Ava Settis is right. Dee had befriended Yvonne, gotten her into the country club, introduced her around, and now Yvonne was betraying her. Dee's got a temper—"

"She wouldn't *kill* anybody!" Amory insisted. "She's not like that at all. You are just—"

"That is enough." Aunt Mary held up one hand in a manner

she could have learned from Queen Elizabeth the First. "I have here a bank report on Mac Marriot. His balance is a modest one—"

"Modest by your standards, or everyone else's?" Sheila asked.

But it was to Amory's horrified "Hey! Where did you get those?" that Aunt Mary replied.

"I have a friend who's able to secure them for confidential purposes. I must warn you, however, that nothing in them must leave this room."

Spluttering, he collapsed against his end of the couch. Sheila hid a grin. Was he more upset that Aunt Mary had the documents, or that she had warned *him* that they were confidential?

"You were saying that Mac's got a modest bank balance." Sheila brought them back to the original topic. "Is his modest bank balance enough to support him, a wife, a huge house, a full-time maid, a doorman, a Continental, a driver, and enormous weekly parties?"

Aunt Mary nodded. "Oh, I think so, if they live frugally in other areas."

Sheila, trying to picture Mac living frugally, was astonished by Aunt Mary's next remark. "He also owns that house next to his, through a corporation. He bought it before he built his own home, and leased it privately to a couple of his employees. When they moved out, the corporation put it on the market."

"At an exorbitant price," Sheila added. "Oh, I almost forgot! I met Mac's mother Friday night, and she said she knows you. Diane Hardwick? No, Yvonne was a Hardwick. It was . . ."

Aunt Mary's charcoal brows rose to nearly meet her hairline. "Diane Harlow, dear? My goodness, I thought she was dead! We lost touch many years ago, after—" She broke off and stared into space. "Oh, my goodness," she murmured to herself. "Oh, my goodness."

"Are we to be let into the secret?" Sheila asked her.

Aunt Mary began to shuffle her papers. "There's no secret,

dear, just a bit of unpleasantness." She pursed her lips and looked at Amory, then back at Sheila, a ploy Sheila interpreted to mean "Not in front of the company, dear." Amory might be a Travis, but he was not a Beaufort.

Aunt Mary then chose a blue sheet and peered at it through the half glasses she had taken from the table beside her. "Alex Divesty has almost no bank account to speak of. He withdrew his savings, two hundred thousand dollars—"

"Oh!" Sheila was enlightened. Of course! *M* in Yvonne's little date book must be simply the Roman letter for one thousand. She was trying to add some of the numbers preceding those m's when Aunt Mary continued, unperturbed. "—on April twenty-third—"

"Yvonne's birthday!" Sheila exclaimed. "He gave her a loan, and she claimed it was a gift!"

Amory whistled. "There's our man! That would be enough to make *me* do murder."

Aunt Mary pursed her lips to think it over, then nodded briskly. "It's the best motive we have found so far."

Once a financial motive came into the picture, both Aunt Mary and Amory were after it like hounds on a scent. While they commiserated with poor Alex for being conned, Mildred came in with a final round of coffee. "How's Forbes?" Sheila asked.

"Sound asleep," Mildred told her. "Poor child still hasn't said anything about that man Amory says took him at Stone Mountain, but tonight he couldn't stop talking about his grandmother. Fell asleep still chattering about his momsy."

Amory yelped. He'd spilled hot coffee in his lap.

While Mildred ran for a dish towel, Aunt Mary sipped tea and explained. "We've had a series of visits today. Sunday afternoons always used to be like that when I was a girl. I remember—"

"Remember Forbes's grandmother," Sheila prodded her. "I assume you mean old Mrs. Hardwick?" Before Aunt Mary could protest the appellation, she asked, "Where did you find her?"

Aunt Mary touched the envelope she held. "Charlie. He learned that she's living over on Juniper Street in a retirement home. The one where Mavis Brown lives. Mavis and I are such good friends that I called her—"

"Are you and this Mavis really friends, or did you make that up, too?" Amory demanded, mopping his trousers.

Aunt Mary spoke severely. "I never make things up, Amory. Mavis and I have played bridge every Wednesday for nearly thirty years, so I asked her to let Mrs. Hardwick know that I had her grandson for the afternoon and he wanted to see her. Mrs. Hardwick called me right back and came for dessert after dinner. Forbes was delighted, and so was she."

"I hope between expressions of delight, Aunt Mary, you managed to ask her if she still thought Yvonne murdered Dr. Hardwick?"

"Oh, yes, dear, she was more than willing to speak about that when Forbes went down for a short nap. She said she was absolutely certain Yvonne was responsible for her son's death. She would go so far as to say his wife drowned Martin in his bath! But Yvonne threatened that if she prosecuted and lost, she would never see her grandson again. He's her only one. She did not exactly say so, but I think she moved to Atlanta right after Yvonne did to be near young Forbes. Yvonne took him to see her every Friday afternoon until the week before she died."

"But Forbes said his mama never let his momsy come to their house." Mildred was rigid with indignation. "And she threatened to whip him if he told anybody his momsy lived in town. When he went to bed tonight, he was terrified he'd get in trouble for telling you, Amory, where she lived." Mildred's gray uniform fairly crackled with indignation.

Amory half rose. "Should I go talk to him?"

Mildred waved him back. "He's sleeping. I told him you never said a word—Miss Mary found her. He thinks Miss Mary's terrific."

"She is," Sheila agreed, "most of the time."

Aunt Mary cleared her throat delicately. "Yes. Well. There is one more thing. On the Friday before she died, Yvonne called Mrs. Hardwick and told her the visits were over. She didn't have time, she said, to drive downtown each week. Mrs. Hardwick was devastated, as you might imagine."

Amory brightened. "Devastated enough to kill her or hire someone else to do so?"

"Amory!" Sheila rebuked him. He sounded far too cheerful.

"He has a good point, dear." Aunt Mary sipped her sherry, dark eyes sober. "Losing Forbes after losing her son could have given Thelma Hardwick a strong incentive for murder."

Sheila sighed. "Where Yvonne Delacourt was concerned, several people had strong incentives for murder. Almost everybody who knew her, in fact—except Walt."

"Thank God Walt never knew about her past before today," Amory rumbled, "or he'd have had the best motive of all—self-preservation."

*In Dunwoody, Monopoly is a serious game.
Everybody starts with at least three
properties and one hotel, and when they go
to jail, they don't roll three times—they hire
a lawyer.*

MONDAY

"I hate to call so early," Frank McGehee said at
seven, "but I thought you'd want to know that he knew."

Sheila had been on her deck, enjoying her first cup of coffee
and reading the paper—which, she was glad to see, had nothing
new about the Delacourt case. Now she struggled to bring her
mind back from the latest situation in Sarajevo and another
earthquake in Mexico. "Who knew what?"

"Delacourt knew about his wife's past. While you were gone
yesterday, Drake searched Delacourt's desk again. He'd found
an envelope of clippings on top the day of the murder, but hadn't
paid it a lot of attention. When yesterday's article came out,
though, he remembered one of the clippings had the same picture of Mrs. Delacourt and her second husband. Drake's memory
is legendary, Sheila. If he said he'd seen that picture, he'd seen
it. So we went back yesterday and found the envelope stuffed in
a bottom drawer under some other mail. It had all the clippings
someone sent to the *Constitution*. Delacourt swears he never
saw the envelope, but his prints are all over it. He knew, Sheila
—no doubt about it. Drake is pleased as punch."

Sheila pressed her head against the kitchen cabinet. "It could
have been planted. Check the mail carrier, Frank. I took in some
mail Wednesday night. Find out how many days mail had been

left in the box. The murderer could have left that envelope on Walt's desk, and after he found Yvonne, Walt just stuffed it in the drawer."

"You're stretching, Sheila. You know that."

"Hey, Frank, when it's a friend, you stretch. Walt would never have killed his wife for that reason. I just know it!"

"How about for greed? According to the records, Mrs. Delacourt has collected over five million dollars in insurance these past ten years, and she must have gotten a good bit from 'friends,' too. Yesterday's article was picked up in Memphis, and we've already gotten three calls from men, testing the waters. They each claim she conned them out of amounts ranging from a thousand dollars to over five hundred thousand, but they don't want their wives to know. Her story, apparently, was 'I've got some debts to pay and I don't dare tell my husband, but I know you will help me.' They fell for it, forked over a loan, and never got a penny back. It's not likely she spent it all. Drake's looking for it, and he's going to find it. When he does? Well, she and Walt made wills leaving everything they had to each other." He paused, then said in a voice charged with confidence, "Face it, Sheila, your friend did it."

At nine that morning, on Running Ridge Road, Paula Divesty raised tear-reddened eyes to her husband. "Do you hate me?" She pulled her terry-cloth robe close around her for warmth. She felt as chilly as if it were December, not June.

Sunday Alex had been busy and she had not been ready to talk to him. First thing after breakfast this morning, however, she had drawn him into the den, sat him down in a chair, seated herself on the couch nearby, and told him everything. Now she felt strangely hollow—and utterly terrified that he would leave her.

He wasn't able to meet her eyes yet, but he reached out and

touched her gently. "No, honey. I hate *me*, and Steven, and maybe even Craig just a little. Not you. But you're finished now? No more?"

"No. I went by last night and got all my things. But I don't know what I'm going to do instead of dancing, Alex. I can't earn that much money as a secretary. I can't possibly pay Craig's bills by myself—"

"You don't have to," he told her. "You weren't the only one busy on Saturday night."

His expression took her attention off herself, made her ask anxiously, "Oh, Alex, what did you do?"

His grin was as wide as the Cheshire cat's. Even his green eyes danced with mischief. "Went to see old Steven. I did! I'd gotten tired of how exhausted you were, how hard you were pushing yourself for Craig. I thought you were at the shelter, of course." He ran his hands through his red hair and shook his head. "Shelter! No wonder you told me I couldn't ever phone you at work! But whatever you were doing, Paulie, I always knew it was too much. Craig's his kid, too."

"What did Steven say?" Her eyes were huge, her voice a whisper.

Alex chuckled. "Well, first he asked me to leave. He had a new girlfriend over, a woman about half his age, and he had a different kind of evening planned. But after a while he saw it my way."

"What . . . what did you do?" she stammered. His expression frightened her.

Alex rubbed the knuckles of one hand against the palm of his other. "Oh, just chatted a bit about my boxing days at Georgia, mentioned your daddy a few times. . . . He tried to send his girlfriend away, but I suggested she hear all about how he treated his first wife and son, in case she was planning to become his second. She decided on her own to stay."

"Third," Paula corrected him. "She'd be his third wife." Her eyes gleamed appreciatively. "I wish I could have been a mouse in the corner, Alex. I'll bet you were terrific!"

"Oh, I was!" His grin widened. "I pulled out all the stops. How you were working yourself to the bone for the kid's doctor bills, how much the state objects to fathers who don't pay adequate child support, what our lawyer has advised us to do—"

"You even talked to a lawyer? Oh, Alex!" Now her eyes shone.

He knelt before her, took her hands in his. "I couldn't have you killing yourself, could I? I love you, Paulie. I promised you I'd think of something."

She held him tight for an instant, then drew away. "So what did Steven say?"

"We're to have our lawyer call his lawyer, and they'll work something out. I told him if it's not enough, we'll talk again. Are you impressed with your old man?"

"Definitely!" She engulfed him in her arms. "Oh, honey," she murmured, "you're terrific. How can I thank you?"

"Come upstairs and we'll think of something. The hell with the office. Nobody's coming in this early anyway."

Sometime later, as he dressed for work, he threw his checkbook onto the bed. "Go shopping this morning, Paulie. Get yourself some clothes with style and color. Let everybody see what I've known all along—that my wife is a gorgeous woman."

"Can we afford it?" she asked, swinging her long legs off the bed and heading for the shower.

"Oh, yeah, that's the other thing I did Saturday—talked with Walt. Told him about the loan to Yvonne, and that she never paid me back. Showed him the canceled check. He said he'll make it good. Wasn't that terrific?" He slung his jacket over his shoulder. "You don't have to worry anymore, Paulie. I've taken care of absolutely everything." He clomped downstairs, whistling.

But Paula sat quickly on the bed, suddenly too weak to stand.

"Everything, Alex?" she whispered. Then she pulled the spread up around her. She was very cold again.

Sheila reached Walt at his office about ten. "Of course I didn't know about Vonnie," he told her, exasperated that she would even ask. "And I still don't believe most of it. Her mother must have treated her terribly for Vonnie to leave home. She loved her mother, Sheila—kept her picture on her desk. And Vonnie had no money when I married her, either. She showed me her checkbook, and it had less than two thousand dollars in it. She was worried about how she was going to make her next house payment. That's why we moved into her house, in fact—because I'd already taken up her payments. We were planning to find something else later. There's no way she had millions stashed away. I'd have known. I did all our finances."

"What about that envelope?"

"What envelope?"

"I told you, Walt, the envelope with the clippings in it. The police found it in your bottom desk drawer with some other mail."

"I never saw it."

"It has your fingerprints all over it!" Had Walt always been this dense, or was it a developing condition? "Did you open it, Walt? Think! Had you seen that story before yesterday's paper?"

"I never saw it," he said obstinately. "Now, look, Sheila, I've got work to do here."

"I've got work to do here, too, Walt," she replied sweetly. "And *I* don't have the police accusing me of murder. Maybe you'd better think about that envelope and how it got your prints on it."

She hung up wondering why she was doing all this. Then she smacked the side of her head at her own stupidity. She had meant to ask Walt if he had seen Mac since Friday night, and if Mac had mentioned his prowler.

Aunt Mary called a few minutes later to say her friend Charlie had located Yvonne's bank accounts—in her maiden name—and they held not five but nearly six million dollars. Sheila gasped, then told her about the envelope the police had found and Walt's reaction to it. She concluded by asking rather nastily, "Aunt Mary, what difference does it really make to anybody if Walt goes on trial? Walt doesn't care. He's got a top-notch attorney who could persuade a jury that guinea pigs have tails. Why don't we just give up and let his lawyer handle his defense from here?"

Aunt Mary's reply was crisp and immediate. "Because it will kill Rip if his son is tried for murder. That's why."

Sheila sighed. "It will take a miracle to prevent that now."

"I," Aunt Mary said with vast dignity, "am not above praying for miracles. Meanwhile, you think, dear. Surely there is something we have failed to see or do."

With a sigh Sheila picked up three message slips and dialed the number. She would love to let Nan Quentin leave messages until Judgment Day, but just maybe the writer had found something of value.

Nan had to be paged at the hospital. She came to the phone with excitement in her voice. "I know where Mrs. Delacourt's mother-in-law is living! She's in a retirement home right here in Atlanta, on Juniper Street!"

Sheila didn't have the heart to dampen her enthusiasm, so she asked for the name and number. She was disgusted to find later that she was such a creature of habit that she had actually scribbled them down on the corner of an important report.

"Did you ever get a chance to read my first article?" Nan asked before they rang off. "I took it over to the *Time* magazine office. They said they'd let me know. Wouldn't it be wonderful if my first story appeared in *Time?*"

It certainly would, Sheila thought. As she went into the outer office to fetch herself a fresh cup of coffee, she wondered if there was ever a beginning writer who didn't expect to hit the big time without all the years of effort other writers put in.

Her attention was caught by the mournful expression of Masako Nanto, her executive assistant, bending over something on top of her desk. "What's the matter, Masako?"

Masako held up an earring. "I broke the red bead off the bottom."

Sheila took it, examined what remained. "It's still pretty."

"But now it's merely navy and white. I bought them for the Fourth of July. How will anyone know they were once red, white, and blue? I wanted to look so patriotic, show America I am proud to be here. Now I will look ordinary." Masako was close to tears.

"Wear them with a red dress," Sheila advised. Masako brightened.

As she returned to her desk, she marveled at the difference between Masako, devastated over a broken earring, and Walt, who wasn't even worrying about his own life. But as she tackled her correspondence, something Masako had said pricked her memory. If she could just remember what it was—and why it was important—perhaps Aunt Mary had her first small miracle!

The second miracle came through the unlikely person of Amory, who called just before noon. "Could you come take me to see Forbes on your lunch hour? Mildred called and said it's an emergency."

"Oh?" Sheila, buried under work, had not planned to go out for lunch. Maybe Amory's emergency was minor enough to keep.

"Yeah, he's broken one of your aunt's soldiers, and he's real upset. He's afraid your aunt will hit him."

"Nonsense! Aunt Mary might fuss a little, but she would certainly never hit a child. What would make him think she would?"

"I think—" Amory hesitated, then said in a rush, "I think his mother must have beaten him, Sheila. He hinted as much when we were out together the other day. Anyway, I think we ought to go over. Miss Mary's out for lunch, and Mildred says the poor kid won't stop crying."

Sheila shoved back her work at once. "Poor darling! How about if I go right away? It would take me an extra half hour to come get you."

When she got to the penthouse, Forbes lay on his stomach, face burrowed in his pillow, his black curls as wet with sweat as his heart shaped face was with tears.

Sheila pulled him upright gently. "Tell me about the soldier."

"I br-br-broke it." He hiccuped and pulled away from her.

"Show me." She sat down beside him, but not too near. She had the feeling if she made one wrong move, the child would bolt.

After a moment he fumbled beneath his pillow and reluctantly brought out Nathan Bedford Forrest, minus a saber point.

"It broke," he said unnecessarily, putting a grubby finger on the rough edge. "I was trying to stick Lee . . ." Fresh tears erupted.

She took the little soldier and examined it carefully. It was certainly damaged, possibly beyond repair. "Why was General Forrest sticking Lee, Forbes? They were friends."

"I know, Miss Sheila," he said, eyes wide and earnest, "but Miss Mary doesn't have any Yankees."

Miss Mary certainly didn't.

"Well"—Sheila set the wounded soldier on the nightstand—"I think the best thing you can do is tell Miss Mary when she gets back. Tell her it was an accident, and you are sorry."

He began to tremble. His skin was so pale, Sheila felt a blaze of anger toward his dead mother. What had Yvonne done to him? "She'll hit me!" he cried.

"She will not hit you," she assured him softly. "She may make you put the soldiers away until you are older, but she won't hit you, I promise you. I stayed here sometimes when I was a little girl. Did you know that?"

He nodded, but his eyes told her he was not convinced there ever had been such a distant past.

"Well, Miss Mary got angry with me sometimes, but she didn't hit me, not once. She made me sit in a chair, or go to bed without supper, or once when I wrote on the wall she made me wash the wall with soap and water. But she never, ever hit me. Do you believe me?"

Again he nodded, still uncertain.

"Did your mother hit you sometimes?" she asked gently.

"Just when I was bad," said the four-year-old, fiercely loyal.

"But she wouldn't have hit you for having an accident, like breaking off the point of that sword, would she?"

When he hesitated, Sheila wished she had bitten her tongue. What did she know about how Yvonne had disciplined this child? Nothing—except that the memory left him pale and trembling.

"I bent sumpin' by accident once," he whispered. "She hit me then."

Sheila hated to pry, but his whole trembling body pleaded with her to talk about it. "Was it something valuable?"

His head drooped. "It was Walt's. He kept it on his desk. My dresser drawer got stuck, so I took Walt's special thing and tried to open my drawer. But I bent it. Mama was very, very mad. She hit me hard."

Sheila didn't know whether she was angrier with Yvonne for inflicting such pain on this child, or with herself for not learning how to help a child deal with pain. "If you didn't mean to do it . . ." she began.

He raised dark, stricken eyes to hers. "It was Walt's most special thing, Miss Sheila! He got it on their hummymoon."

Suddenly Sheila could scarcely breathe.

"What did it look like?"

"A knife, but on the handle it had a little bird."

"What color was it?"

"Gold," he said reverently. "It was made of pure gold."

Sheila kept her voice carefully calm. "When did you bend the gold knife, Forbes? Do you remember?"

He started to shake his head, then he nodded. "The church day before I went to Corny's. I 'member, 'cause Walt was watching golf and I was trying to get a Micromachine out of the drawer to take to Corny. Walt just watches golf on church days," he added knowingly. "Other days he plays."

"Was Walt's special thing *badly* bent?"

He nodded again and traced a J with one finger. "Like that."

"What did Walt say?"

A ghost of a smile flickered on his face. "Nothing. He didn't know. I hid it after Mama hit me, so Walt wouldn't hit me, too."

She drew back, aghast. "Walt hits you?" She couldn't picture it.

Forbes shook his head "No," but added with the practical logic of a child, "But I never broke sumpin' that was his, before."

Sheila leaned over and gave him a big hug. "I don't think Walt would ever hit you, Forbes, and I've known him a long, long time. But where did you hide his special thing? Do you remember?"

He reached behind him for the stuffed gray elephant on his pillow. "Inside Ellie, where I keep my jammies." He offered the pale zippered stomach to Sheila.

She trembled as she unzipped it. Inside, beneath rumpled pajamas, lay a brass letter opener. It looked just like the one the police reports had described—but this one had a very bent point.

Sheila lifted it out, held it reverently. Such a small, pretty thing to save a man's life. "I need to keep this for a while, Forbes, but I promise you Walt will not be angry when he finds out you bent it. Do you believe me?"

He gave her a long, grave look. Then he nodded.

"And how about if we ask Mildred to be there when you tell Miss Mary about General Forrest. Would that help?"

His face lit up as if dawn had occurred inside. "Yes! She won't hit me if somebody's with me!"

Sheila went back to work feeling both elated and a bit sick.

She couldn't reach Frank McGehee until nearly three. "I've got Walt's brass letter opener, Frank, with a positive identification." She explained. "So either Walt and Yvonne had two, or whoever killed her brought their own. Can you find out who else had one?"

He called her back about ten that night.

"We sent the hotel in Hawaii a list of everybody involved in this case, and it seems to be Dunwoody's home away from home. The Divestys stayed there on a trip he won selling real estate four months before Yvonne and Walt got married. The Marriots were there last summer. Dee Ivy's kid Lori went with her dad and his mother over spring break. The manager ran a check to see who else from Dunwoody has been there in the past year, and he found fifteen couples, including one guy who works for Hosokawa. Tom Settis?"

"I think we can scratch him as a suspect," Sheila told him. "The day Yvonne was killed, Tom and I were in a meeting together all afternoon."

Frank laughed. "That lets you out, too, then, I guess. At the rate we're going, we won't solve this thing by the Fourth of July!"

Sheila hung up and had started toward bed when what Frank had said finally jogged her memory. She sat on the edge of her mattress, remembering and thinking. Was it possible?

She went to her dresser and rummaged through her notes, pulled out one sheet and read it again. She considered all the angles. Then, hoping they could get the information they needed, she went to call Aunt Mary. It would take them several days to get everything, but with any luck they could have this murder solved by the end of the week.

*How many Dunwoody housewives does
it take to change a light bulb?
Three. One to hold the tennis racquets,
one to mix the martinis, and one to
call the electrician.*

THE LAST FRIDAY

Light streamed from the Marriot house. Party noises engulfed the small group of people waiting in the cul-de-sac.

"Do I look all right?" Nan Quentin looked down anxiously at her black dress. She was pale and nervous, as might be expected. Not every Friday night did she travel in a chauffeured silver Cadillac to a Dunwoody party. "Are you sure it will be all right if I come?"

"Of course," Aunt Mary told her crisply. "You must be there. You have been involved since the beginning, dear."

"You look fine," Sheila reassured her for the fifth time.

Normally Sheila would have been unhappy about her own appearance. Last week's ruination of her good black silk had made a hole in her wardrobe she had not yet had time to fill, and she never looked her best in navy blue. Tonight, however, she had no thoughts to spare on how she looked. She was too busy worrying about being at the Marriots' house at all.

"It is by far the best place to get everyone together," Aunt Mary had insisted when Sheila had objected to the plan.

"But if Richard has told Mac I was one of his prowlers . . ." Sheila didn't finish the sentence. She didn't want to imagine what might happen—or why Mac hadn't already gotten in touch with her.

"That's one of the mysteries we have to solve," Aunt Mary had replied airily, as if it were of little importance. "I have already called Diane, Mac's mother, and gotten myself and a few friends invited. Wear your navy dress, Sheila, the ugly one Tyler bought you. That Richard person probably won't even recognize you."

Sheila was less sanguine. Richard had last seen her ragged and disheveled, and he had called her by name. She doubted that an ugly navy blue dress would be a more effective disguise.

She jumped when Amory rumbled in her ear, "What are we waiting for? If we are going in, let's go in."

"We sure look funny just standing out here," Harley Sanders agreed. Sheila caught Nan giving him an appreciative look. He *was* a beautiful boy, his broad shoulders covered by a navy blazer and his blond hair freshly cut for the occasion.

"We must wait for Detective Drake." Aunt Mary altered the hang of her silver wrap. "After all the trouble Sheila had persuading him to come, we certainly cannot go in without him."

"Next time," Sheila muttered, "you can persuade him yourself."

Aunt Mary wasn't listening. She had looked away to return the polite greeting of another arriving guest.

When Sheila saw who it was, she was annoyed to feel her cheeks growing warm. So what if she had not seen Yvonne's gardener since their adventure last Friday night? So what if he looked splendid tonight in a black suit with a gleaming white shirt? Was that any reason for a woman nearing forty to feel as tongue-tied as a thirteen-year-old with her first crush? He did not seem similarly afflicted.

"Good evening." He gave her the nod of one who has not been formally introduced and doesn't care to be, passed them, and ran lightly up the steps without a trace of nervousness about entering the front door of a house he had left by an upstairs window. To Sheila's astonishment, Norris welcomed him like one of the family.

"All right, let's get this show on the road."

They heard Jake Drake's growl before they saw him. The detective had slicked himself up for the occasion: He wore a red tie with his customary baggy gray suit, a white carnation in his lapel. Behind him, Frank McGehee looked quite handsome in charcoal pinstripes.

Aunt Mary took Drake's elbow and inclined her head in a gracious nod. "Shall we go in?" Her dainty elegance made Drake look more like an eccentric escort and less like a cop.

At the door Norris stepped forward to block their way. "This is a private party," he said stiffly.

Aunt Mary drew herself up to her full five feet. "I am Mary Beaufort, a guest of Mac Marriot's mother, Diane Harlow." A duchess couldn't have said it better.

Norris gave her a courteous bow. "Of course, Miss Beaufort. I was told to expect you, and to take you upstairs when you arrived."

Amory came up from the rear. "Good evening, Norris." He socked the butler lightly on one arm. "What happened to those Phillies this week?"

"They could use some improvement, Mr. Travis," Norris admitted gloomily as he stood aside to let them in. "Fill yourself a plate, Miss Beaufort, then come back here and I'll take you upstairs."

No one took any notice as their party separated and drifted through the various rooms. The band was loud, food and drink flowing copiously, and voices shrill. Deciding that a frontal attack was better than suspense, Sheila approached her host with a smile. "How's it going, Mac?"

His cheery smile was just the same. "Couldn't be better! How's it with you? Gotten anything to eat yet? There's plenty." He waved her toward the buffet. Across the room Jaqui Robinson waved a crab claw in welcome.

Relieved but puzzled, Sheila drifted into the dining room. Richard was once again carving ham and roast beef. When she held out her plate, he ducked his head as if he dreaded this meeting more than she did, and served her a generous slice of beef without a word. More puzzled than ever, Sheila moved toward the bowl of iced crab claws.

"Guess what, Sheila!" Jaqui glided over to join her. Jaqui had to glide. Her gold dress was too tight to permit much walking. "Paula Divesty and I are going to start playing tennis Monday morning!"

"That's great! Some Saturday, find one more person and let's play doubles. I could use the practice."

Jaqui grimaced. "It isn't nice to murder your friends. Let me practice first. And speaking of murder, Slade's been playing in San Diego this week and Cornelius and I went along. What's been going on here? Any more news on who killed Yvonne?"

"They're working on it." Sheila took a fifth claw and decided that was enough for the time being.

Jaqui looked worried. "It's taking a while, isn't it? I really hate to let Cornelius out of my sight these days."

"Any day now," Sheila assured her.

"See you later!" Jaqui slithered to join her husband. Sheila watched her put a possessive hand on his arm.

Rilla drifted by, a thin young man in tow. ". . . my roses."

Sheila nodded to Frank McGehee, who headed toward the front door.

A ripple of excitement pulsed through the crowd. Sheila, joining Ava Settis, looked to see what had happened.

Alex Divesty stood in the doorway, head high with pride. Beside him walked the most gorgeous woman in the room. Her body was draped in chiffon that shaded from red to green to purple to smoky gray as it clung to her body, giving her the look of a living flame. Short, gleaming chestnut hair fell straight to her chin, then curved under her delicate jaw.

"Paula! You look wonderful!" Ava hurried to give her a hug, then stepped back to take another look.

She did indeed look gorgeous, but Sheila noticed Paula's smile did not reach her eyes. They roamed anxiously as she stood clutching her husband's arm. When they reached Sheila, she gave a quick flicker of a wider smile, then looked away. Sheila understood. Confession may be good for the soul, but it is hard on budding friendships.

Norris pressed a note into Sheila's hand and returned to his post without a word. Edging her way to a corner, she read: *Meet me upstairs!* written in an unfamiliar masculine hand.

Without knowing she did it, she scanned the rooms for a tall, dark figure. He was giving a short blond woman his full attention.

She fingered the note uneasily. Who could have sent it? She hoped it wasn't Mac! No, she could hear him laughing and joking in the dining room. Slade and Jaqui were talking with Alex and Paula in a music room just off the front hall. Harley was charming two older women near the buffet. Richard was carving roast beef. Tom Settis was chatting with two friends by the living room fireplace. Amory was wrangling with Dee on the sofa. If Sheila needed help, would he take time from debating their latest historical battle to come to her aid? Probably not. If Amory had lived in the 1860s, she reflected, he'd have been too busy reliving the Revolutionary War to notice the War Between the States.

She waited until Norris accompanied a woman in green out the front door, then nipped up the staircase, hoping she was not being foolish.

The hall was empty, the den door open, the room empty, the bathroom door ajar. As she crossed the den, however, Richard pushed the bathroom door open and gestured with his hand— and a short revolver. "We have some unfinished business."

She stepped back, startled. "But I just saw you downstairs!"

"Back staircase," he said briefly. "Come in here." He waved the gun again.

The bathroom was small for effective self-defense—as Sheila well knew. She stayed where she was. "I get claustrophobia. Come out here."

"In!" he ordered.

She obeyed. He closed the door and she heard the lock click.

"Okay, Mrs. Travis, what's your game?" He leaned against the door and relaxed his arm, aiming the gun at her left toe.

"Game?" She tried to think of a clever way to get out of this situation. She was abysmally short on clever ideas.

"What were you and that fellow doing here last week?"

"What were you doing in the house next door?"

As soon as she'd said it, she knew she shouldn't have. His body tensed, and he raised the gun. Whatever he'd been doing was clearly not Mac's business—and he was terrified Mac would find out about it. Until then Sheila had not been seriously afraid of Richard. She had not believed he would really hurt her in Mac's upstairs bathroom with the house below crowded with guests.

She believed it now.

His eyes narrowed. "I'm asking the questions! Why were you here?"

If he shot her, he would never get away, of course. Would that make any difference to her?

She shook her head to answer her own silent question.

Richard moved the gun a bit closer. "Don't shake your head at me, missy. Why were you here? And who was your partner?"

Something moved just beyond the window. Someone was climbing the magnolia again! Was it someone who already knew that route from previous travel?

Now she was as terrified that Richard would notice the climber as she was that he would shoot her. Willing her eyes not to look toward the window, she shifted slightly—forcing Richard to turn.

In spite of the air-conditioning, Sheila felt sweat begin to trickle down the bodice of her dress. Desperation brought inspiration. "He wasn't my partner!" she said with all the indignation she could muster. "I'd had too much to drink and got dizzy, so I came upstairs to lie down. I must have fallen asleep. When I woke up, I thought I'd wake Rilla or Mac's mother and ask them to let me out—but I ran into that man. He forced me to climb out the window with him."

"Who is he?" he demanded.

"I don't know who he is," she said truthfully. "I assumed he was one of your guests. Wasn't he?"

"I didn't get a good look at him," Richard growled. "He kept his head down, and then you . . ." He took a small step backward, as if remembering what had happened next.

From the corner of her eye Sheila saw the branch nearest the bathroom window shudder with weight. Recklessly, she tried a desperate gamble. "Maybe you could persuade him to tell you why he was here. He's downstairs tonight, you know."

Richard's eyes narrowed. "Here? Tonight? I didn't see him."

She nodded. "A short man in a wrinkled gray suit."

He chewed his lip, considering. "Red tie? Bald? Sleepy eyes?" *Hooded* was the word Sheila would have used, but she wouldn't quibble. She nodded. Richard nodded back, as if they had sealed a pact. "I noticed the fellow," he said. "Never saw him here before. He looks too short, though. You're sure it's the same man?"

"I don't forget somebody who forces me to climb down a tree."

To her relief, Richard put the gun in his pocket. "Okay, Mrs. Travis, I'm going to find him. *If* he's here. In any case, I'll be back. And to make sure you're still here. . . ." He opened the door of the linen closet. "Inside." He waved the gun meaningfully. "I said, get in!" He pulled a vanity chair from under the counter and waved her to the small space beneath the shelves.

She had little choice but to obey.

After she heard Richard bar the closet door and leave, she waited to give him time to get downstairs, then pounded on the door and shouted. Nobody came. Why should they? The upstairs was off limits to guests, and Mrs. Harlow was far down the hall visiting with Aunt Mary. Sheila's only hope was the man in the tree. Was he even now climbing closer? Would he swing in like Tarzan, shattering the window, and tear the door from its hinges? "Grow up," she told herself. "Mac cut the branches. Besides, grown men don't climb trees in good black—"

"Hey, you!" Someone shouted in the room next door. Sheila heard a yell outside, then silence.

"I think I got him, Mary!" Though muted, old Mrs. Harlow's voice was clearly excited.

"I hope you didn't kill him, dear! That could cause so many complications."

Sheila pounded on the door. "Aunt Mary! Mrs. Harlow! Help me! I'm locked in the bathroom closet! Aunt Mary! Mrs. Harlow!"

"Sheila? What on earth are you doing in there?" The silvery voice was on the other side of the door.

"Move the chair, Aunt Mary."

The chair scraped, the door swung open, and Sheila almost tumbled onto the feet of the two elderly women. Mrs. Harlow peered down at her, Super Soaker poised to fire.

"Don't shoot!" Sheila hauled herself to her feet and stumbled toward the window. "Did you already shoot somebody else?"

"A burglar, dear!" The fat old woman jigged with excitement. "Climbing the magnolia! He fell, but don't worry. He won't get away. The dogs will get him."

Sheila shuddered and peered down into the dark yard. Nothing moved—especially, thank God, not dogs.

Aunt Mary, meanwhile, was asking in a mildly curious voice, "What were you doing in that closet, dear?"

"Mac will be very angry," Mrs. Harlow told them. "The upstairs is off limits—"

"Usually." Mac himself stood in the doorway. "What the hell's going on?"

"I shot a burglar in the tree, dear, and he fell out. He shut Mary's niece in the closet."

"Not exactly—" Sheila began, but Mac had already shoved her aside, raised the window and screen, and leaned far out to peer down.

"Where are those damned dogs?" He whirled, about to rush out.

Aunt Mary stopped him with a hand on his arm. "Mac Harlow! I haven't seen you since you were three years old, but I'd have recognized you anywhere! Diane, he has your father's eyes!"

"Yes, doesn't he? Although his chin is decidedly Harlow."

Aunt Mary peered up at Mac and nodded. "Yes, I remember Mr. Harlow used to have a dimple just there." She lightly touched Mac's dimple with one shell-pink nail. "And that jutting lower lip was old Mrs. Harlow's, wasn't it?"

"Well, my mother's lower lip also jutted a bit. . . ."

Sheila bit her own lip to keep from laughing at Mac's chagrin. Once two old southern women start discussing the facial genealogy of one of their offspring, they can go on for hours. Family eyebrows are to white southerners what ethnic origin is in other parts of the country.

Aunt Mary saw the glint in his eye, however. She stepped back and sparkled up at her frustrated host. "I just came up to visit your mother, Mac. I hadn't seen her for a coon's age, and we've had a pleasant little visit." Supremely in charge of the situation, she led the way out of the bathroom.

Frank McGehee and a uniformed officer stood in the den doorway, blocking it.

Aunt Mary turned to her old friend. "Diane dear, I think you should go to bed. I enjoyed our visit, and I'll come back for another soon."

Mrs. Harlow looked anxiously from Mac to McGehee, then back to her son. "Mac? You haven't done anything wrong, have you?"

Mac was suddenly engrossed in the tips of his shoes.

"This time I shall not lift a finger to save you," she told him firmly. Without another word she turned and hobbled down the hall, her hunched back rigid with dignity and unshed tears.

"Mac Marriot . . ." McGehee began the familiar ritual of the Miranda warning. The uniformed officer pulled Mac's arms behind him and fastened cuffs on his wrists, then they all started downstairs, McGehee in front of Mac and the uniformed officer behind him.

Harley stood in the front hall, looking like he wondered when he could go home. Norris was ushering a couple out the front door. The man was very drunk, and Norris was encouraging him, "Come on, fellah. One foot in front of the other."

"Need some help?" Harley offered.

"We'll be all right." Norris maneuvered the man with finesse and told his wife, "You go ahead and bring the car to our drive. I'll get him inside." Harley closed the front door behind them.

They were halfway down the stairs when an officer appeared from the back of the house, Rilla's bright head bobbing by his shoulder. Her hands, too, were cuffed, and the officer steered her by a hand at her elbow. "Take your hands off my wife!" Mac demanded. "Don't you dare touch her!"

Guests nearest the hall looked up with one large, inaudible gasp, moved a fraction closer while trying to pretend they were still conversing normally.

The officer dropped his hand but stood by Rilla's side. Her eyes were wet and red. She gave Mac a startled, frightened look. Tragedy sat strangely on a face so deeply etched with laughter.

"Come here, honey." Mac pushed past McGehee and descended the last two steps to join her. She lifted her face and he kissed it. "It was a great ride while it lasted, doll. Sorry it's over."

Tears streamed down her tanned face from under closed lids.

"What's going on?" Alex Divesty moved forward.

McGehee hesitated, then replied. "We're charging these folks with selling drugs, and concealing them in the house next door."

"Nonsense!" Alex objected. "That house is kept locked. . . ."

"They own the house," McGehee informed him.

Alex swiveled to gape at Mac. "So that's why the price was kept so high!"

Mac shrugged, the ghost of his usual grin on his lips. "Sorry, buddy. Maybe now we'll lower the price."

Voices swelled in a quick, hushed babble, then died.

Rilla looked over her guests, her eyes pleading with them to understand. "We sold only what people wanted, and only to people who could afford it." Mac made a move to quiet her.

Sheila, still on the staircase, noticed several guests moving slowly toward the back of the crowd. "Better cover the back way," she called softly down to McGehee.

"It's covered by the whole narcotics division," he replied. "They've had an agent watching this place for weeks. They were about ready to close in, anyway."

So she had been right about who was in the tree. He had been covering the back door, not coming to her rescue. Why should she feel disappointed?

Rilla was still talking. ". . . weren't hurting anyone," she concluded.

"No one?" Aunt Mary spoke from the step above Sheila. "What about your mother, Mac? She sold everything she had to pay your attorney fees the last time you got into trouble. She won't live to see you get out of prison this time. Is that nothing?"

Mac did not reply.

"Let's go," McGehee told them, but before they could move, the front door opened. Norris, seeing Mac and Rilla surrounded, stopped on the threshold.

Mac jerked his head. Norris flung the door wide and threw

himself between Mac and the officers. *"Run!"* Mac roared at Rilla. She obeyed—he followed.

"Halt, or we'll shoot!" cried the young officer with McGehee, drawing his gun. Norris's hand flew to his jacket, but Harley tackled and sat on him.

From the rear of the crowd another uniformed officer pushed past the shocked guests and bent to cuff the fallen doorman. "Good work, fellow. You ought to play football!"

"Yeah." Harley got up, flushed with embarrassment.

From the commotion outside Sheila could tell that Mac and Rilla had not gotten far. McGehee had not been foolish enough to leave the front unguarded.

Guests began to surge into the hall. "Everybody go back inside," McGehee ordered. "We'll have a few questions to ask you."

That sobered even those as bourbon-happy as Amory.

McGehee looked around, puzzled. "Where the hell is Drake?" he asked the officer at his side. "I expected him to have everything under control down here."

The other man shrugged. "Haven't seen him all evening."

"Can you carry on without him, Frank?" Sheila murmured.

"What do you think I've just been doing?"

Aunt Mary touched his arm and gestured toward the crowd. "Perhaps while you finish up here, our party could go next door. It would be less hectic."

"Next door's full of police and drug-sniffing dogs, ma'am."

"Oh, I didn't mean to the vacant house, dear. So uncomfortable, with no chairs. I meant Walter Delacourt's, on the other side. He's Sheila's friend. I'm sure he wouldn't mind."

McGehee looked at the milling guests, then back to Aunt Mary. "Maybe you're right, Miss Mary. I'll join you in a little while."

"And may we invite a few others, Mr. McGehee?"

In fifteen minutes Walter Delacourt's living room was full.

Slade and Jaqui shared a love seat at one end, puzzled but willing to be there. Paula and Alex huddled on one end of the couch, clutching each other's hands but not meeting each other's eyes. Nan effaced herself in a distant corner on a dining room chair and pulled a tiny notebook and pen from her bag. Harley leaned against the doorjamb, refusing to sit. Amory filled one large wing chair. Dee had dragged a small chair next to him and kept her small hand tucked securely in his. Sheila shared the couch with the nervous Divestys.

Walt, their bathrobed host, sat in a wing chair by the hearth, baffled and a bit belligerent. Clasping his glasses with his left hand, he peered at Sheila. "I still don't understand why you are all here."

"You will," she assured him. He looked unconvinced.

Perched on a fireplace chair, Aunt Mary smoothed her skirt and smiled around the room. "Well, I believe we are ready. Mr. Divesty, why don't you begin?"

Alex put his hands on his knees, getting ready to stand. "I'm ready to call it a night, ma'am. It's been a dreadful month on this street, and I hope it's over."

"Almost," Aunt Mary agreed, "but before you go, what time did you come into this house the afternoon Mrs. Delacourt was killed?"

Alex's face deepened from pink to deep red. "I—I don't know what the Sam Hill you're talking about!" Paula clutched his arm so tightly, Sheila feared she'd cut off his circulation.

"Of course you do," Aunt Mary said in her best no-nonsense tone. "You left a Perrier bottle on the sink. You hoped to retrieve it the next morning, but Sheila was here, so you wiped your prints off it instead."

"I . . . I . . ."

"We don't think you killed Yvonne," Sheila told him. "But it will help immensely if you'll just admit you were here."

Divesty looked quickly around the room, found every person there waiting to hear what he had to say.

"Okay. I was here. I'd given Yvonne an ultimatum about"—he stopped, looked at Walt—"a business matter, but she'd made herself scarce all day. I came over early that morning—"

Nan nodded triumphantly in her corner.

"—but she didn't answer. I knew she was here, dammit! But I had an appointment to show a house, so I couldn't wait until she came out. About—oh, probably three or three-fifteen, I ran by on my way from one appointment to another. The front door was ajar—"

"Ajar?" Walt was baffled. "Who left it ajar?"

Alex shrugged. "I don't know, but since it was—and I damn well knew Yvonne wouldn't come if I rang—I went on in and called. She didn't answer." His eyes moved nervously around the downstairs, reliving those moments. "I went into the kitchen, set down my bottle without thinking, and called again. Nothing. Then I got mad! I thought she was in her office upstairs, waiting me out. I stomped up the stairs loud enough to put the fear of God into her, calling 'I want my money and I want it now!' At the top of the stairs—"

He stopped.

"Yeah? What?" Amory urged him impatiently.

Alex swallowed. "I didn't know which room was her office. I turned right and went in the first one I came to . . ."

This time he could not go on.

Sheila spoke gently. "She was already dead?"

He nodded, studying the hair on the back of his hands.

"Honey!" Paula cried sympathetically. "What did you do then?" Sheila, beside her, felt Paula's relief.

Alex shrugged. "I went home, locked the door, and had several stiff drinks. I couldn't decide whether to call the police or wait until Walt got home. I put off deciding so long that Walt came home first." He looked from Slade to Walt. "You know the rest."

Sheila had one more question. "You shut the front door tight when you left?"

He nodded. "I didn't want anybody else walking in."

"Thank God," Jaqui breathed. "Cornelius told me later that he and Forbes tried to get in about four to pick up something. They couldn't, because the door was locked. I'll be grateful to you, Alex, to my dying day."

He gave her a small, embarrassed smile.

"Oh, honey." Paula snuggled into his shoulder. Only Sheila heard her whisper. "I was so afraid you'd done it!"

"Me?" he yelped. "Why would I have killed her?"

Now everyone was waiting for what Paula had to say.

She sighed and straightened. "Yvonne had, uh, asked me for some money to tide her over a rough spot." She reached for Sheila's hand and squeezed it, a silent plea for forgiveness—or silence? "I told her I didn't have any extra money, so she said maybe Alex could help her. When I heard she was dead and knew you'd been here that afternoon, I thought she'd made you too mad, honey. I was so scared—!" Again she squeezed Sheila's hand, then released it.

Alex leaned over and kissed her. "You shouldn't have been scared, sweetheart. Why should I kill her? She owed me money!"

"A miser after your own heart," Sheila told Aunt Mary, adding, "After Yvonne Delacourt's, too, apparently."

Walter rose from his seat. "That's a *lie!*" he roared. "She was the sweetest, most generous—" He caught Sheila's eye and sat back down, tears steaming his glasses. "Find out who killed her!"

Sheila gave him a weary smile. "We have, Walter." Ignoring a rustle of unease that rippled through the room, she went on. "Most of that day was carefully recorded by the woman in the corner there. Nan Quentin wants to be a writer. She wanted to interview you, Slade, for an article, but she was timid about asking."

"Why?" the ball player rumbled. "Nobody else is."

"I'm just starting out," Nan said with a deprecating shrug.

Sheila continued. "So Nan watched this neighborhood for one whole morning—the important morning. She even talked with the Robinsons' yard man."

"I told you, Sheila," Jaqui said in exasperation, "we don't *have* a yard man right now."

"No?" Aunt Mary raised quizzical brows at Slade.

He gave a rueful little laugh and turned to Nan. "Would you know this yard man if you saw him again?"

She flushed. "I don't know. He was big, and—" She stopped.

"Black?" he suggested. "Scruffy clothes? Drove a little gray pickup with Fulton County tags?"

"Slade!" Jaqui protested, eyes wide. "You *didn't!*"

"Didn't what?" Amory was thoroughly puzzled.

Slade chuckled. "Put on some old clothes, drove to my daddy's place down in East Point, borrowed his truck and mower, and came back up here to cut my lawn. I've never understood," he told the room at large, "why men pay somebody to cut their grass, then play golf or work out to get exercise. I *enjoy* mowing a lawn, but it's not the done *thing* in Dun-*woody*. I figured, though, that in old clothes and a pickup, most people up here wouldn't be able to tell one black man from another."

"I gave you *tea!*" Nan spluttered. "Slade Robinson drank *tea* out of *my* glass!" she told the others, eyes alight.

"And I'll give you an interview whenever you're ready," he told her, smiling. "I owe it to you."

"First," Aunt Mary told them, "let's talk about the death of Yvonne Delacourt. Please continue, Sheila."

Poor Walter looked so weary, Sheila wished they could all just go home. They could, before long. It was almost over.

"One odd thing about this case was the way Yvonne was found. Her body had recently been rubbed with lotion—"

"She'd played tennis that morning and taken a shower," Dee contributed. "I always put on lotion afterward. My skin is so dry."

Sheila nodded. "Yes, that may be it. But Yvonne was found in her underpants lying on a bed as if asleep—or laid out for burial. She had taken a mild muscle relaxant before lunch, so she may have been dozing when she was stabbed." She ignored a cry of dismay from Walt and hurried on. "There were also two sets of lunch dishes in the dishwasher, but Walt told me he didn't eat lunch."

"Because I didn't," he reminded her.

"There was also an envelope on your desk that you swear you didn't put there."

"Because I didn't." He was getting truculent. "Look, Sheila, you're going over old territory."

"But put it all together, Walt: muscle relaxant, lotion, underpants, dishes, envelope—what do you get?"

"How the hell should I know?" he protested. "If I knew, don't you think I'd have told the police?"

"Does anyone else see a pattern?"

After a moment's silence Jaqui spoke hesitantly. "This may be far out, but it sounds to me like Yvonne went for a massage after tennis, then had a friend in for lunch. But no—she'd have had the massage after lunch. That's why she was undressed!"

Sheila nodded. "Whoever gave her the massage killed her while she was dozing afterward, put an envelope on Walt's desk, and left the front door open to make it look like anyone could have come in. He or she couldn't know that Forbes would come home before anyone else,"—she heard a quick, suppressed gasp—"that Alex would slam the door behind him, or that Walt would shove the envelope unopened into his desk drawer the same way he shoved in the mail I brought in another evening. I asked the police to check with the carrier. Monday's mail was collected, but not Tuesday's."

"I didn't get the mail Monday," Walt objected. "Who could think of bringing in mail after—"

"No one," Sheila assured him. "But someone did bring it in. Yvonne, or someone who was here before Forbes got home. The carrier gets to this street about two—right?"

Several heads nodded.

Aunt Mary cocked her head and asked, "*Is* that right, Nan?"

Nan was bent over her lap, fiddling with a contact lens. "I left about one, ma'am. I don't know." She peered up at Walt. "Could I use your bathroom? My lens is off center." He nodded and gestured toward the hall. She stood.

Aunt Mary held up a hand to hold her. "But you came back, didn't you? To see Yvonne Delacourt?"

"No, ma'am. I didn't know Yvonne Delacourt." She was hurrying toward the door, one hand pressed to her eye.

Aunt Mary said, at her most imperious, "You knew Yvonne Jones, Nan Jones Quentin—and killed her, too!"

Nan dashed for the hall.

Harley caught her neatly, pulled her back into the room. Amory flapped a large hand in distress. "Hold on! I think we're making a mistake here!"

Caught in Harley's arm, Nan could not move. Her green eyes, contact lenses in place, were fixed on Aunt Mary's stern brown ones.

"We can prove it, dear. Sit down." Aunt Mary nodded toward Nan's empty place. Harley escorted her back to the chair and sat her in it, then returned to block the exit again. Nan sat unmoving except for her eyes, which darted wildly about the room. She didn't say a word.

Aunt Mary looked at Sheila. "Tell them, dear."

"The wound went cleanly to the heart. Only a trained person, such as a surgical nurse, would know how to place it that well. The letter opener came from a hotel where you spent two nights when you were stationed in Hawaii years ago, Nan. Did you really not know that Yvonne and Walt went there for their honeymoon until you found that newspaper article? Or did you know before you chose the opener for your weapon?" Nan's eyes flickered, but she didn't reply.

"You called the police about that opener, dear," Aunt Mary reminded her crisply. "Were you trying to implicate Walt?"

"I told them it must have been Yvonne's!" Nan insisted. She licked her lips nervously.

Sheila shook her head. "Walt had already told the police it was his." She gave Walt a rueful smile. "You didn't know, but Forbes bent yours the day before his mother died, and hid it. The police now have both of them, and a copy of the hotel register with Nan's name on it. They also have a copy, Nan, of the rental agreement for the blue car you used that day to come to lunch, having taken care to be seen earlier in your own brown one. Once we knew what must have happened, it was not difficult to find the rental car." She turned to Jaqui. "I think you are right about the massage. Nurses give wonderful massages."

Nan sat like a frozen woman. "What made you think it was me?"

Sheila gave her a sad smile. "You told me so yourself. I just didn't realize it until my assistant lost a bead off her earring. 'How will anybody know it used to be red, white, and blue?' she asked me. Something jarred in my memory. Later I knew what it was—your story about this house after the murder." She turned to her nephew. "Amory, bring me the front-door wreath." When he had done so, she held it up. "What color is this wreath, Nan?"

Amory answered for her. "Pink and purple."

"Pink and mauve," Sheila agreed. "Yet Nan's cutline said it was pink, mauve, and blue. How did you know it used to be blue, Nan?" Nan licked her lips in a face so white that her freckles glowed. Sheila answered her own question. "Because when you first saw it, the day Yvonne died, the most noticeable thing about it was a huge blue silk magnolia. You took your pictures in black and white, and wrote the cutline from memory. But the morning after Yvonne died, Walter pulled the blue flower out and crushed it. He stuffed it in a vase on the mantelpiece. Amory, is it still there?"

Amory peered into the vase. "Yep, it's there."

Walter suddenly spoke. "You killed Vonnie? Why? Tell me that —why?"

Now pink flooded the spaces between Nan's freckles. "She killed my brother! And Harley's father, and a sick old man. Nobody would believe me, but she did! She *did!*"

"Her brother?" Amory looked from Aunt Mary to Sheila, confused.

Sheila nodded. "Henry Jones. Nan is the sister Edna Warton's mother mentioned, the one Yvonne telephoned the day after Henry died—"

"—asking if we'd seen him!" Nan raged. "Acting like she had no idea where he was. Sweet as pie and so, so *worried!* And all the time, Henry . . . Henry . . ." She slumped forward and covered her face with her hands.

"Oh, honey!" Jaqui reached out and touched her with one long red talon. "I'm so sorry."

Nan jerked back. "Well, *I'm* not sorry! I'm glad she's dead!"

"Tell us, dear," Aunt Mary urged. "Let out all the poison."

Nan straightened. Tears ran unheeded down her cheeks. "When Henry died, I didn't think Yvonne had done it—not at first. But I started to hate her. She didn't act like she'd loved him at all. She just took his insurance money and started living fancy." She swabbed her tears angrily and continued. "You want to know why I put a lily on her body? Because she bought white lilies for his funeral. A huge showy blanket that made everybody else's look little and cheap. But not because she loved him. It was just because she wanted people saying how wonderful she was. Then she rented an apartment on the water, bought herself beautiful clothes, and started going out with a man she'd met at work—a man who drove a big car, wore nice suits, and took her to expensive places."

"My dad," Harley Sanders muttered.

Nan's eyes flicked him lightly, then returned to Aunt Mary. "When they got married, I clipped the announcement out of the paper, with her picture. Then I joined the navy. Another sailor saw the clipping one day and said, 'That woman lives in Memphis. Her husband was just shot!' I asked her to call her mother and have the paper sent down. There was Yvonne again, and another dead husband! After that I subscribed to the Memphis paper. No matter where I went, I got it sent to me—even after I moved here. I knew when she got married again. When her third husband died, I wrote the Memphis police, but they must have thought I was a crank. They never even replied."

"Very unwise," Aunt Mary murmured.

Nan went on, her voice now low and hurried. "I didn't know where Yvonne was for nearly two years. Then early this month I saw her picture in the paper *here*, pouring tea at some fancy party."

"Me, too!" Harley agreed. He shot her a timid smile. She was past seeing it.

"So I called her and told her I was in town. I just thought I'd warn her that I was watching her, tell her she'd better not try anything with her latest husband."

Walter gave a short, strangled gasp.

Nan ignored him. "I was pretty aggressive, but she was sweet as pie—didn't even seem worried. She invited me to lunch on Monday. Then she asked if I'd give her a massage when I came, like I used to. Can you believe that? Invite somebody to lunch, then ask them to give you a massage afterward!"

"Tacky!" Dee agreed indignantly.

"I'll tell *you* something else," Nan told her. "That whale necklace Yvonne gave your daughter and told her she'd ordered especially for her? I gave it to Yvonne the first Christmas she and Henry were married. I was so proud to have her in our family. . . ." Her voice trembled.

"When did you decide to kill her, dear?" Aunt Mary asked. "Surely you didn't spend a hot morning in your car at the corner and bring a letter opener to lunch without a good deal of thought."

Nan gulped, and raced on like an animal followed by a swarm of bees. "On Saturday I drove up here to see where she lived.

The more I saw, the madder I got. Why kill Henry if this was what she wanted? Why didn't she just divorce him and marry a rich man?"

No one had an answer. Nan's eyes flicked to the front hall. Frank McGehee stood just inside the door, listening.

"And that's when you decided to kill her, dear?" Aunt Mary prodded. Eyes glued on Frank, Nan did not respond. "It was a very good idea to spend the morning watching the street," Aunt Mary tried again, "so you would know who was about."

Sheila gave her a stern look. Aunt Mary did not need to sound so approving. Besides, Sheila herself had a bone to pick with Nan. "You deliberately put yourself in Amory's way, didn't you? I should have suspected something at lunch, when you had that convenient copy of your notes in your purse. You used us, didn't you?"

Nan shrugged. "I wanted to stay close to somebody who knew what the police were finding out—so I could write a story," she added, one eye still on Frank, who had moved to stand by the fireplace.

"You wanted to be sure people knew about Yvonne's past, too, didn't you?" Aunt Mary asked. "That's why you left those clippings on Walt's desk. Then—when nobody seemed to have read them—you sent copies to a reporter. How did you know the reporter, dear? Did he speak to one of your journalism classes?"

Nan looked from one set of accusing eyes to another. "I'll admit I had the clippings and sent them to the paper, and rented a car. But I could have rented that car to go to the mountains for the afternoon. I'm not confessing to *anything!*"

"What's to confess?" Jake Drake—more disheveled than ever —stood in the doorway, clutching someone by the arm. There was a large bruise on his left cheek.

Sheila's stomach gave a lurch. Drake held the Delacourts' yard man, but he was no longer immaculate. His pants were torn and soaking wet, his feet were bare, his eyes looked a bit unfocused, and one shoulder was strangely lower than the other.

"I found this guy unconscious under a tree in the Marriots' backyard," Drake announced. "Anybody know who he is?"

"Crispin!" Nan exclaimed. "What are you doing here?"

"Crispin?" Sheila and Amory spoke simultaneously, but it was Nan toward whom he looked with a weary smile. "Hi, Nancy. Good to see you again." He staggered toward the only vacant chair in the room and fell wearily into it.

Sheila looked from him to Frank McGehee, puzzled. "Isn't he your agent from the narcotics division?"

McGehee chuckled. "No, their agent was a woman, name of Sue Ella. She's been working as the Marriots' cook, and I think she gave you a jolly time last week." His eyes twinkled.

Remembering the Dover men with pinchers, Sheila had the grace to blush.

The Delacourts' yard man groaned. "Water!" As every eye turned toward him and Dee hurried toward the kitchen, Nan made one last dash toward freedom. This time Harley stopped her with a flying tackle just inside the front door. They crashed to the ground, along with a large vase that had stood beside the door.

"Are you okay?" Harley asked Nan anxiously. She groaned. "I'm sorry about the vase," he added to Walt.

Walt was past caring about vases.

As Harley helped Nan to her feet and again escorted her, limping, to her seat in the corner, Jake Drake repeated sourly, "What's to confess?"

Aunt Mary inclined her head toward the corner. "That young woman stabbed Yvonne Delacourt, and we can prove it."

Crispin jerked his head up and stared at Nan. Drake nodded at McGehee, who started toward her, already rolling out the Miranda warning. When he had finished, Aunt Mary held up a hand. "Don't take her out quite yet, please. Let her tell us what she knows about this man Crispin before she goes."

Sheila silently seconded that idea.

"He's Yvonne's brother or something," Nan said, her burning eyes on his face. "We were both in Henry and Vonnie's wedding. He's—I don't know what he does, but he's rich, I think."

Sheila recalled Yvonne's almost monthly entries: *C1000, C1500.* Crispin? But there were things she wanted to know about him besides his bank account. For once Jake Drake spoke words she wanted to hear.

"What were you doing under that tree tonight?" he growled.

Crispin groaned again. "Trying to rescue someone who needs rescuing about as much as a five-hundred-pound gorilla. And I got shot for my pains. Some old fool with a water gun . . ."

"Young man!" If Aunt Mary had had a lorgnette, she would have whipped it out. "The woman to whom you are referring as an 'old fool' happens to be a friend of mine."

"She shoots a mean water pistol, ma'am. The shock made me fall nearly two stories. She could have killed me!"

Aunt Mary gave him a glacial look and raised her chin. "Diane uses a water gun because she's got arthritis. If it had been me—"

For an instant his familiar grin flashed. "I am heartily glad it wasn't. As it is, I think I've broken my shoulder. Thank God somebody had already tranquilized the dogs."

Sheila reminded herself to take McGehee or Sue Ella out for steak. But why did Crispin not so much as look her way?

Amory shifted in his seat and thrust his heavy jaw forward. "Why did you kidnap Forbes?"

Crispin shook his head. "I didn't. One reason I came to Atlanta was to make sure Forbes was all right. Yvonne had a temper, and I was worried she might get carried away and—well—hurt him."

Walt half rose in protest, but sat down again when Amory grunted and Paula said, "I think you had good reason to be."

Her eyes held Crispin's for an instant, then he looked around the room and settled on Walt as the person most deserving his explanation. "My sister wrote that she thought there was something fishy going on next door—"

As Paula stiffened and Alex reached out and took her hand, Crispin shook his head. "Not on your side, on the other one. She'd seen lights in the vacant house, and had rigged up a mirror so she could watch the Marriots from her guest room window. She'd seen Mac Marriot going between the lots as if he were passing through the fence. From what she wrote, I suspected drugs at once. Looks like I was right." He gave McGehee a brief smile.

This time Sheila's thoughts were voiced by Dee. "So you *are* a detective?"

Crispin laughed. "Hardly. But I thought if Vonnie got to know too much, she could get in bigger trouble than she knew." He shook his head at Nan. "I would have never imagined—"

She met his glance briefly, then looked away.

"So what did you find out about the Marriots—and how?" Aunt Mary was speaking to Crispin, but her eyes were on Sheila.

"If you don't mention last week," Sheila sent him a silent promise, "neither will I."

His eyes never moved in her direction. "Nothing worth knowing, actually. Their security was pretty tight."

Aunt Mary gave him a shrewd look. "The newspaper sources never mentioned Yvonne having a brother."

He grinned. "I'll present all my credentials when I come to visit my nephew, Forbes. Will that satisfy you, ma'am?"

Aunt Mary held his eyes for a long moment, then nodded. But her voice was huskier than usual when she asked, "If you are Yvonne's brother, are you also her next of kin?"

"I'm her only kin," he told her. "And if you're wondering if I am Forbes's legal guardian, I am. I am also executor of her will."

Walt gave a start. "Her will? Our lawyer has her will!"

Crispin shook his head. "If you look at the wording of the will you have, you will see it pertains only to the property of Yvonne Delacourt. Vonnie put all her other assets in her maiden name, and explains that in the will my lawyer has. But don't worry." He held up a hand to forestall their question. "It all goes to Forbes. All I get is enough to take care of him until he's grown."

"You aren't a fit guardian," Amory objected. "You tried to kidnap him! What's to keep you from killing him and taking the money?"

The pirate's grin was back. "Nothing—except Forbes's friends here in Atlanta. You'll have to keep an eye on me. But I told you, I didn't kidnap him. I—whatever it's called when you put somebody back. I was following you in the park to make sure he was all right. He saw me getting off the train and followed *me*. I had a devil of a time persuading him to wait for you—but he did, didn't he?"

"You didn't even stick around to see!" Amory was flushed and beginning to sweat, and his nose twitched violently. As Dee put a restraining hand on his arm, Sheila gaped at him in astonishment. Was Amory getting attached to a four-year-old boy? For the first time, it occurred to her that her large nephew might one day make somebody a terrific father.

"Oh, but I did," Crispin assured him. "I waited behind the Whistle Stop until you arrived, limping down the track and bellowing like a steer."

"I was not!" Amory retorted. "I was merely—"

"At least you know I was there." Crispin stood and held out his good hand to Aunt Mary. "If you don't mind, ma'am, I think I'll go see about this shoulder. May I visit Forbes tomorrow?"

Aunt Mary did not immediately reply, and Sheila saw that the small woman's hand was trembling. "You don't plan to take him immediately, do you?" she asked, her voice not quite steady. "I believe he and my housekeeper have some plans. . . ."

Her housekeeper, indeed! Sheila made a small motion of rebuke. For the first time Crispin acknowledged her presence. "I am glad to see *you* looking so well, Mrs. Travis." He gave her a small formal nod. "We have a few things to discuss. I will see you later." He went to drop a comradely hand on Nan's shoulder. "You, too."

After he'd gone, a frozen-faced Nan accompanied Drake and McGehee to a cruiser. Amory walked Dee home. The Divestys and Robinsons left. Walt went into the kitchen and Sheila heard him drawing himself a glass of water. Harley went to ask for one, too.

She sat on the sofa in a weary but not altogether unpleasant haze. Aunt Mary spoke crisply. "I wonder if Nan Jones needs a lawyer?"

Sheila roused herself and reached for her purse. "Do you plan to ask yours to try to get her off?"

"No, dear. I do not approve of murder. And a woman who nurses hatred for as long as that woman did certainly has no business nursing the sick. But under the circumstances, Ms. Jones deserves a better trial than she can probably afford." She got up with a bit of difficulty. "Now, you wipe that silly smile off your face, dear, and let's go home! It's getting later every minute."

It was. Remembering what Crispin had said to her as he left, Sheila suddenly found that a comforting thought.

Jake Drake was waiting for them in the street. "Mrs. Travis? Miss Beaufort? May I speak to you for a moment?" His voice was smooth as snake oil—and as unpleasant.

Sheila hesitated, but Aunt Mary trotted over and put a hand on his sleeve. "I hated to ask inside, Captain Drake, but whatever happened to your poor face?"

He touched his cheek. "Just a scrape, ma'am. I had a bit of trouble with Marriot's bodyguard. He took me for someone else." His slitted eyes turned in Sheila's direction and he smiled. Sheila shivered. His gaze made her feel like she'd stepped inadvertently under a cold shower. "He'll be away for some time. In addition to the drug charges, he'll be up for assaulting a police officer. It's a serious offense."

He added, pleasantly enough, "So is inciting someone to assault a police officer."

"Now, who would do a thing like that?" Aunt Mary's lashes fluttered, and she stepped back in indignation.

"I am naming no names, ma'am. But I hope we'll get all the evidence we need in this case without any trouble from anyone. I just hate publicity seekers. I surely do." His voice was as bland as salt-free butter.

"Oh, I'm certain everyone will cooperate to the fullest, Mr. Drake, and you will get all the credit you deserve." She raised her hand and beckoned to a silver Cadillac parked down the street. As the Caddy purred toward them, Aunt Mary inclined her head to the detective. "Now I must go persuade Diane Harlow to come home with me for a few days. Good night, Captain Drake!"

"Good night, Miss Beaufort. And good night to you, Mrs. Travis, until we meet again."

Sheila had absolutely no intention of ever meeting Jake Drake again. She turned toward Aunt Mary's car resolved to send McGehee everything she had on this case before tomorrow noon.

*What is a Dunwoody matron's
favorite position?
Facing Neiman-Marcus.*

The sky was perfectly white. From Sheila's deck the trees, grass, and pond looked like a drawing a child had forgotten to complete. Soon it would rain. Sitting in a wicker chair, Sheila felt incomplete, too. Her hair was beginning to frizz. She really ought to go inside and start packing for tomorrow's flight to Tokyo, but she couldn't summon the energy. She winged a prayer for Nan. Did she still think that murdering Yvonne was worth what came afterward?

Lady at her feet, a cup of coffee at her elbow, it ought to be marvelous to have the mystery solved and a few hours of solitude. So why was she so restless?

Amory had been gone three hours, but surely she wasn't missing him! She had wished often enough these past two weeks that he would leave. Still, without Tyler to worship, Amory had turned out to be not half bad. She had invited him back, if he'd call first. But she was glad to get her apartment to herself. She had already performed the small rituals to reclaim it: stripped his bed, put away books he'd left lying about.

While he was making breakfast and packing, she had written up all her notes and called Frank. He would stop by for them sometime later today.

Was that what she was waiting for? She was certainly waiting for something. Even Lady dozed uneasily, her nose rising from time to time to test the air for change.

It would have been hard to determine which was more relieved when they heard the doorbell, the mistress or the dog.
Both stood with alacrity. Lady pranced to the glass doors and
waited to be let in, then trotted to the front door and sniffed the
crack beneath.

"It's probably Frank," Sheila told her. Lady wagged her tail
but did not move her nose. Sheila shoved her gently with one toe
and opened the door.

Crispin held up a large box and tried to avoid Lady's dance
around his ankles. "Special delivery, ma'am. Where shall I put
it?"

"What is it?" She meant to sound cool and distant, but her
sudden dash from the heat outside into the cool had left her a bit
breathless. With a grin he entered and headed without invitation
for the living room.

"Something I decided last night you badly need." He set the
box on the coffee table and took the big wing chair. Lady
promptly settled herself with her chin on his foot. He bent and
patted her absently, then looked around. "Nice place. Needs a
few plants, though. And where's old what's-his-name?"

"Amory? He flew back to Tupelo right after lunch." Sheila
settled herself into one corner of the couch and eyed him warily.
If he thought he could ignore her one night, and the next day
come barging in without one word of explanation—

"Without Dee Ivy? After last night, I thought they would soon
be living happily ever after."

His eyes twinkled. In spite of her best resolutions, Sheila's
twinkled, too. "Poor Amory thought so, too. He even worked up
his nerve to ask her. But when push came to shove, Dee wasn't
ready to leave Dunwoody. She surprised the socks off Amory,
and I think she surprised even herself. After all these years of
thinking that all she needed was a good man, she found she isn't
ready to give up her independence. She's going to fly out to see
him next month, and they may eventually make something good

together—but it won't look like either of them would have thought a week ago."

"Sheila Travis, prophetess." He laughed. To her surprise, she heard a tremor in his voice. Could he be nervous? "Open the box," he invited her, waving his right hand, then wincing.

The remnants of her anger vanished in concern. "You're strapped up! Was the shoulder really broken?"

"Sure was." He patted it ruefully. "Next time I climb a tree to rescue a lady, I'll make certain there's not another lady around with a squirt gun. The doctor says it will be several weeks before I'm normal."

She snorted. "Are you ever normal? What on earth made you climb that tree?"

His jaw dropped. "I like that! I told you—I was coming to your rescue!"

"You never got there," she pointed out, "and I'm surprised you noticed I *needed* rescuing. You looked busy." The memory of the small blonde who'd engrossed him at the Marriots' made her voice tart.

He slid deeper into his chair. "Oh, I wasn't as blind as you thought. I saw Richard hand Norris that note and Norris hand it to you. You looked to see if it came from me—"

"I did no such thing!"

"You did, too. And then Richard hurried toward the back staircase." He smiled ruefully. "But it's a good thing you didn't depend on me to rescue you, as it turned out. I should have known—" He broke off and shook his head. "I will never forget the way you looked kicking that gun out of Richard's hand last week. And I thought I was protecting *you* in that tree!"

"Protecting?" Her eyebrows raised. "Is that what you call it?"

"Well, if I'd known you knew karate—"

"It's hard to defend yourself in a tree."

She spoke without thinking. Their gazes met and held for a moment, dropped at the same time. "Open the box," he repeated.

She bent over the gift, trying not to get prematurely thrilled by the name on the lid. It could be an old box he was reusing.

It was not.

"Oh!" It was a black silk dress, lovelier than the one she had ruined the week before. She held it up and looked at him in astonishment. "It's perfect. How did you know the right size?" She was surprised at how level her voice sounded. The rest of her felt as if she'd just ridden Six Flags Over Georgia's new roller coaster.

He shrugged, then winced with pain. "Ow! When I've been as close to a woman as I was to you in that tree, I know a lot of things. Go put it on. I want to see you in it."

She did, too—but not yet.

She folded the dress back into its box. "First tell me why you pretended not to know me last night."

"I didn't pretend not to know you, I pretended not to know you well. What would you have done if it had been *my* aunt sitting there? Would you have called me darling, and discussed our flight down the tree and away from Richard's gun?"

"No," she admitted, "but there might have been a happier medium."

He stroked his jaw with his good hand. "There might have been, but I wasn't able to think too clearly. I just knew. I didn't want your reputation, like your dress, in shreds."

That reminded her of something. "Speaking of Richard's gun, I take it your wound was a flesh one?"

He nodded. "It had almost healed before I got this one." He touched his arm. "Give a poor hurt man a treat, woman. Put on your new dress and let me see how you look in it."

As soon as she returned, she could tell from his face that it was perfect. "You ought to always wear black or white," he told her, "or that combination of burgundy and champagne you had on earlier. Get rid of the blue thing you wore last night. Unless it's your favorite?"

"Not even in the top ten," she assured him, preening in the foyer mirror. "This is gorgeous! I ought to simper and turn it down, but I won't. If you thought I would, it serves you right."

"Serves me right," he agreed, coming up behind her. In the mirror their eyes met and held, then he took a step back and jerked his head toward the kitchen. "Do I smell coffee? Can I get us both a mug while you change?"

They drank in what Sheila supposed was a companionable silence. At least it was comfortable. Outside, rain began to pitter on the leaves of a tulip poplar just outside the window.

When they had finished, she set her mug on the coffee table, settled more comfortably into the corner of the couch with her feet tucked beneath her, and demanded, "Tell me about Yvonne."

He stretched out in the chair, head resting on its high back. "What do you want to know?"

"How you are her brother when Mrs. Warton didn't know you. What Yvonne was really like. What made her do the things she did. Anything you want to tell me, really."

"I am her brother because my old man played around. It's that simple. He owned a good bit of the town I grew up in, and he thought that included some of the women. Most of them, if some people are to be believed. But Yvonne was the only kid I ever knew to come out of his affairs. I first saw her when I was twelve and she was two."

"A very impressionable age," Sheila murmured absently, doing arithmetic. That made him about two years older than she.

"It was for me," Crispin agreed. "Yvonne was a cute, chubby toddler. I felt—I don't know what. Guilty as hell for what Dad had done to Mary Jo, sorry for Vonnie, mad at Dad, but also a little secretly glad to have a sister. Mother had died that year, and I was an only child, pretty alone most of the time."

"Your dad didn't consider marrying Yvonne's mother?"

Crispin shook his head and looked, for just an instant, young and very vulnerable. "He probably wouldn't have considered marrying *my* mother if her father hadn't owned the town when Dad got there. I don't think Dad gave Mary Jo another thought after that visit. And I certainly will never know why he took me along."

"Maybe he thought you'd think it was a routine visit to a friend," Sheila suggested.

He shook his head. "Don't try to defend him. Any fool could have seen that while Mary Jo was blond with green eyes, Vonnie looked more like Dad than I did. I played with her while they talked, then Dad gave Mary Jo a check and suggested she move to Pensacola. I didn't see them again until I was twenty-one."

Sheila knew instinctively what he wasn't saying. "And inherited a great deal of money. Then you went to see them. Offered to help them out."

His smile was rueful. "Do you read tea leaves? Unfortunately, you're right. My mother's father died and left me his half interest in the family business. Dad died later the same year, and I suddenly had it all. I remembered Yvonne and Mary Jo, and thought I could be Lancelot and Galahad rolled into one. But Mary Jo turned me down. Flat. She never would take a penny from me—even when she was dying." He stopped, his eyes distant and sad.

The rain grew suddenly harder, fell in sheets. Sheila rose to pull down the window. "And Yvonne?" she asked, her back to him.

She was glad to hear him chuckle. "Oh, Vonnie wrote me the next week and asked for money for an Easter dress. After that we sort of got into the habit of her asking and my sending money."

"More and more money." Sheila nodded. "And no, I'm not clairvoyant. Amory found her little green record book."

He was startled. "Do you still have it?"

She rose and brought him the copies she had made. He looked through them, whistling several times in dismay. "It was worse than I thought. I knew she'd put the bite on a few people. A couple she ran into at the Four Seasons in New York, for instance. He was a gynecologist and she was the wife of a senator. Vonnie got a good bit out of both of them, I fear."

"And a good bit out of a lot of other people. What will you do about it?"

"What do you think? Should I pay them back out of Forbes's estate, or consider they were justly paying for their sins and forget it?" Without waiting for a reply, he thumbed through the rest of the notes, then tossed them onto the coffee table. "Poor Vonnie. No matter how much money she got, she never had enough."

Sheila digested that for a few minutes while they both listened to the rain, then she asked, "Did you suspect she was killing people?"

He nodded. "After Edna Warton died, I talked with one of the others who got sick. She told me that Edna ate Vonnie's dessert, giving each of them a bite. Do you realize they could have all died and she wouldn't have cared?" His eyes were haunted.

"Why didn't you turn her in?" But she already knew. A lonely boy who finds a beautiful baby sister doesn't turn her in.

What he said, though, was "She denied it, and I couldn't prove anything. The best I knew to do was hang around—try to protect her from herself, and other people from her, too. But when I heard about the Marriot setup, I knew she was in deeper than she could handle. Funny that it was little Nancy Jones who got her instead. Nancy was the skinniest bridesmaid . . ." He closed his eyes. "God, I'm so tired!" It sounded like a prayer.

"You can rest if you'll tell me one more thing," she promised. "How did you get so chummy with Norris? He let you into the Marriot house like a relative."

"Maybe I am. Can't you see me with caterpillar eyebrows?" He wiggled his slim black ones at her. "In fact, somebody ought to pick up the Marriot family business. How about if you and I . . ."

"Stick to the topic. How did you know Norris so well?"

"Beers in the bushes. Servants together and all that. Mac and Rilla were gone a good bit, and Richard drove them. Norris liked to sit in the front seat of his car and have a beer. I had a few with him. Told him I was from an old family. If he got the idea that the family was Mafia—well, it was his own idea. I certainly never said so."

"I will have my work cut out, keeping you and my aunt Mary apart," Sheila told him. "There's not an ounce of scruples between you."

"Ah, but there *is* a child between us, and I got the feeling last night she's most reluctant to surrender Forbes to my tender care. What do you think?"

Sheila considered. "I don't think she'll be sad to surrender his day-to-day care. Aunt Mary likes to travel, and she's used to setting her own schedule and having Mildred at her beck and call. Forbes has put a crimp in all that these past weeks. But she'll probably want a lot of say-so in his upbringing, and she won't surrender him at all unless she thinks you're fit to raise him. Beneath that crusty exterior, she has grown very fond of him."

"I'm glad. Do you think she might consider keeping him for a while? Sort of a foster-home arrangement? We'd have to work out suitable fees, of course. Will you come with me after dinner tonight to ask her?"

He hadn't asked her to dinner, but Sheila wouldn't quibble. She could wear her new dress. Besides—she turned her head so he couldn't see her expression—she wouldn't miss being there when he made his proposal, not for the world! Aunt Mary's exquisite penthouse a foster home?

Across the room Crispin stretched, squirmed in the chair to get more comfortable. "God, I am so tired!" he said again.

"Here." Sheila got up. "Take a nap on the couch. I need to do a few things at my desk in the other room anyway."

He was asleep almost before he stretched out. For a few minutes she stood in the doorway, contemplating that lean, almost-handsome man. She didn't know much about him, and had no idea how far she wanted to travel with him, but in the few times they had met, he had never been dull.

What was it she had almost said to Amory his first night in town? Something about wanting to meet a middle-aged intelligent man who made her laugh? "I didn't ask for a four-year-old," she reminded whoever might be listening in Higher Places. "I don't know anything about small boys."

On the floor beside Crispin, Lady shifted and sighed a most contented sigh. Dogs have a right to make a few requests, too.